EVEN THOUGH IT'S BREAKING

A PSYCHOLOGICAL SUSPENSE THRILLER

SHANNON JUMP

To Alysson –
xo

ALSO FROM SHANNON JUMP

My Only Sunshine

Contemporary Fiction

Copy Editing by Librum Artis Editorial Services
Cover created by Shannon Jump

First edition published October 2021
ISBN: 978-0578977065 (Paperback)
ASIN: B09B7WSSGC (Kindle Edition)

This book is intended for readers over the age of eighteen and contains mature content that may be unsuitable for younger audiences, including: child adoption, domestic violence, drug use, self-harm, stalking, sexual assault, and (implied) rape.

For the ones who embraced the sunshine

For happiness one needs security, but
joy can spring like a flower, even from
the cliffs of despair.

Anne Morrow Lindbergh

PROLOGUE

I remember the sounds.

Panting.

Grunting.

An IV dripping.

The constant beeping of a machine.

My screams.

Things have come to me in bits and pieces, but I have no way to differentiate fact from fiction, and the police are no closer to finding the man who did this to me. Nothing I've shared with them has brought us any leads.

"All evidence points to a stranger attack," they say.

As if that makes everything less traumatizing.

As if that makes me feel safe.

The smells are coming back to me, too. They linger, as if the memories are buried just deep enough that I can't quite reach them.

Sweat.

His breath—tainted with alcohol and mint—warm and labored as he hovered over me.

The copper-like sweetness of blood.

There are many things I don't remember that somehow still manage to haunt me. Like the look on his face, the feel of his calloused hands—the ones that groped my body hard enough to leave bruises. His teeth on my neck—when he bites me so hard he draws blood, the wound requiring four stitches.

The moment he invades my soul.

These are just a few of the unimaginable things law enforcement wishes I could remember; that they have tried to coax out of me since the moment I came to, after several days in a medically induced coma to reduce the swelling in my brain caused by the innumerable hits I took to the head. They say that if I can recall these *significant* details—as if the ones I have managed to remember are of *no* significance—they may be able to locate and arrest the man who raped me before beating me senseless and leaving me for dead.

I can see him there, in my mind. But he has no face. He has no body. He is nothing but a dark figure lurking in the shadows.

I've been awake now for a couple days, responding to questions I don't actually know the answers to, taking medications I'm not even sure I need.

Dissociative Amnesia.

The apparent diagnosis that explains why I can't remember anything.

And leaves me feeling like nothing but a failure.

In time, my recollection may improve. There are methods to aid the memory's recovery process, to coerce the information from the depths of my brain. I'm being asked to give those methods a try, to agree to a course of treatment that is not even guaranteed to bring my attacker to justice and is likely to traumatize me more than I already am.

Sounds delightful, right?

He could be anywhere by now, the forty-eight-hour window of opportunity long gone. Or he could be close… somewhere out there.

Waiting for me.

Watching.

CHAPTER ONE

Allie

Wednesday, June 24, 2015

A darkness washes over me as I slip into a state of unconsciousness. It's quiet, almost peaceful. I don't feel anything anymore, in this dream-like state I'm in, but I think I'm okay with that—the pain was too much to bear anyway.

I'm sinking, but when I reach the bottom, I hear birds chirping, the rustling of a soft breeze against the trees, the warmth of the sun on my face. I tilt my head up toward the clear sky and wonder if this is it.

I'm dead, and this must be heaven.

"We're losing her. Charge the paddles."

I'm shaken from my illusions, the sound of a nearby voice startling me. I want to react, but my body fails me. My arms won't move, the muscles no longer in service, and I can't open my eyes. Fear prickles the back of my neck and brings the hairs on my arms to a stance.

A shock wave jolts through me, the electrical current

thrashing through my veins, and I think my heart is about to explode, but if I'm already dead I suppose that's okay.

"I've got a pulse!"

The darkness returns as if by the flick of a switch.

I no longer feel a thing.

"Allie…baby?" I hear his voice, the soft rasp taunting me, and I can't tell if it's close by or far away. He's begging me to wake up, to squeeze his hand if I can hear him.

I try to squeeze, but my fingers are merely foreign objects adhered to my hand, and I'm not sure I actually manage to move them. Before I can give it too much thought, I hear the reassuring sound of Tarek's voice again.

"Oh, thank God," he whispers, and I feel his head lower next to mine as he nestles into the crook of my neck. "I've been so worried, baby." He caresses my cheek, his thumb grazing my lips.

With exhausting effort, I pry my eyes open. It's dark in this room, so it doesn't take but a moment for my eyes to adjust and spot the shadow of a man at my bedside. I have no idea where I am, but I recognize this face, this voice. His green eyes blink away tears, and they roll slowly down his cheeks. He looks disheveled, wearing gray sweatpants and a navy Twins shirt that's seen better days. I can only assume that's because of me and whatever reason I have for occupying this bed.

I want to speak but can't, the tube down my throat rendering me silent, and once I realize it's there, I gag. Tarek kisses my forehead and jumps to his feet, forgetting to let go of my hand until he's practically dragging me along with him. I groan and he releases his grip, my arm thumping back down by my side. "I'm going to get the doctor," he announces, the door slamming behind him, and it's then that I realize we're in a hospital.

I'm definitely not dead.

A nurse enters the room before Tarek gets far, the incessant beeping of my heart rate monitor having alerted the nurse's station to my duress.

"Okay, dear, hang tight. Try to relax. We'll get that tube out for you in just a minute," she says, reaching over my head for something. "I'm Darcy," she continues. I imagine the fear in my eyes, how my face must be contorted with confusion. "Just a few more minutes and we'll have you comfortable again."

When the tube is removed, I cough violently, and everything hurts—my throat, my stomach, my chest. I try to speak, and all the letters of the alphabet are there, but they're jumbled up in my brain and won't form a cohesive word, let alone a complete sentence.

"Tar..ek?" I croak, each individual letter barely audible. I'm so thirsty, my mouth the equivalent of a spoonful of sand.

"I'm here, baby," he says, squeezing my hand. I wince as if I'm expecting his touch to hurt, but my fingers are numb and I hardly feel him.

"Wa…wate…wat-er."

The sterile room suddenly makes me queasy. My brain pounds against my skull, my body producing a constant ache like I've never felt before—the muscles don't want to work, but I know they're in there.

Something is wrong.

I'm disoriented.

I'm so tired.

My eyes flutter closed.

Just for a moment, I tell myself.

When I come to again several hours later, Tarek stirs next to me. He's dozed off in the chair, and his head rests on the side of my bed, his hand still gripping mine. I do my best to wiggle my fingers, and somehow they move and alert Tarek to my wakeful state.

"Oh, sweetie. You're awake," he says, groggy from sleep. I don't trust my voice, so I just nod in response. He rubs the sleep crusties from his eyes and yawns before he stands and kisses my cheek. His lips are warm against my cold skin. "I'll be right back. Don't fall asleep on me this time," he teases, making his way to the door.

I feel myself fluttering back to sleep, but the clock on the wall is ticking so loudly, and I want to find something to throw at it. Not that I'm naive enough to believe I have the strength to throw anything, but one can dream. I still don't know why I'm here or what could have possibly happened to me, but before I can generate a conscious thought, the door swings open again.

Tarek lingers in the hallway while the doctor enters, white lab coat and all. He's older—maybe in his fifties, with salt and pepper hair—and I hope for his sake that it's nearing the end of his shift, because he looks about as exhausted as I feel.

"Miss Mason, I'm Dr. Nelson," he says with an unexpected boom to his voice. "I'm glad to see you're awake. How are you feeling?" He smiles, and then flips open the chart he carried in with him, making a note on the page before looking up at me. Not waiting for my answer, he says, "You've been in a coma for a few days."

"A coma?" I echo, my voice still scratchy.

"A detective with the Maple Grove Police Department has

been waiting to speak with you. He's on his way in now and should be here shortly."

A detective?

"Do you know why you're here?"

I shake my head slowly, and the confusion I was riddled with a moment before quickly turns to fear.

Have I been in an accident?

Did I suffer a brain hemorrhage?

Is it cancer?

Have I killed someone?

"You've survived a pretty brutal attack, Miss Mason. You're very lucky to be alive." He moves to the foot of my bed, lifting the white blanket and exposing the hospital slippers that cover my feet. He taps my heel with a reflex hammer. "Can you feel this?"

"Yes," I admit gratefully, nodding through the kink in my neck.

He works the blanket back over my feet, tucking it underneath, but I'm growing warm, and I no longer want the blanket. Nor do I want to be lying down. I bring my hands under me and try to push myself up, but my right arm buckles at the elbow and I flop down onto my back.

"Whoa, whoa…slowly, Miss Mason," the doctor warns, coming to my side. He places a hand on my shoulder and another behind my back, helping me sit forward before raising the headrest with the remote control attached to the bed.

I wince at the flash of pain in my abdomen and bring my hand to my stomach. "You suffered a couple broken ribs," the doctor informs. "Not much we can do for those, unfortunately, but we'll do our best to keep you comfortable."

I don't know what to say, so I nod, my mind reeling with all the information. I see Tarek in the hall, his cell phone raised to his ear as he paces back and forth. *"Yes, she's awake. The doctor is in with her now..."*

I hope it's my mom on the other end of that call.

"All right, I've ordered some tests. A nurse will be in shortly to collect some blood samples and check your vitals. Is there anything I can get you?"

"Um...I'm...sorry, doctor—"

"Nelson. Dr. Lee Nelson."

"Thank you. Dr. Nelson," I say. My throat is stinging, but I need answers, so I continue. "I'm...confused. You said I survived...an attack? What kind of attack?"

"I think it would be best to wait for the detective. I'm sorry, but while I know your injuries, I'm not privy to the details of what happened. I've been asked to alert the authorities as soon as you came to." I nod, unsure why the police are involved but beginning to worry that I've done something wrong. "I'll have one of the nurses bring you some water."

I muster a "thank you" and Dr. Nelson leaves the room, my chart in his hand as he holds the door open for Tarek, who pauses at the threshold.

"How are you feeling?" he asks, returning to my side. I rub my temple, applying pressure against the pulsing in my skull.

"I...don't know...how—"

"It's okay, baby. Don't try to talk too much. Here, I got you some water," he says, placing the plastic cup on a dinner tray and wheeling it over my lap. I reach for the cup, but my arm is weak and I knock it over, the water spilling everywhere.

"Oh, shit. I'm so sorry, honey." Tarek rights the cup and grabs his sweatshirt from the chair to sop up the liquid.

"...my fault," I manage, the words slightly more coherent despite the continued dryness in my throat.

"I'll grab you some more. Be right back." He darts from the room and I'm left wet and cold, still unbearably thirsty. I sigh and lay my head on the pillow behind me, already anxious for whatever nightmare this is to be over.

There's a knock at the door, and it opens before I have a moment to answer. A tall African American man enters, dressed in dark-washed jeans and a button down flannel, a shiny police badge adhered to his belt loop. His dark skin glistens with sweat in response to the layers of clothing he wears, but he flashes a bright, toothy smile. His brown eyes are warm but cautious as he closes the door and makes his way over to me. I sit up again, my efforts slightly embarrassing, but somehow I power through.

"Miss Mason, hello. I'm Detective Feeney with the Services Division, Maple Grove. How are you feeling?" He offers me his hand and I take it, his handshake firm and confident, unlike my own.

"Okay, I guess. I'm…a bit confused." I admit, tucking a loose strand of hair behind my ear. I haven't even looked in the mirror yet—I must look a mess.

"That's to be expected. Do you remember anything about the night you were attacked?"

"No. Nothing. This is all a bit of a shock, and Dr. Nelson didn't tell me much."

"Well, let me tell you what we know. Stop me at any time if this becomes too much, okay?" I nod as he continues. "An intruder broke into your apartment. It looks like they used the fire escape and broke in through your bedroom window. You were found unconscious on the bed, bleeding and severely injured. Do you remember calling 9-1-1?"

His words hit hard, the weight of them crashing against

my chest. I draw in a breath, disbelief wafting in the air around me.

How could this happen?

"No," I finally reply. He's patient, giving me a moment to take it all in, and I'm grateful. He smiles gently before continuing.

"Your cell phone was on the nightstand, still on the line with our dispatch team. Transcripts show you never spoke a word during the call. Miss Mason, I understand this may be difficult to hear." He pauses and drops his brow. "Evidence suggests that you were sexually assaulted. We've collected semen samples from an unknown male, along with blood from the window sill and some prints. But we're still processing the evidence."

My heart drops. This can't be happening—it's…impossible to imagine.

And I don't remember?

"Who did this to me?" I whisper, clasping my hands together in front of my face.

"A couple witnesses reported a male suspect lingering around your apartment building over the last few months, usually dressed in black and always after dark. We have reason to believe this man—whoever he is—was stalking you. Sightings go back to about two months prior to your attack, but no one ever saw him enter the building or reported it to police. CCTV footage shows the same; we have him on camera, but can't get a visual of his face. The DNA evidence we've collected hasn't returned any matches yet, so he's likely not in the system."

It takes a moment for me to digest this information. My head is still foggy, but even if it weren't, I don't think any of this would make sense. I shudder at the thought of someone

—a stranger—watching me. That I never saw them in the first place.

"A stalker? How...how is that possible?"

"Have you noticed anyone following you?"

I shake my head, the motion leaving me dizzy. "No."

"How about an online dating profile?

"No. Tarek and I have been together for six years, and we met through a mutual friend in college. I've never even tried online dating."

"I didn't think so. We looked and weren't able to locate any active profiles for you."

"Who would do this?"

"We're still waiting on some evidence from the crime scene. Hopefully that'll bring us some leads. Until then, do you have a place you can stay once you're released?"

"Why would I need a place to stay?" The question is out of my mouth before I realize he's already told me why: I was attacked at home.

My home is a crime scene.

How could I have forgotten already?

Detective Feeney pinches his eyebrows together, and I see the torment on his face. His dark eyes are pained, and he tilts his head as he waits for my response.

"I…I'm sure I can stay with Tarek. Or my parents."

"Or me." I turn and see my best friend, Courtney, step through the door. She drops her purse to the floor and runs to my bedside, her arms outstretched and ready to embrace me. She squeezes too hard and I wince, but I don't care.

"I'm so happy to see you," she says through a few sniffles. "How are you feeling?"

Detective Feeney clears his throat, reminding Court of his presence. "I'm so sorry I barged in," she says, backing away but still holding my hand. “I just…I heard she was awake and needed to see her.”

“It’s all right, miss.”

“I’ll be back in a bit, okay?” she reassures me, giving my hand another squeeze. She scoops her purse up from the floor and exits with a little skip in her step. My heart swells at the sight of her—she must have been worried sick.

I turn back to Detective Feeney, and he’s pulled out a small notebook and a pen. He flips the page and looks down at me. “Miss Mason—”

“Allie,” I correct him.

“Allie,” he continues, and I like the way my name sounds coming from his mouth. “Is there anything you can tell me about the night of the attack? Anything at all. Even if it seems insignificant, it could be helpful to the investigation.”

I shake my head again, and frustration hits me.

How do I not remember a single thing?

“When did it happen?” I ask.

“Last Saturday, the twentieth,” he says after referring to his notes.

“And today is?”

“Wednesday, the twenty-fourth.”

I try to recall what I might have had planned last Saturday, but not much comes to mind. I don’t get much time to think on it, though, because I spot Tarek in the hall. His arms are loaded up with vending machine snacks and bottled waters. He stops abruptly when he looks in and his eyes land on Detective Feeney. He stands still, staring in at him. I don’t think he sees me watching him, and I’m not sure what to make of the look on his face, but I know I’ve seen that look from him before.

It hits me then, and I manage to pull my eyes away from

Tarek and over to Detective Feeney, who's staring at me with concern.

"Miss Mason?"

Suddenly it's hard to breathe, as if the wind has been knocked out of me. I'm gasping for air, reaching for the detective, and I know I'm having some sort of panic attack, but I can't catch my breath long enough to explain why. The words are stuck in my throat, so I point and frantically turn back to the window that overlooks the hallway as Detective Feeney presses the call button for the nurse.

Tarek is gone.

"It's okay, just breathe. I've got you," he assures me. He didn't see what I saw, and he doesn't know what I think I know, so he's calm and he's holding my hand instead of bolting out the door after Tarek like I think he should be doing.

I'm not even sure why Tarek was here in the first place, because even though I'm still foggy from the coma, and even though I seem to have forgotten how to get air into my lungs, I am fairly certain of one thing.

Tarek and I broke up last month.

BEFORE

CHAPTER TWO

Allie

My mother always says happiness is relative. It's like her slogan, her motherly advice set to repeat any time my younger brother Linc or I experience an upsetting life event. It's a simple mindset, really, but easier said than done. I get it—when I'm down, getting back up should be as simple as a quick lather, rinse, repeat cycle. According to my mother, anyway.

I'm struggling to put her expert advice to use these days, though.

It's not that I'm the type to wallow in my sorrows—truly, I'm not. Life is good…for the most part. It's just that lately I'm struggling to find reasons to be happy. I'll check my privilege in a minute, okay? I know I don't have much to be sad about, nothing that should be holding me down for long, but tell that to my brain and then we'll have this conversation again.

I can't help the way I feel.

I've been down more than usual the last few months, my

moods an offset of daily stressors every young adult experiences, I'm sure. When put that way, perhaps I'm able to downplay it a bit. But the truth is, I'm unhappy.

Don't tell Mom.

On the surface, everything is great—I smile plenty. I laugh boisterously, which I've been told is endearing. I do things—like my weekly happy hours with my best friend, Courtney. I drive home to Brainerd to see my parents and Linc every couple months, and I work a full-time job that I actually love—for a boss that I don't entirely mind.

And then several nights a week I see my boyfriend of six years, Tarek.

It's a simple, repetitive cycle that should be carefree and fulfilling—if you're one who appreciates routine and every day feeling just like the last, which I don't. I'm bored.

I feel like Ariel from *The Little Mermaid*—sans the long, flowing red hair, fish-like tail, and the ability to breathe under water. To put it simply: I want more.

It's not that there's anything wrong with my life per se. But some days I think my childhood love of fairy-tales may have tainted my views on the world. I used to dream of happy endings—not of the sexual nature, although those are nice, too—and all things happily ever after. Hunky dory and skip-to-my-lou be damned. I've always been a dreamer, it's why I love all things fiction—of the fantasy worlds we can create with our imaginations; a reader of feel-good love stories and a true believer in romance. I'm like the Midwestern, white-girl version of Oprah, standing on a couch and giving out free love to everyone in my make-believe audience.

My idealistic views of the world have been singed into my brain, permanently branded by love stories like *Cinderella* and *The Sound of Music* and rom-coms like *The Notebook* or *How to Lose a Guy in Ten Days*. I was that young girl picking wildflowers in the field—which is apparently illegal in some states, a fact I wish I never learned—and skipping through a meadow in a sundress while a subtle breeze blows through my hair.

Even into adulthood, I'm a firm believer that no one is too old for fairy-tales, and eventually we all find our 'happy everything'. That good things come to those who wait and all that fuzzy feel-good stuff.

But lately?

Lately it feels like that's all a bunch of crap.

I grew up thinking there is no suffering, no heartache, and nothing bad ever happens simply because "that wouldn't be fair."

No, little girl, it sure wouldn't.

What I wouldn't give to go back and slap that kid across the face.

So, I've spent my entire life—including the majority of my adult years—as naive as one can possibly be. Truth be told, I've spent the last several years of my life under the assumption that I had everything I ever wanted: a loving family—great parents and a younger brother I don't mind; the stereotypical best friend—the yin to my yang, the one who takes crap from no one except me; and a doting boyfriend who loves me more than life itself. We're sure to get married and drive off into the sunset one of these days.

See? A hopeless romantic, I am—er, was.

It's bullshit, really, to think such happiness can exist. That it can't be tainted. When you grow up the way I did, it's easy to overlook all the non-happy things. The suffering, the agony. The heartbreak.

My life *was* perfect.

I *was* happy.

Until I wasn't.

It'd be easy to look back and blame everything on one single event that changed the course of my life forever. But I won't. I'm not that little girl dreaming of fairy tales anymore. I know the reality is a bit harsher than the make-believe stories we tell ourselves.

I know the end of my 'happy everything' started long before that night. But Mom was wrong. Happiness isn't relative. It's nothing more than a chemical reaction, a serotonin effect that can be tampered with. We all want to drink the Kool-Aid, but not everyone has a cup. So sometimes we drink directly from the bowl. We get our germ-filled hands in there and tamper with it. We mix in.

We unintentionally change its makings.

And then we have to learn to live with the consequences.

CHAPTER THREE

Allie

Thursday, May 14, 2015

"Babe, did you grab the bag from the bathroom counter?" Tarek asks as he shoves his wallet into the back pocket of his jeans.

"Yep, it's already in the car," I reply. I meet Tarek at the entryway of my apartment and sling my cross-body purse over my neck. I'm tempted to grab my laptop off the kitchen table, but Tarek has requested we get through the long weekend with as few distractions as possible. A four-day weekend at a bed and breakfast in Duluth. The only rule? No devices. I eye my laptop and sigh outwardly, audibly chastising Tarek for banishing me from nearly all means of communication. He sees me playing coy and reaches over, taking my hand.

"It's just a few days," he says, pulling me to him. His arms wrap around me, and he leans in for a quick kiss. "I'll do my best to keep you busy." He winks and wiggles his eyebrows.

I return his kiss and relax against him. "I know. It's just that Franklin isn't happy about me going off the grid for so long. You know how he is."

"Right. And you know you're entitled to actually *use* your vacation time, correct?"

I shove his arm playfully, well aware that I'm acting like a child who's just been told they can't bring their favorite toy on a long car ride.

But damn it, I want the toy.

"Trust me, everything will be fine. And you'll be nice and relaxed when we get back. The work will still be there, and you'll still have a job." Tarek takes the car keys from the hook by the door and jiggles them. "You ready?"

I nod and make my way to the door, slipping my feet into my shoes. I can't help but think I've never dreaded a four-day getaway so much in my life.

Tarek and I have been together since college, both having attended Minnesota State University in Moorhead and graduating with honors. He was a different person then. I was, too, I suppose, but Tarek especially. He was funny, goofy in his own way but never over the top. Never too serious. A charmer of sorts—which he still tries to be some days, but his attempts don't land the way they used to. He was a dedicated student who was active on the football team and even took the time to buy his girlfriend—me—flowers and chocolates on Valentine's Day, even though our anniversary is the day after—when everything is fifty percent off.

He doesn't do that anymore. Now I get the day-after

reject flowers that nobody wanted, slightly wilted and clearly picked through. Not that I expect flowers or extravagant gifts from Tarek, truly I don't. But why change things now, after all this time?

Some days, I swear it's his family that ruined him.

After graduation Tarek took a job as an investment banker working alongside his father, Steven, and brother, Tristan. The three musketeers, as they're often referred to. Inseparable both in the office and on the golf course. Trusted members of an elite cigar club—whatever the hell that is.

Tarek never cared about the money he came from until he took that job. Financial security be damned, I often wish he'd never accepted the offer in the first place, but let's face it, he was molded for this job since birth. Everyone knew he'd follow in his father's footsteps.

I admit, I knew that going into things. I knew what his father and everyone else in his family expected of him. But the Tarek I knew then never would have gone down that path when all was said and done.

College Tarek wanted more out of life.

I sit here now, my painted toes in the sandy beach overlooking the expanse of Lake Superior, wondering if he'll ever be that young man again. The carefree, happy guy who wanted nothing more than the clothes on his back and his woman in his arms.

I miss that guy.

"Allie, look!" Tarek yells from down the beach. He jogs over, pointing to the pier behind him. In his hand is a glass bottle. "Look what I found!"

I push my sunglasses to the top of my head and squint, cupping my hand in a rainbow arch over my brows. "What is it?" I ask. He holds up the bottle for me to see. A small piece of white paper is stuffed inside. "A message in a bottle?"

"You've always wanted to find one," he says, a smile on his lips. He's sincere, a genuine sparkle in his eyes. "Should we try to open it?"

I turn back toward the water where the sun is setting. "Maybe we should leave it for someone else?" I say. I don't reach for it, but I can tell it's new, lacking the decades-old secrets and romance of the waters before us. "It looks like it just washed up and never made it far."

"Aren't you going to look at it?" Tarek pouts, extending the bottle in my direction. I wave him off and drop my sunglasses back over my eyes.

"It's not like it's hundreds of years old, Tarek. Throw it back and let someone else find it."

He scoffs, his frustration evident, and I know I'm being a snot, but I don't have a choice. I can't read the note I know is inside that bottle.

I can't.

"Fine. Whatever, Allie." He turns and pitches the bottle into the lake. It smashes into a wave and bobs up and down for a moment before floating away into the glowing sunset.

Tarek is already walking back to the car, his hands stuffed in his pockets, his head hung low. He never even looks back to see where the bottle landed.

I stand, brush the sand from my legs and gather my bag. I take one last wishful look over the crisp blue water, the setting sun reflected in its surface, and then start walking up the beach toward the car. My bare feet are cold against the sand, but all I can think about is the piece of paper inside that bottle and the square-shaped lump in Tarek's pocket.

I ruined his perfect proposal.

On purpose.

CHAPTER FOUR

Allie

Monday, May 18, 2015

I pour steaming coffee into my favorite Rae Dunn mug—my typical go-to on a Monday morning for the simple fact that it has the word *ugh* splattered across the front in big, bold letters. Adding a splash of sweet cream before bringing the mug to my nose, I inhale the heavenly aroma and let the steam warm my nostrils before indulging in the first sip. An exaggerated "ahh" escapes my lips.

Coffee.

Because Mondays.

But my perfect cup of coffee doesn't change the fact that it's my least favorite day of the week. This being the reason Mondays were the first day I asked for when I started working remotely.

I've grown to distrust anyone who likes Mondays.

It's kind of my thing.

Also, anyone who can wake up at the ass crack of dawn

with a smile on their face. Mega distrust of the ones who do so without the help of a caffeinated beverage and still manage not to stab someone.

So despite my love of fairy tales, Mondays can suck it.

And this morning? Even though I work from the IKEA-designed comfort of my own home, I'm late for work. Because in addition to requiring large quantities of caffeine to start my day, I'm also kind of a head case at the start of the workweek—something my mother swore I'd grow out of but never actually did.

I dash across the living room of my apartment and open the curtains before making my way to the massive oak desk in the corner of the room that overlooks the walking trails outside. Jabbing my finger into the power button, I groan to myself.

My company-issued laptop whirls to life, and I punch the passcode in with my pointer finger before setting my mug down on a coaster. A stack of paperwork stares back at me, a sight I once dreaded, but today I welcome the distraction with open arms.

Jed Franklin, my boss at Franklin Books & PR, who really only ever goes by the name Franklin, is oddly obsessed with paper. You'd think in today's world he'd have moved everything to electronic record copies, but no. He's kind of an old fart set in his ways and likes to complicate my life with mounds of recycled paper, despite the fact that we live in a digital world—despite the fact that *books* also now coexist in a digital world.

I work from home as an editor and book promoter three days out of the week, the other two from Franklin's office off Hemlock. My preferred editing method is electronic, yet he still faxes me paper copies of every manuscript I review, and they stack nicely next to the pile of red correcting pens he keeps making me take home that I never use. One of these days I'll pop over to the elementary school and donate them, but today's not that day.

Today, I drink the coffee.

I shake my head and sigh, ready—but not really—to start the day. I log into my Outlook account and scan through the nearly two hundred emails in my inbox—a hazard of the four-day weekend I just spent with Tarek—and already I know it's not going to be a good week. I'm behind on deadlines for two book projects, one of which I never wanted to take on in the first place. The other, I have no excuse. It's a great manuscript, complete with a murderous vengeance and all that jazz, but the author—Brian Wilson—is a nightmare to work with, and I already penciled in a headache for the two-week period we'll be working together on edits.

At a quick glance, I see Wilson's name on at least a dozen of the emails littering my screen. Apparently, there's no rest for the wicked.

My cell rings across the desk, and my best friend's goofy face illuminates the touchscreen.

"Hey, Court," I say a bit groggily, the frog in my throat not yet awake.

"Hey, honey face! How goes it?" she chirps back. She's perkier than anyone should be this early in the morning, but she happens to be one of those people who don't mind Mondays.

Tragic, I know.

A car horn blares in the background, and I make the assumption that she's on her way into the office. She's on site the days that I'm not—Franklin's doing, of course. I should mention that we work together. Cliche, yes, but we wouldn't have it any other way. "My money will be better spent keeping you two apart," Franklin once told us. While it's entirely possible he may have been on to something, Courtney and I have yet to abuse company time beyond the extended bathroom break or coffee run, but I digress. At least we get Fridays together.

"Just livin' the life over here. Getting ready for the workday. You driving in?" I ask.

"Yep. I'm doing my best not to flip the road rage switch. What the hell is wrong with people on the roads this morning? I'm already five minutes late." I neglect to call out the fact that we live in suburban Minnesota, about a half-hour northwest of the Twin Cities, in Maple Grove. Sure, there's traffic. But it's not like we're in New York.

"What happened to Minnesota nice?" I tease, well aware that Courtney would never practice kindness on the road. She's a classic "angry bitch" behind the wheel, one of the many reasons I avoid riding in with her on the one day a week that we're both on site. "I'm already thinking we need happy hour tonight."

"Oh, God, yes. I was worried you were calling to tell me you wouldn't be in today, and I'd have to take your place." I laugh. "I need it after the weekend I've had." I jab the speaker button with my index finger and set the phone on my desk before taking another sip of coffee and turning back to my laptop.

"Oh boy. Trouble in paradise? How was the trip?"

"Okay, one, I never said I was in paradise. And two—yes. It was a *long* weekend."

"Well, I can't wait to hear all about it," she teases with a sigh. "Oh, come on, jackass!"

"I'll let you go—I hope you're hands-free over there. You know texting and driving isn't cool, right?"

"Yeah, yeah. I know. I'm on Bluetooth. But, I'll see you tonight. Five o'clock?"

"Five o'clock," I confirm.

We end the call, and I can't help but chuckle at Court's brazenness. But that's who she is, that sister those of us without sisters always wanted. We met by chance, in one of those weird ways that almost makes you question the makings of the universe. She was a stage-five clinger, and I couldn't stand her. Once she figured out I didn't like her, though, she stopped being nice. We made deli sandwiches together at Subway and always argued over who got to take the veggie side on the assembly line. She sucked at closing the subs, and all the veggies would slide off as she wrapped it, yet she thought she deserved that spot. "Who the hell cares?" she had said the day I verbally questioned her skills as a sandwich artist. "It all squishes back together when it gets wrapped anyway."

"It doesn't," I said flatly. "And people are starting to complain." I pointed to the family of four in the corner booth of the lobby. "I had to remake two of their sandwiches." She rolled her eyes and walked back into the kitchen, slamming plastic containers around and mumbling to herself.

When I took my lunch break later that day, she refused to help the customers who had walked in, and since we were the only two on the schedule, I abandoned my complimentary six-inch meatball sub and snack-sized dill pickle chips to take and make their orders.

I returned to a smashed bag of potato chips and a plastic fork sticking out of my smushed sandwich. I never would have imagined we would have become the friends we are today, but I learned a week or so later that Courtney's boyfriend at the time wasn't as loyal as she had hoped. We bonded when I found her crying in the bathroom and haven't looked back since.

Today, the woman has a heart of gold, but only if she

likes you. I chuckle to myself at the memory and return to my email, an audible groan escaping my lips.

When the workday ends, right around five o'clock, I change into my favorite jeans and T-shirt combo, slapping on a bit of concealer and swiping black mascara over my lashes to make myself look more human. I pop a couple extra-strength Tylenol, hoping to get rid of the headache pulsing in my brain as a result of Brian Wilson's endless arguing over commas and all things punctuation.

Wilson is often the reason I require happy hours on Mondays.

While the Maple Grove area doesn't have a shortage of bars, Court and I prefer the small-town feel—fewer people, less trouble—so we typically head over to Ditto's in St. Michael, our former karaoke stomping grounds back when we used to still go out on weekends. We have a no-drama-till-we-get-there motto, so our time in the car is reserved for music—not to mention I'm always the driver thanks to Court's previously mentioned road rage issues.

I pick Court up across town and when we pull onto the freeway, we blast the radio with the windows down and sing like idiots to Prince's *Purple Rain*, as passersby stare at us and shake their heads. Our ritual is really more for stress relief than anything, but it's a tradition we've managed to keep up with for several years, and it's really grown on me. And, oddly enough, it kinda works to shake the crazies out.

Today's stressor? Tarek.

I nearly broke up with him yesterday afternoon when we returned from our trip to Duluth, and he didn't take it well. Truth be told, I'm not surprised, and I can see how he would think it was a bit out of the blue. It kinda was, at least to everyone but me. After crying and pulling me close, he quickly started singing a different tune and accused me of seeing someone else. I didn't do the best job convincing him otherwise.

Not that there's someone else—there isn't. I just…fell out of love. Or grew out of it, perhaps.

If I'm being honest, I think I checked out of the relationship months ago.

"So, enlighten me, oh wise one. What's the news with Tarek?" Courtney asks as our drinks arrive at the table. A Sex on the Beach for her and a Rum and Diet Coke with lime for me.

I suck down half my drink and then release a drama-filled sigh. I know Court won't be on the same page with what I'm about to tell her, but that's what balances us out and keeps our relationship interesting: we rarely agree on anything, and she truly believes Tarek and I were made for each other.

"I think he was going to propose." Court's eyes go wide, her face frozen in place.

"Really?"

"Really," I confirm.

"So…what's wrong with that? Why would that be so horrible?"

"He wants kids. Like, right now, five minutes ago, what have you." I wave a dismissive hand in the air and set my drink down on the table.

"I thought you wanted kids?"

"I do. But…not yet."

And not with him.

"Okay, but that's it? That's the whole reason you're

breaking up with him? Because he loves you too much and wants to start a family?"

"Well, when you put it that way, it doesn't make me sound too good, does it?" I chuckle and take another sip of my drink before continuing. "But no, that's not the *whole* reason. Tarek and I have been together for six years, and it was great at first—it really was. But now? Now, it's just...I don't know. Boring? Mundane? Same shit, different day?"

"Okay, yeah, I get it..."

"I know that sounds selfish, I really do. But Court, there's no spark anymore. Nothing. None. Nada. Zil—"

"Yeah, okay. Gotcha, sparky," she says, leaning back in her seat and folding her arms across her ample chest. "So," she smirks, "Mr. Preppy Gorgeous Pants can't get'cha off anymore, huh?"

"Court! Keep your voice down!" I blush, despite the laugh that sneaks out. As I do, I realize she's not necessarily wrong. "I want passion, you know? Like a relationship that sweeps me off my feet. That's never been what Tarek does for me. He's...comfortable."

She nods, and she's spent enough time with Tarek and me to know what I mean. "Do I really want comfortable at this stage of my life?"

"I get it, I do, but Tarek's a great guy, Allie. You and I both know those are hard to come by." She flags down the waitress and sets her menu on the edge of the table. "Ready to order?" she asks.

I nod, jumping right back into it. "I don't think I'm ready for shitty diapers and crying babies and over-the-top dinner parties with neighbors we don't even like—you know the type." I pause. "PTA moms," I whisper, as if PTA is a swear word and nearby children need to cover their ears. "We're twenty-six; why can't we live a little first?"

"Wait, so you're not ready to become a bit of a bore?" she asks, the sarcasm practically dripping from her chin.

"No, I'm really not. Plus, you know Tarek. He may be a hardworking man who would do right by a family, but outside of the nine-to-five hustle and bustle, he's a lazy ass. And his mother is going to be the death of me. I swear she's ruined him."

Ah, one of my chief complaints—Tarek's laziness, which is probably more of a Momma's Boy issue than general laziness, but still an issue nonetheless. His idea of a fun Friday night consists of a six-pack and a pizza while stationed in front of his sixty-five-inch flat-screen watching whatever sporting event is currently live, and then wooing me into the bedroom just before the buzz wears off in hopes that he'll get laid before he passes out. Tell me that doesn't sound wonderfully romantic.

I'm confident the only reason we've lasted six years is that we don't live together yet. He's asked, of course, but I always find a reason to shut him down—unintentionally at first. Now I have a whole list of reasonable excuses. I don't want to break my lease, the commute for work is too far, yadda yadda. Those excuses are running out, though, and it's time for me to shit or get off the pot, as Court would say.

"I'm sorry, Allie. I really don't know what to tell you other than you really need to…"

"…shit or get off the pot," we both say in unison. So predictable, my best friend and her catch phrases. "I know." The waitress arrives, and we order wings and fries, along with another round of drinks, before Courtney runs off to the restroom and I'm left alone to ponder in my thoughts for a few minutes.

The 'yes girl'.

That's me, or so I've been told. I have a hard time saying

no to people, especially anyone I don't want to disappoint. Like when my next-door neighbor Mrs. Mayberry asked me to grab her some butter the next time I went to the grocery store. Or when my brother, Lincoln, asked me to show his new girlfriend, Sophie, around town as a favor, when really he just wanted to go golfing with his buddies and she had nothing to do in the meantime. Or when Franklin asked me to work two Saturdays ago because some author needed a last-minute edit and his usual editor was on vacation.

I say yes to things, sure. I'm working on it, though. In fact, Tarek was one of the people who mentioned how I need to start looking out for myself, to start saying no. I should have pointed that out to him when I tried to end things with him yesterday; I hate when I think of good points *after* an argument.

I'm tired of doing everything for everyone else and never worrying about what I want. And while I may be ready to end my romantic relationship with Tarek, I still care about him. I still have love for him and don't want to hurt him.

So, why am I left feeling guilty about it?

CHAPTER FIVE

Owen

Monday, May 18, 2015

She's always on my mind, consuming my thoughts. Every damn day all I see is her beautiful face. I hear her angelic voice and long to feel her breath on my neck, her tongue slithering across my skin.

But I know that won't happen, at least not anytime soon. There's still work to do.

I slam my fist into the drywall for the third time this week, a guttural roar erupting from my throat as my knuckles collide with the wall, my frustration getting the best of me again. I know I have anger issues and need to dial it back, but she's supposed to be mine, and every day that she's not just makes me that much angrier. She's supposed to want *me.*

How can she not see that?

Ungrateful.

That's what she is. No, wait, not my Allie.

How could I think that of her?

I shake the chalky remnants from my hand, surprised to see blood as I draw it back from the wall, my knuckles now split open and a chunk of skin dangling. I pluck it off and toss it to the floor, annoyed that I'll need to clean up another mess. I hate mess.

I need to see her. I'll feel better once I do.

I know where she'll be tonight though, my angel. Ditto's —of all places—where I've visited her many times of late. Personally, it's not my favorite hang-out spot, but as long as I get to see her I don't really give a shit where we are.

Such a coincidence that we both venture to the same bar on the same night of every week, isn't it?

I glance at the watch on my wrist, catch the time displayed in the window—half-past three. Happy hour starts at four o'clock, so I don't have much time to pull myself together before then. They usually arrive around five, and I like to get there before them.

I just need to see my girl—she'll help me relax, she always does. Her weekly happy hour with her friend—Courtney, I think her name is—is the highlight of my week. I always make sure to sit across the room, far enough away that she doesn't see me and can't hear me when I place my order with one of the trashy bartenders that double as waitresses.

She's not like the others, my Allie. She's…different. Beautiful in that she-doesn't-know-how-beautiful-she-is kind of way. That's the perfect kind of beauty, if you ask me.

My dick hardens at the thought of her, and I adjust myself in my jeans.

"Not yet," I mutter, pointing to it as if I'm scolding a child and then chuckling to myself under my breath. "I'm losing it," I say.

I need a distraction, something to take my mind off her until it's time to head out. The true-crime show I've been watching flashes on the TV screen across the room, but I make my way to the window instead of parking my ass back on the couch. The blackout curtain is drawn, like always, and I pull it aside, spotting a parcel on the concrete doorstep.

The binoculars I ordered.

Like a small child on Christmas morning, I flip the deadbolt and swing the door open to retrieve the Amazon box, my pocket knife in hand, ready to cut into it. But my cell phone rings from the coffee table, and I quickly scurry back inside and lock the door.

I know that ring tone.

I *dread* that ring tone.

My feet are heavy as I move toward the sound, drop the Amazon package onto the couch, and palm the device before raising it to my ear.

"Hi, Mom," I mutter.

"I need some money," she demands, not even bothering with the niceties this time.

"For what?" I ask. I sense the lie before it even comes out of her mouth.

"The cable is out again."

"I bet." I sigh, well aware that simply ending the call won't make a bit of difference. She'll just keep calling until she gets what she wants.

"Well?"

I sigh again, already sick of the sound of her voice, sick of her constant demands. "How much?" I snap back.

"I dunno…like five hundred or something?"

Yes, Mother, I'm sure your cable bill is a whopping five-hundred fucking dollars.

"Fine." I end the call and jab my finger onto the icon for my banking app, quickly going through the motions and sending her the drug money she's requested. "What'll it be today, Mother? Cocaine? Heroin?" I say to no one but myself.

A never-ending cycle of drug abuse, that's my mother for you. Dad left her for it, dragging me with him after meeting his current wife, Amber—twenty whole years and some odd change his junior, of course. Sure, she's hot and all, but in that cheap stripper kind of way.

She's nothing like my Allie.

And certainly nothing like my mother, whose addiction I'm clearly enabling, since my father stopped funding her habits years ago, but I don't give a shit anymore. Maybe one of these days she'll overdose and finally be out of my fucking life for good.

One can dream, right?

I glance at my watch again and realize it's time to go. I'll have to open my package later; it's time to see my girl.

There she is.

I see her, my Allie. She's laughing at something her friend said, and the sound of her voice makes me want to run across this dirty bar and scoop her up into my arms. She's at a high-top table in skinny jeans and a white V-neck T-shirt, a silver necklace with a heart at the end of it hanging loosely in her cleavage. It's such a simple ensemble, one that would leave any other woman looking less than attractive, but not her.

I want nothing more than to walk by her table and take in the fruity scent of her chocolate brown hair, but I know better. Even though it's obvious she styled it just for me, because it's exactly how I like it—loose and flowing across her shoulders, curled at the ends so it has just a little bounce.

She smiles, and it's intoxicating. God, those lips…if I could just—

"What can I get ya?" an overly chirpy voice echoes in my ear.

"Hmm?" I mumble back to the waitress who hovers over the table. She's startled me, the bitch. Didn't even see her coming, and I'll be damned—that's not like me. I'm usually very well aware of my surroundings, trying to blend in without being noticed. "Uh, whatever's on tap," I say.

She doesn't write it down, just nods and saunters away as if she knows I'm about to check out her ass.

I wasn't going to, but I do, anyway. Out of spite, really.

She turns and looks back over her shoulder, the cap of her pen in her mouth as she winks at me. I consider it—taking her home and fucking her senseless—for about half a second before I remember that I'm on a date and it's rude to check out another woman when you're on a date. Even ruder to imagine her naked, her tits bouncing while I—

No.

Stop it, Owen.

Allie wouldn't appreciate these thoughts very much.

Shame on me.

I risk another peek over to her table just as Allie shoves a fry into her mouth. It's incredibly sexy, the way she eats. The way her lips curl around her fingers, her dimple popping as she chews. If I hadn't seen her in the gym, I'd find myself wondering how she keeps her great figure with all the fries I've watched her eat.

I divert my eyes, careful not to overindulge. French fries have become an aphrodisiac thanks to her, and I can't afford that level of excitement in a public establishment.

Little Miss Cute Ass returns and sets a frosted mug of beer on the table in front of me. She tears a sheet of paper off from the notebook she never seems to write in and grabs my hand, tucking the slip into my palm.

"I give good head," she says, motioning to the beer mug. Her plump red lips curve into a smile and send a current straight to my dick. She heads to the table next to me with a flip of her bleached blonde hair, and I unfold the note she's given me.

There's a phone number and a name written in bubbly purple ink.

"Millie," I say aloud to myself before reaching for my beer. I take a cold sip and look back over at Millie. She's tall and lean, but not overly so on either point. Probably around five-foot-eight, a nice contrast to my six-foot-two stature, if I do say so myself. Her brazenness caught me a bit off guard, but I'm not sure why. Women hit on me all the time; I'm used to it.

I don't blame them, if I'm being honest. I'm a bit of a catch, at least in the looks department. Who doesn't love a tall bad-ass with a sleeve tattoo, blue eyes, and a full head of dark hair?

Allie, that's who.

"Have a good night!" I hear, and my eyes dart across the room. Allie and her friend wave to the bartender and exit through the front door, the dingy overhead bell announcing their departure.

"Fuck!" I mumble, slamming the mug down and jumping to my feet. The amber liquid sloshes all over the table. I pull a twenty from my wallet and toss it into the foamy puddle —*good head, my ass*—and grab my coat from the back of the chair.

Little Miss Cute Ass just ruined my date with Allie.

Fucking bitch.

I don't want to cause a scene—because all that does is

make me memorable and I'd rather no one recall that I was here—so I snatch a roll of towels from the bar and use them to wipe up the mess on the table. Millie sashays over, her hand on her hip.

"Ya know, we're hiring bartenders if you're interested," she says. "Although, you'd have to actually keep the beer in the mugs a little better." She chuckles to herself, and even though I almost want to smack her, I smile.

"You're sassy. I like that in a woman," I say despite myself. For some reason, I even wink and smile at her.

"I hoped you might," she teases with a flirtatious laugh.

"What time are you off?" I sneak a peek of her cleavage before I can stop myself, and she catches me looking, but it's her own fault and I know she likes it, so I don't look away.

She leans over and swipes the twenty off the table, stuffing it into the pocket of her apron before pressing her body to mine and bringing her lips to my ear. Her breath is warm on my neck as she whispers, "I'm off at nine o'clock. Text me your address," and then slicks her tongue along my ear lobe before she turns and walks away.

I smirk and make my way over to the exit, shaking my head.

This wasn't the evening I had planned, but a night with Millie will be better than tapping into my spank bank photos of Allie again, and even though I love her, sometimes you just gotta have the real thing.

I can only hope she'll forgive me for my transgressions.

CHAPTER SIX

Owen

Wednesday, November 12, 2014

It wasn't hard to find her, my Allie.

She wasn't mine yet, of course. She still belonged to *him,* but I knew right then and there I would find a way to remedy that. I was attending court-ordered therapy sessions with a woman who, by most definitions of the word, was a fucking bore.

Dr. Mariëtte Simms.

Apparently when you fail out of anger management but continue to harbor unresolved anger issues, the courts like to take it upon themselves to send you to the crazy doc. As if that will solve all your troubles.

As much as I despise Dr. Simms for her overly pretentious ways, I'm nothing but glad I met her. I'm glad I was forced to sit across from her in an oversized chair and share my deepest thoughts and darkest fears with her.

Therapy is my favorite time of the day.

Of course, I lied about everything just to get it over with. Isn't that what everyone does? The only reason I gave two shits about Dr. Simms and her psychoanalyzing is because it was during my first session with her, somewhere between her first condescending question and last, that I laid eyes on Allie.

Not in the flesh, no. Not on that first day.

She was smiling like an angel, in a photo that was secured in an ugly silver frame that sat on Dr. Simms's desktop, her arm around some preppy asshat in a golf shirt.

When I spotted it, Dr. Simms's gaze followed mine, and her eyes lit up with pride. I hoped she was beaming about the beautiful woman in the picture, but I should have known better.

"My-daughter in-law, Allie," she said, pointing to the frame. "And my son, Tarek." Her mouth stretched into a smile.

"Hmm?"

She's married?

To that guy?

"Well, not officially. Yet." She chuckles to herself. "But the proposal is coming soon, I just *know* it." Her face lights up, and I stifle the comments that swim around aimlessly in my head. It sounds to me like her *precious* son held onto his mommy's teat for a little longer than necessary.

"Are you in a relationship of your own, Owen?" she asks, smiling again and watching me intently.

"Yes," I say.

"I'd love to hear about it…" She leaves the sentence hanging, and her pen hovering over the page.

"It's recent," I say. "Practically brand new." I look over at the picture again. I can't seem to take my eyes off her, and I don't want to either.

"New relationships can be exciting. Stressful, too, in some ways."

"Sure."

She pauses for a beat, seemingly aware that's all she's getting out of me on that topic today. She clicks her tongue on the roof of her mouth. "Well, let's put a pin in that and come back to it, shall we?" She crosses her legs and leans back in her chair. I can see she's doing her best to appear relaxed, but it's obvious I make her nervous. She doesn't know what to expect from me, or enough about me and why I'm here, to really gauge where to take this session.

She's a good therapist in that regard, but it doesn't make me want to talk to her any more than I did when I walked in twenty minutes ago.

"Tell me about your childhood. Did you have any siblings?"

"No, just me." I remain stoic, composed.

"And what are your parents like?"

"Gone. They died in a car crash when I was eighteen," I lie. It's easier that way.

"I'm terribly sorry to hear that, Owen. That must have been hard for you."

"It was."

We continue like this for the remainder of the session, another thirty-five minutes, give or take. Not once do I give her an open-ended response. I can tell she's frustrated, but that's how I want her to feel, so this session is a success on my end.

She'll probably go home crying to husband later. They'll be in bed, and she'll turn to him and say, "I just can't get through to this one." And he'll roll his eyes with his back turned to her because he won't give a flying fuck about another one of her patients, and he just wants her to shut up.

I schedule my next appointment with the receptionist—a leggy brunette with a Cindy Crawford mole next to her upper lip—and practically jog down out of the building to my car.

I unlock it with the key fob and sit in the driver's seat, but don't stick the key in the ignition yet. I do my best to burn the image of Allie into my brain, to savor it in the few ways you can commit a single photograph to memory.

A car horn across the parking ramp jolts me back to reality, and I start the car.

What I'd really like to know, though, is how a therapist can be dumb enough to offer up personal information to a patient? Doesn't she realize the danger she's opened her family up to? Any psycho could destroy them with that little bit of information.

Dr. Simms should really be more careful.

I didn't like that she spoke of Allie so carelessly, and I decided I would get a look at her for myself—just to make sure she was safe, and that no one was bothering her.

It wasn't hard to find out who she was, not that I thought it would be. Dr. Simms is on Facebook and not well hidden; I found her profile after just a couple attempts. You'd think she'd do a better job of keeping her profile private, maybe set up a business page or some shit, but women her age don't seem to understand social media so I'm not all that surprised. Plus, she looked hot in her picture, and I think she knew that. It probably made her feel better about herself.

Once I found Dr. Simms, it was easy tracking down her son, Tarek. A simple link was direct path to his girlfriend, tagged as "in a relationship." Allie Mason.

In a relationship, it said.

Not *engaged*, not *married.*

I made a fake profile and sent the asshat a friend request to keep tabs on him—just a simple John Smith type with a random picture of an old dude, as different from me as humanly possible. Nobody questions a John Smith. Everyone knows a John Smith. And of course they'll accept the friend request because God forbid they deny an acquaintance the pleasure of accessing things like their whereabouts and pictures of the homemade pasta they cooked last week. Fucking society has gone to shit, but who am I to complain?

A few years ago I may have done things differently, maybe been a little more willing to go up and talk to the pretty girl like a normal person. But with Allie I need to do things the right way. I need to be ready for her.

I masturbated that afternoon, her pretty face playing a lead role as I imagined her plump lips around my cock, her eyes sparkling and intense as she looked up at me, my dick blocking her airway.

I would never forget her face.

She would be mine.

CHAPTER SEVEN

Owen

Thursday, May 21, 2015

The first time I saw her in person I almost couldn't believe my luck. I mean, it's not like I ran into her by chance, but still. It was almost *too* easy. After seeing her photo in Dr. Simms's office, I couldn't stop thinking about her.

I tried to tell myself to let it go, that there are plenty of fish in the sea and that my efforts would be better spent going after a more available woman—someone like Millie, perhaps.

But I couldn't get Allie out of my mind, and the more I thought about her, the more I convinced myself to go out on a limb for her.

And really, I don't know how to explain it. It was more than a simple attraction, more than wanting to fuck her and move on, like with all the other women. There was an unexplainable connection from the moment I saw her face—a gravitational pull. A force of nature or some crap like that.

So, like the grown-ass man that I am, I actively sought her

out. I researched her and observed her in her natural habitat. I followed her. I vigorously tapped out details about her into the Notes app on my phone, and I pieced together a typical day in the life of Allie Mason.

I found out where she worked—it was linked in her Facebook profile—but quickly realized she works remotely from home most of the time. That made things easier. Still, I tracked her to an office building in the Arbor Lakes area and then followed her from a safe distance when she got off work.

That led me to her apartment.

I watched her every night—rain or shine—for nearly two weeks. I stole glances of her where I could, it didn't matter where or how as I long as I could see her, feel close to her. But nothing was better than watching her at home. Most nights she sat wrapped in a blanket on the couch, her legs tucked under her as she read by the lamplight. There's something about the way her skin glows in those moments, the simplicity of her beauty when she's alone and free to be her natural self.

I could watch her like that for hours.

Sometimes I do.

All this watching, all this time I've invested, the work I've missed that I don't mind missing—I'm freelance, so it works out—has led me here, to Redstone American Grill, where I'm knocking elbows with strangers at the crowded bar, sipping my drink and pretending I'm not as pissed off as I actually am.

I took time out of my day to be here, to spend time with her. And she's here with *him*.

It makes my skin itch, watching them together, and even though I don't want to, I watch him lean in and whisper something in her ear. She laughs, throwing her head back as if that asshole could have possibly said anything worth laughing over. But she laughs, nonetheless.

It's not genuine, and she doesn't mean it. Her smile doesn't even reach her eyes, and that's a tell for her. I know because I've seen her genuine smile, and this isn't it.

For the life of me, I can't figure out why she's here with him.

I throw back the rest of my whiskey ginger ale and signal to the bartender for another. I know I shouldn't, but I can't just sit here staring at them, either. Such a thing would cause alarm, and I'm not here to cause alarm. I'm here to observe. I'm here to watch—because I'm not yet ready for anything more than that.

I didn't plan to stay so long, and I know I shouldn't have. I'm not even sure why I subject myself to this shit, but here I sit, a lonely man pining over a woman who doesn't know he exists.

A woman who doesn't have a clue what a piece-of-shit her boyfriend is.

I should tell her.

That would surely put an end to their relationship and leave me with the perfect opening to introduce myself, maybe ask her to dinner, and demonstrate my many charming qualities.

I could woo her.

But, I won't. Not yet. There's still work to do on my part. Plus, despite the fact that this boyfriend of hers is a complete tool, it would be weird to show up at her doorstep with printed copies of the photos I took of her boyfriend feeling up some chick at Cowboy Jack's last Friday night.

Completely weird.

"But, Owen, how did you know he was my boyfriend?" she'd ask innocently. "How do you know where I live, and what my name is? How do you know my bra size and that I had a Lean Cuisine for lunch today?"

That line of questioning would be damaging. Trust me, I'm no idiot. So, no, I will not make this mistake, and subsequently, scare her—and scar her—for life. I'm a firm believer a cheater always gets caught eventually, anyway. No sense in being the unnecessary bearer of bad news.

Although, I could leave her a note…maybe send a random text from a burner phone; I suppose those are easy enough to come by. I make a mental note to pick one up on the way home.

Just in case.

The second drink appears in front of me, and my mother's face flashes before my eyes before I can manage to take the first sip. I can't bring myself to do it.

The one-drink limit wins again.

Anything to avoid turning out like Mother Dearest.

I grab my wallet from my back pocket and pull out two twenties, sliding them under the glass and popping myself up from the bar stool that's caused my left ass cheek to go numb. I flip my hood over my head and start walking, my feet heavy against the tiled floor.

I can't watch this anymore; this fucker needs to go.

CHAPTER EIGHT

Allie

Thursday, May 21, 2015

My feet pound the treadmill, the hum of the track putting my mind at ease as I run. It's exactly what I needed to clear my head. After a solid three miles, my thighs are burning, the muscles loose like jelly. I push the cool-down button on the machine and my pace slows, the drum of my heartbeat in my ears. I take a sip from my water bottle and reach for a hand towel. Sweat drips from my face, and my yoga pants stick to my thighs like taffy on the roof of your mouth.

I'm spent, but in all the right ways.

I hop down from the machine, taking a quick moment to wipe it down, and then head to the locker room for a shower, towel drying my hair and then twisting it into a bun on top of my head. My cell vibrates from the side pocket of my gym bag, and I pull it out and glance at the screen to find a text from Tarek.

Redstone American Grill, 7:00

How original, I think to myself.

Tarek and I *always* go to dinner on Thursday nights. Or I cook, which truth be told I don't mind all that much. But when it's expected of me it's a bit less enjoyable and more like a chore.

And Tarek tends to expect it.

I text back a thumbs up emoji and slump my bag over my shoulder, mentally preparing myself to relive the same Thursday night I've had every week for months, perhaps years. Tarek means well, I'm sure, but this mundane predictability is really starting to get to me. With a huff, I push through the locker room door and wave a quick goodbye to the front desk receptionist, Britney. She smiles and waves back, but then jogs over to me as I reach the main door.

"Allie, one sec!" she calls. "Someone left this for you."

"Oh, thanks," I say as she hands me a small piece of paper. Curious as to who would leave a note for me at the gym, I read it once I step outside.

You're just as beautiful covered in sweat as you are stretched out on the couch with a book.

Stuffing the note in the back pocket of my jeans, I can't help but smile while I walk to my car. My eyes scan the parking lot, but I don't see Tarek anywhere, and for some reason that makes the coy delivery of his note even sweeter.

Perhaps this won't be just like every other Thursday.

By the time our food comes, Tarek's already had a few too many drinks. I push my wine off to the side and use my fork to pick at my grilled chicken salad. The restaurant is packed, typical for a Thursday evening, and I'm grateful for the distraction.

"Do you not like the wine?" Tarek asks when he sees me set aside my glass.

"It's good, actually," I admit. "I'm not really in the mood to drink though."

He considers that for a moment before throwing back the rest of his drink. I think he's had a rough day at the office, but he hasn't said as much. In fact, he's quieter than usual tonight, and I don't know what to make of it. He sets his empty glass on the edge of the table and signals the waitress for another, his eyes lingering on her backside as she walks away.

I let him look, and watch as he does, but he doesn't notice. His attention is too focused.

"Mother is expecting you for lunch on Sunday," he says a few minutes later. "So, I'll pick you up around eleven?"

"Actually, can I skip it this week? I have a lot on my plate at work and—"

"Allie," he interrupts. "We've been over this. Sunday lunch isn't optional anymore. It's rude of you to skip it for work."

I inhale a deep breath and then nod to avoid an argument.

"What's up with you tonight, babe? Lighten up a bit." He smiles and reaches across the table to place his hand over mine. It's warm—comforting—and I relax against my seat.

"You're right, I'm sorry. It's just been a long week, and I'm a bit tired."

Abruptly, he slides his chair next to me and pulls me to him, his arm lazily looped across my shoulders. I feel his breath on my ear, and he kisses my ear lobe, sending a jolt of electricity straight to my nipples.

"Mmm," I accidentally moan. Tarek chuckles, and I slap a hand over my mouth, giggling at my public arousal.

"Ready to get out of here?" Tarek asks, and I nod, sucking my bottom lip in anticipation.

We barely make it into my apartment before Tarek's hands are all over me, roaming my body. He slides the strap of my maxi dress off my shoulder and his hand hovers over my collar bone, his fingers teasing the sensitive skin. He presses his lips to mine and his kiss is urgent, his arousal evident against my hip.

I drop my clutch on the floor and return his aggression, the need for release urgent and intense.

We stumble together to the bedroom and make love with a fervor I haven't seen from Tarek since college. His kisses are full of passion, and my body responds in all the right ways.

When he enters me it's primal, so unlike our usual love-making, and afterward, as I lay on his chest while he snores softly, I wonder if the spark between us has somehow been reignited.

If perhaps we'll be okay after all.

The next morning I meet Court for breakfast at Caribou Coffee before work, tired and sore from the night's unexpected events.

"Looks like someone had a late night," Court teases, sipping her vanilla latte. She smirks, knowing Tarek and I had plans for dinner, and I kick her gently under the table. She laughs, and I toss a napkin at her.

"How did you know?"

"Ah, hello! Your face is a dead giveaway. You got laid." She cups her hand to shield her mouth and leans over the table. "*And* you got off!" she whisper shouts.

"Courtney!"

"Tell me I'm wrong," she challenges.

And I can't help it, I smirk, and instantly feel a fire under my cheeks.

"I knew it!"

"Okay, *yes,* fine. You're right." I roll my eyes as if I'm annoyed at how well my best friend knows me, but the truth is, I'm not. I knew she'd see right through me the second we sat down for coffee.

"Tell me, tell me!" she hisses, quietly banging her fists on the table and bouncing in her chair. I swear, Courtney lives for a good sex story.

I spill the juicy details, not shying away, but gloating quietly enough that the *yentas* at the table next to us don't hear.

"Ugh, I'm so jealous," Court whines.

"I honestly don't know what came over him, Court. He was a like a new man. Attentive. Mysterious. Gracious. It's *never* been *that* good between us."

Court sits back in her chair and scrunches her nose.

"What?" I ask, knowing she's up to something.

"I have a bit of a secret…" she admits.

"Spill it," I say.

"I may have mentioned something to Tarek about the, um…'lack of passion' in your relationship." She uses air quotes to emphasize my own words, throwing them back at me while I wish like hell I could un-say them. She sinks into her seat, as if the chair will protect her from the anger bubbling inside me.

"You…did…WHAT!"

"I'm sorry! Look, he reached out to me, okay? A few days after your trip, and it was right after you mentioned, you know, the lack of passion…to me." She does the air quotes again. "He was miserable, Allie, trying to figure out what the hell's going on with you all the time."

"It wasn't your secret to tell, Court."

"I know. But Al, you have to admit—without my meddling you would have been missing out on something beautiful! I helped, and you know it," she says, pointing a finger in my direction.

She's right, to a point. I know she is. But it doesn't change the fact that she went behind my back, that she shared something so private with my boyfriend. The sex with Tarek was amazing, yes, but it was so out of character, and now I know why. He didn't genuinely *want* to make love to me the way he did, he did it because he felt like he *had* to, and now I wish it never happened.

"I trusted you, Court," I say.

"I know, and I'm sorry. Truly. I didn't mean to hurt you, and honestly, you were never supposed to find out anyway. I just wanted to help."

Despite my annoyance, I let Courtney off the hook, because like she said, she just wanted to help. That's who she is, and I know there were no ill intentions behind what she did.

What bothers me more is that Tarek betrayed me, too. Like a desperate teenager, he went behind my back and asked *my* best friend for help getting our relationship back on track instead of talking to me like an adult.

I can't help but think his betrayal stings a bit less than it should.

CHAPTER NINE

Allie

Sunday, May 24, 2015

It's Sunday afternoon, and Tarek's family is gathered at his parent's place for lunch, just as we are every Sunday. It's Memorial Day weekend, but apparently because we don't have a boat or own a family cabin in the woods somewhere, there's no excuse to miss Sunday lunch. The Simms family is very routine and likes to stick to tradition. Never mind the fact that I have my own family, and that sometimes I like to spend time with them too. But not on Sundays, of course, because Sundays belong to the Simms family.

And they're sticklers about it, like church people are about church.

The Simms come from money: trust funds and stocks and bonds and investment banking. It's all a little over my head, really, but the money is there. The Simms are loaded.

And I couldn't care less.

But the main reason I tried to bail on today's lunch—the

prickliest thorn in my side at these lunches—is Tarek's mother. Dr. Mariëtte Simms, licensed therapist, or whatever her title is these days. She's a bit much; overbearing, if you want to know the truth. Demanding. Condescending. She sits on a fairly high horse—and I'll admit, she's earned it for the most part—but one word I'll never use to describe Mariëtte is humble. And for some reason she adores me.

I haven't quite figured out why.

Perhaps because I'm the Yes Girl.

Tarek's mother talks about me as if I'm already her daughter-in-law, which didn't bother me in the beginning; I was quite honored back then, actually. But after six years with her son and no engagement to celebrate, no expensive wedding to plan, she's become a bit relentless. And I get it, really, I do. She wants her son to be happy, and she thinks I'm the one to do that.

Mariëtte Simms operates under the assumption that her son and I will get married, produce no less than three point five children, and live nearby in an expensive home equipped with a pool and a live-in nanny.

Just like she did.

So, to say I'm a bit on edge today would be an understatement. I don't want to be here, sipping pretentious wine with my not-quite-in-laws. I'd much rather be doing something else I hate, like filing my taxes or cleaning the toilet. But because I'm expected to be here—as Tarek said—I refrain from pouting and take a large, un-ladylike sip of my wine instead. It's tart on my tonguc, kinda like the mood I'm in, because no more than two minutes after Tarek and I arrived at Mariëtte and Steven's, Mariëtte took my hand and dragged me through a thirty-minute tour of their newly remodeled guest house. She even made sure to point out all the high-end changes, not shying away from announcing prices as she did so. The updates look great, don't get me wrong, but it's a bit too fancy for my liking.

And the guest house rarely gets any use. I can think of about a million other things she could have done with that money, but I'll let that subject rest for now.

After the tour, everyone moved out to the poolside patio, where we were served expensive salads and perfectly cooked filet mignon, prepared by the Simms's catering chef. It was fucking delicious, and I almost hate myself for loving it.

"Did you hear Mother's question, Allie?" Tarek asks once we've moved to the sitting area. He nudges my arm, and red wine spills from my glass onto my lap, making a wet spot on my sundress. I sigh under my breath, dabbing at it with a cocktail napkin and then look over to Mariëtte with a lazy smile.

"I'm sorry, no. What was that, Mariëtte?" Everyone's eyes are on me, and I choke down a sudden rush of nerves. It doesn't matter how many of these lunches I sit in on, the Simms still manage to rattle me.

Tristan, Tarek's older brother by two years, and a spitting image of their father—preppy and clean-cut, with gorgeous blond hair he doesn't even know what to do with—mumbles something to Steven, and they chuckle to themselves like the rich assholes they are. They are the two members of the Simms family I tend to avoid more than Mariëtte, never to be left in a room alone with them, because they love a good, old-fashioned sexual innuendo, and both seem to have less of a filter the more you get to know them. They'll talk your ear off about politics and religion as if you give a damn, but disagree with them you shall not.

Mariëtte sits across from me wearing a cocktail dress and heels. She smiles kindly, but I know I've disappointed her with my inattentiveness. As a therapist, she's always trying to get to the heart of everything. She'll want to know what's distracted me today; why she hasn't managed to capture my undivided attention.

It's kind of her *thing,* trying to get through to me. I'm struck again by how different she is from my own mother, a homemaker even after her adult children left the nest.

"Dear, I asked if you'll prefer navy or burgundy for the bridesmaid dresses," Mariëtte asks—apparently for the second time.

I'd say "I told you so" but I'm sure you already knew that was coming—the unsolicited wedding talk and assumptions that I'll marry her son and change my last name, proud to become the wife of a Simms man. That I'll give up my body to the art of baby-making, only to name one of them after her, my dearest mother-in-law.

Allie Elizabeth Simms, so nice to meet you.

Okay, fine—I'm whining. I know. I suppose it doesn't sound *that* bad, and I'm probably just pre-menstrual today. I'm grateful for Tarek's family, I really am. I just don't think I fit in with them, that's all.

I try not to roll my eyes, but frustration booms like thunder in my chest, and I know the words are about to fall out, that there's not much I can do to stop them. Still, I force myself to remain civil.

"I really haven't given it any thought. Tarek and I aren't even engaged." I try to say it politely—matter-of-factly—but my annoyance drips from my tongue, and there's *tone.* There's always tone. "Excuse me a moment," I say, standing abruptly.

I beeline to the sliding glass door off the patio and place my wineglass on the kitchen counter, surprised it doesn't shatter at the stem from the force. I stomp down to the lower-level bathroom, locking the door behind me and leaning against it.

Drawing in a few deep breaths, I do my best to calm down. To relax, and try to enjoy the lovely afternoon Mariëtte has put together for her family. A family she desperately wishes I'll be a part of soon. I feel like she knows something I don't, and it hits me in that moment that Tarek must be gearing up to propose again. I ruined his first plan last weekend, and apparently now it's time to try again.

Mariëtte probably even helped him pick out the ring. Something astronomically large and shiny that'll catch on everything and snag my favorite sweater.

I know I should be grateful that a wonderful man wants to marry me and make babies with me. But I can't help feeling suffocated. I'm not ready for such a domesticated life, and I'm certainly not ready for babies.

Something is off, and has been for some time. It's suddenly clear to me that I need to end things with Tarek before he proposes. I can't keep putting this off. We want different things. Him, a giant house full of children and a wife who stays home with them and attends all the PTA meetings, drives the carpool, the soccer van.

I don't even like soccer.

And me? I don't know what I want out of life yet, but it's certainly not that. I want more (remember Ariel?). I pull my phone from the pocket of my dress and shoot a text off to Courtney that lets her know we're having a girl's night tonight.

At her place, where Tarek can't show up uninvited.

She replies immediately, the dancing dots that signify she's typing barely flashing on the screen before her response comes through. "Bring the wine," it says, which is Courtney Code for you-better-bring-something-stronger-than-wine.

Sounds like my BFF had a rough day, too.

A knock at the door startles me. "Allie? You okay in there?" Tarek asks. I adjust myself in the mirror and take another deep breath. I wish I'd brought my wine in with me, maybe the entire bottle, but I suppose beggars can't be choosers, huh?

"I'll be out in a minute," I yell back.

I text Court again, take a deep breath, and then head back out to the patio without stopping for my wine glass.

Court calls my cell phone ten minutes later—on the dot—with an "emergency." Something about being locked out of her house, and of course, I happen to have the only other key. I excuse myself and thank Mariëtte for lunch. The look on Tarek's face when he hands over the keys to his BMW tells me this breakup won't come easy.

I consider stopping home to pack a change of clothes and an overnight bag before heading to Court's, but I decide I'm too angry to care and find myself inside the liquor store instead. I don't peruse. I don't ask for suggestions or leisurely sample the display wines like I usually do. Instead I march straight to the whiskey aisle and swipe a medium-sized bottle of Crown Royal from the shelf. I turn and take a few steps toward the register before stopping abruptly and heading back to exchange the medium bottle for a much larger, more serious one. Economy size, I guess you could call it.

I pay for the liquor and drive across town to Court's single-story rambler, parking Tarek's BMW in the driveway and stuffing the keys in my purse. He's texted four times already, even though I left less than a half hour ago. I roll my eyes and ignore the alert indicating another text has come through, and shove my phone into my purse next to the keys.

I'm over it. I'm done playing nice today.

I swipe my giant bottle of liquor from the back seat—now covertly hidden inside a brown paper bag—and slam the door closed. Court's already at the front door when I make my way up the sidewalk, a "poor you" expression taking over her face. Truth be told, I'm still a little upset with her for sharing my secret with Tarek, but I swallowed most of that bitterness on the drive over here. Court tilts her head to the side like a bird and looks at me as if I showed up wearing a chicken suit. Like me, she wears her emotions smack-dab in the middle of her face, which is nice because I always know what I'm going to get with her.

Also, *not* nice because I always know what I'm going to get with her.

"Oh damn, girl. What happened?" she asks, reaching out and taking the brown paper bag from me. I grumble and step into the house, dropping my purse on the entryway floor. The thud echoes in the airy space. "That bad, huh?" she asks when I walk straight past her toward the living room.

"Yeah," I huff. I plop down on the gray love seat while Court heads to her newly remodeled kitchen—courtesy of her annual bonus—to mix our drinks. She knows how I like mine, and I trust she'll make it extra strong in consideration of my mood.

"I can't do this anymore, Court," I say, well aware that it comes out sounding like the whine of a toddler. "I *have* to end things with Tarek…with his family. I'm drowning here."

"Sunday Funday was that bad?"

"Yes."

"Do elaborate..." she teases as the ice maker kicks on. She fills the glasses and sets them on the counter, adding a heavy double pour to both before topping them off with Diet Coke and lime wedges and making her way to the living room.

I take the glass from her hand and suck down half of it before wiping my mouth with the back of my hand. Classy, I'm sure.

"Thirsty?"

"Mariëtte has our entire fucking wedding planned," I spit out, ignoring her jab.

"No..." Her eyes go wide and she shakes her head. Court has always had a flair for the dramatics, and while it usually drives me slightly crazy, today it's just what I need.

"Yes," I continue. "At this rate I'll be married by next fall."

"Wait. Did he propose again?" she asks, sipping her drink, her eyes still oddly wide.

"No. Not yet, anyway. Stop looking at me like that," I wave in her direction and her face returns to normal. "But I have a feeling it's coming sooner than later with the way Mariëtte's acting. She's not even being subtle anymore." I roll my eyes again, this time falling back against the couch in the process. I'm being ridiculous, but because I'm well aware of my theatrics, it's okay.

So I tell myself.

"Okay, let's back up a second. There's more here than what you're saying, and I know this isn't the first conversation we've had about your soon-to-be mother-in-law"—she winks—"but come on, Allie. What gives?"

She's right. I know she is. Mariëtte certainly isn't *that* bad and any woman would be lucky to have a mother-in-law as invested as she is.

But I'm not *any* woman, and I don't feel all that lucky right now.

"It's too much, Court. I don't want to marry Tarek. I don't want to be a Simms, and there's no way in hell I can deal with a helicopter mother-in-law like Mariëtte for the rest of my life."

My phone beeps from my purse and I gesture toward the entryway where it still sits haphazardly on the floor. "See? That's probably Tarek *again*, calling to bitch about me leaving early and embarrassing him."

"Are you gonna answer it?" she asks. When I make no effort to get up, she sets her drink on the table and leans forward, placing a hand on my knee. "Al, I think it's time to cut this off before it gets worse. Put your big girl panties on and just do it."

"Just do it, huh?

"Yeah, be like Nike. Or whatever."

She jogs to the entryway and shoves her hand into my purse, pulling out the phone I wish didn't exist and peeking at the screen. "You took his car?" she asks.

"I took his car," I confirm, raising my drink in the air and then throwing back the final sip.

"He wants to come pick it up. Says he'll take an Uber and wants to know where you are."

I roll my eyes, and Court takes the hint. "Got it. Not telling the BF where we are." She clicks her tongue and throws back the rest of her drink. "I would have come to get you, you know."

I nod. "I know."

"Another?" she asks, taking my empty glass.

"Indeed."

"All right. I'm over the moping. Let's do something fun." She takes our glasses to the kitchen and mixes another round, rattling off ideas as she does. “Wanna go dancing? We haven’t done that in forever!”

“Meh. I’m not really up for dancing. Plus, you and I both know we always end up leaving early when the wanna-be pimps start grinding on us.” She laughs and concedes.

“Shopping? MOA probably has some sales going on.”

“Too people-y. You know I hate the Mall of America,” I argue.

“Oh yeah, good point.” She comes back to the living room with fresh drinks and hands mine over, setting hers on a perfectly placed coaster before slumping down next to me and leaning back against the cushion.

“Ya know, you’re really ornery for twenty-six,” she teases. We give each other a knowing look and lace our fingers together.

“I know.”

This was just what I needed.

“Movie Night!” we say in unison.

CHAPTER TEN

Allie

Tuesday, May 26, 2015

I spend the rest of the holiday weekend at Court's watching 80s rom-coms and eating junk food. She drops me off at home Tuesday morning and then heads into the office. Tarek picked up his car yesterday, a grimace on his face as he climbed into the driver's seat. I handed Court his keys and waited inside while they chatted in the driveway. He wasn't happy I took the car for so long—or that I never went back to Mariëtte's—but I tell myself it's no big deal. It's just Tarek being Tarek.

I've been in a stabby mood all morning, stewing on it. My impending breakup with Tarek is starting to weigh me down, and while Court has been supportive, she seems to think ending things with him would be a big mistake. She thinks I haven't thought things through, that I'm throwing away a future. But I have. I've been teetering this line for months, and my misery is only getting worse.

So I've dodged Tarek for the better part of the week—using work as an excuse to avoid him—even going to the office a couple extra days to drive the point home in case he tries to stop by my apartment.

It's now Thursday again, and if I keep this up, Franklin will get used to my presence and before I know it I'll be back to working full time on site. I can't have that. I need my space at home.

Franklin—the heavy breather that he is—hovers over me like a vulture as he's done for the better part of the morning. We're discussing a manuscript from a debut author, Robert Green, and if it were up to me I'd sign the guy on the spot—his characterization is impeccable—but Franklin the Grouch isn't sure it's "hip" enough to be a bestseller.

I look up at him with a pained expression on my face, certain the man wouldn't know the meaning of the word hip if he'd written the definition himself.

"Franklin, really, this guy has *it.*" I argue, taking a sip of water. I shuffle the pages around on the executive table we're sitting at even though we're the only two people here.

"I don't know, Allie. I don't feel it. The plot needs work."

"Which is where we come in…"

"Developmental editing takes time and money, you know that. We don't have that kinda time. Or money." He slides a page over to me, pointing at a passage with his signature red pen. "Look, here." He circles the paragraph for dramatic effect, or maybe just to make sure I'm looking at the right section, but still, it feels extreme and manages to annoy the shit out of me. "His protagonist gets sent to prison for a crime he doesn't commit, and then gets sentenced to forty years. Forty!" He's nearly yelling now, and I'm not sure that amount of anger is warranted for this situation. "They don't send money launderers to prison for forty years. Not even the worst of them."

He sits back in his chair like his point has been proved. I lean forward.

"I get it, Franklin, I really do. But that's a technicality we can work with." I slide the page back to his side of the table. He sighs and shoves it back into the stack with the remaining pages.

"It's not…truly. Lowering the prison sentence would change the entire time line of the manuscript. It literally changes everything."

His calendar alert goes off, and he quickly stacks the pages and scoops them into his arms before sliding his glasses to the top of his head. The ones he claims he only needs for reading, but any idiot can see that's just wishful thinking. "We'll continue this discussion later," he says, exiting the room. I gather my things and do the same, making my way back to my desk.

I know I can't give up on this story, but I make a mental note to try again in a few days once he's had some time to sit on it. Franklin is clearly stressed about something and is taking his frustrations out on this manuscript.

"Hey you."

I hear the familiar voice and do my best to withhold any negative physical reaction from my face. Tarek stands in the doorway to my office, his back against the frame and his arms folded across his chest. He smiles, and I do my best to smile back and feign excitement.

Why I continue to fake it with this man, I do not know.

"Babe, what are you doing here?" I stop just in front of him, but don't reach for him. He notices, and leans forward to plant a kiss on my lips. I move past him and relieve my arms of the paperwork, setting the manuscript on the edge of my desk.

"I thought I'd surprise you and take you out to lunch."

"I'm kinda busy…"

He huffs, his smile forming into a pout. "You've been busy all week," he whines.

"I know, I'm sorry." I offer nothing more.

"Then dinner tonight."

"What about it?"

"I'll come over."

"Tarek—"

"No, babe, really. I'll come over, and we'll have a nice romantic dinner at your place. I know you're still upset about my mom last Sunday, and that's fine. I get it, she can be a bit much. But don't shut me out, sweetie." He steps in front of me again and takes my chin between his fingers. "I miss you," he whispers.

"Fine," I say, relaxing against the palm of his hand. He presses his lips to mine and lingers longer than socially acceptable for an office setting.

"I'll see you tonight, my love," he says, leaving the room. I sink down into my office chair and wonder how I manage to sit up straight without a backbone.

It certainly feels like mine is missing.

Around five I remove my bag from the bottom drawer of my desk and slip my laptop inside. My phone vibrates with a text from Tarek confirming he'll be over around six. Really all that means is that he's expecting me to cook him a nice dinner—after working all day, no less—and then throw on "something sexy" for him.

Which I won't be doing.

I'll cook, sure, but only because a girl's gotta eat. I tap out a quick response and grab a sticky note and a pen from my desk to make a quick grocery list. He'll expect my signature lasagna, which is arguably the best home-cooked meal on the planet, but doesn't bode well for romance, in my opinion. It's too heavy of a meal and always leaves me gassy.

Which is exactly why it's on the menu for tonight.

I'm a coward, I know this. I'm pretty sure Tarek even knows this, which is why we're still together the following morning, our limbs a tangled mess between the sheets. It's why he's spent another night in my bed, and why I willingly dragged him into my bedroom—while the lasagna baked—and asked for a repeat of last week.

He willingly complied.

CHAPTER ELEVEN

Allie

Friday, May 30, 2015

Armed with a to-go cup of coffee and a glazed donut, I make my way into the office again. I'm starting to miss the comfort of my living room workspace and the lack of interruption it brings, but I sigh—grateful at least that it's Friday. Nonetheless, I'm cranky and under-caffeinated despite my mug of coffee, so the fact that I get to spend the whole day with Franklin does nothing to improve my mood. We still don't see eye to eye on the Robert Green book, and I'm starting to doubt we ever will.

"Morning, Franklin," I chime as I walk by his office toward the one I share with Courtney. He waves without looking up from his computer, already tied up on a conference call despite the early hour.

When I get to my office and open the door, I'm hit with a strong floral scent. A vase of long stem red roses sits on my desk. I set down my purse and laptop bag and then pick the card out of the bouquet.

Dinner, 7:00. I'll pick you up. Dress nice. Love, Tarek

I send a text to Tarek thanking him for the flowers and then another to my Mom telling her I'll call her later; she's already called and texted this morning. I know she's been itching for me to come home for a visit, and I haven't had the energy with how busy work has been. The slew of heart emojis she texts back makes me smile, and I promise myself I'll go home soon.

Once I figure out what to do about Tarek, that is.

After drinks arrive, Tarek seems a bit fidgety. He wipes a bead of sweat from his brow and clears his throat for the umpteenth time.

"Are you okay?" I ask, wondering if he may be coming down with a cold or something.

"Me? Yeah, I'm fine. Why?" he asks, too nonchalantly. I narrow my eyes at him, and that's when I see them.

Violinists.

Heading straight for our table, the romantic first notes of Elvis Presley's *Can't Help Falling in Love* echoing throughout the expanse of the dining room.

Oh, no.

My eyes dart around the room, at the couples enjoying their dinners, a middle-aged woman with a tear in her eye as she watches in awe, waiting to see Tarek drop to a knee before me. I look at him, fear in my eyes, panic knocking in my chest, but Tarek doesn't notice, because why would he? This is his moment, the one he's planned over and over again because of my quiet attempts to stop it from happening. He reaches across the table, taking my hand in his, and now my breath catches in my throat and tears swell in my eyes.

I can't do this.

I can't let this man propose to me, knowing deep down that I don't want this life for us. Slowly, I pull my hand back and he knows.

"Allie?"

"Tarek, I…"

His face falls, and I see it then. The moment he realizes the inevitable is happening.

That this is the end for us.

"Please, no…" he pleads. I drop my chin to my chest, unable to look him in the eye. *Can't he see this hurts me, too?*

"I'm so sorry, Tarek. I can't let you do this," I whisper, my heart hammering in my chest. "I don't—it's not what I want."

"Please, Allie…I wanted to do this a week ago and didn't get the chance. You're my everything. I—"

All the words I need to say, everything that's been on my mind for so long, suddenly gets lost in my head. I can't say them, I can't properly explain to him how suffocated I feel. By him, his family.

When I look up, there are tears in his eyes. He holds the pale turquoise ring box in his hands, but doesn't open it. I reach across the table and place my hand over the box.

"I'm so sorry," I whisper.

He doesn't move. Doesn't even look up at me, as I stand and tuck my clutch under my arm. I lean over and place a gentle kiss on his forehead and I walk away, leaving this man that I've loved for so long alone at the table, heartbreak written all over his face.

When I step out onto the sidewalk, the heavy boulder that has sat on my chest for months finally lifts.

And I breathe.

CHAPTER TWELVE

Allie

Friday, June 5, 2015

After a trip to the gym and a quick shower, I dress in jeans and a hoodie and start prepping food for dinner. Dad and Linc are in town for tomorrow's Twins game, so they're coming for dinner tonight. I've been looking forward to their visit for weeks, and when the intercom doorbell finally rings, I run to let them inside.

"How's my Allie-Gator?" Dad asks, pulling me in for a hug. His are the best, and I don't get enough of them these days. He lets go and pulls a plastic container full of Mom's famous chocolate chip cookies from behind his back.

"I knew there was a reason I love you!" I tease, taking the cookies off his hands. Linc comes in behind him and closes the door.

"Hey, save some for me," he whines, slipping his shoes off.

"What's on the menu tonight?" Dad asks, following me

into the kitchen. He claps and then rubs his hands together like he's trying to start a fire in the woods.

"Kale salads and tofu," I say, my face stoic. "It's time we all start eating healthier."

Linc groans, and I can't help but smirk as Dad nearly does the same. The Mason men wouldn't put kale or tofu near their mouths if you paid them. "I'm kidding!" I say, chuckling at myself as their faces return to normal. I slide a pair of oven mitts over my hands and pull the oven door open, grabbing the Pyrex dish and placing it on the stove. "I made chicken enchiladas; how's that sound?"

"Oh, thank God. I was about to call the pizza place," Linc jokes, feigning to wipe the sweat from his brow. I remove the foil from the dish and the three of us hover over it, inhaling the steam and nearly drooling from the smell. "Ahhh," we say in unison. I grab a spatula and start divvying the pieces.

"Dad, do you want to get us some plates? Linc, the toppings are in the fridge, do you mind grabbing them?"

We dish up our food and take our seats at the table, each of us quietly indulging in the first few bites of our enchiladas.

"Your brother and I are checking out that Rush Creek Golf Course on Sunday," Dad finally says after a few minutes. "You interested?"

"I don't golf, Dad."

"I know, but maybe it's time to start, huh?" He tips his head my way and takes another bite.

"Maybe one day. I don't think I have the patience for it. It doesn't sound like much fun to me."

"Well, maybe some other time then."

"You'd be a terrible golfer anyway, Al," Lincoln offers, speaking with his mouth full. "I'm sure you'd shank just about every ball and you'd get what—at least a quadruple bogey on *every* hole." He laughs at his joke while Dad withholds a snort.

Meanwhile I can't get over the terms he's using right now. "Shank? Bogey? What language are you speaking, Linc?"

He laughs and shakes his head, exchanging a knowing look with Dad.

"Where's Mom when you need her?" I tease, getting up from the table to clear my plate. I cover the enchilada dish with tinfoil and stick it in the fridge before starting on the dishes.

"How are you *really* doing, peanut?" Dad asks, nudging my arm as he comes up behind me with a towel. He grabs a plate and starts drying it, and I stop scrubbing for a moment, exhaling while my shoulders slump.

"You know me too well, Dad," is all I say.

"Yes, and don't you forget it," he teases. "Your mother and I worry about you out here on your own."

"I know, Dad. But I'm not on my own. I have Court and…" I stop myself as I'm about to say Tarek's name, the habit not an easy one to quit.

Dad smiles and dries his hands on a dishtowel. "All right, kiddo." He pats my back and reaches for another cookie. "Talk to your mother," he says. "She'll want to hear whatever it is from *you*, not from your old man."

And I smile, nodding and shoving another of Mom's cookies into my mouth. Despite being a man of few words, Dad always seems to know what to say.

By mid-morning Saturday, I'm about a hundred pages into the first manuscript of the weekend when the intercom doorbell rings and makes me jump.

I push the stacks of paper from my lap and shove off the couch, trotting to the foyer and unlocking the deadbolt. The door swings open and it's not the delivery service.

It's Tarek. Uninvited, and holding a Caribou Coffee bag in his hand.

He pushes it forward and raises a brow. "For you," he says. "One of those lemon cake things you like." I don't tell him I stopped eating those months ago, despite their deliciousness. Instead I take the bag and hold it awkwardly while Tarek tries to peer into my apartment.

I lean against the door, blocking his view for no reason other than I don't plan to let him in. I'll need to speak with the doorman and make sure he's removed from the pre-approved visitors list.

Despite Tarek's near wordless response the night I ended things between us, he hasn't taken our breakup particularly well, based on his presence now, along with the slew of unread text messages and unanswered voicemails he's left on my phone the last few days.

You can't do this to us.

I've done everything for you.

This doesn't make sense, Allie. We're supposed to be together.

We should have had at least one child by now—that's why you're bored. You need someone to mother, someone to love.

Why aren't you answering me? I'm worried about you. Don't do anything stupid.

I hate conflict. Always have, always will. So when the series of text messages started, all I could do was ignore them wholeheartedly and silently watch as they piled up, growing more concerning each day I failed to respond.

I can't believe you're doing this.

How could you be so fucking stupid?

You WILL marry me, Allie Mason. I will see to it.

It hurts me to hurt him, but at this point there's no other way, I refuse to take part in a childish exchange of messages that does nothing but result in the same conversation over and over. Part of me thought he would have taken this better than he has, while another says I had it coming; I should have just responded and asked him to move on. If I had, he wouldn't be standing at my doorstep right now.

Six years with this man and somehow I still can't read him.

But I exhale slowly and drop the tough-girl act once I get a good look at his face. It's obvious he's been crying. It's obvious he's heartbroken. His usually styled hair is unkempt, and he's sporting several days of stubble on his chin. His designer jeans are wrinkled, and the T-shirt I bought him last year on our trip to Mexico sports a stain beneath the collar—very unlike Tarek.

I don't think I've *ever* seen him like this. Not even when his grandmother passed a few years ago. My heart pangs a bit at the sight of him, and I suck in a breath.

"Tarek, I'm not sure you should be here," I say softly, as if consoling a child.

"Please, Allie. Talk to me," he pleads and nudges his way inside. His hands find mine, and we stand there together in silence for a moment. I can't look him in the eye; I can't watch him hurt like this, knowing it's my fault he feels this way.

He leads me to the living room. "Let's sit and talk."

I don't want to talk anymore, I remind myself.

"I think you should go." My voice wavers, even though I'm confident on the inside. I don't want him here, but I've never been able to tell this man no, so the fact that I suddenly am is a bit of a shock to both our systems.

"Allie, this is ridiculous. You and I are great together, and you know that. We have a future planned, for Christ's sakes."

I can't help it, I raise my voice a little when these words register in my ears. *How dare he?*

"No, *you* have a future planned for us, Tarek. Not me. It's always been about what *you* want and what *you* or your mother thinks is best for us."

He pulls me to him and forces his arms around my body. I want to resist, to pull away, but the smell of his cologne wafts into my senses and renders my limbs immobile. There's comfort here, familiarity. His fingers rake through my hair and I inhale a breath, reluctantly wrapping an arm around his torso.

"There's my girl," he coos, taking my head into his hands. His green eyes bore into mine, and I still can't read them. I've never been able to read them, and that's what scares me—to have no idea what thoughts go through this man's head from one day to the next. Tarek is a man of many emotions, but few words.

He places a soft kiss on my forehead and then pulls away, motioning toward the living room. I don't move until he does, but then like always, I follow him.

"We can work this out, babe," he says, his eyes wandering to my cleavage in a scoop neck sweatshirt. Or maybe my neck, I'm not sure. I reach for the television remote for no reason other than to occupy my hands. His stare is starting to make me uncomfortable.

"No, Tarek. I'm sorry, but we can't." I say it softly, but he recoils as if I've slapped him, quickly jumping to his feet.

"This is fucking bullshit, Allie!" The vibrato of his baritone voice echoes in the small space, and I flinch at the sudden shift in his demeanor. "What the hell has gotten into you? We're supposed to be together, a team!" He runs his fingers through his disheveled hair and paces in front of the window. I know I need to respond, but I don't really have the words. Not the ones he wants to hear, and I don't have it in me to keep going back and forth like this. I sit back against the couch, my hands folded in my lap. "Really? You have *nothing* to say?" he barks.

"I've said all I need to say."

And I have—last week when I ended our relationship. I told the truth—mostly—that I've fallen out of love with him. That I'm not ready for a family.

That I need some time to myself.

I left out all the unnecessarily hurtful stuff—about his overbearing family and their 1950s views on marriage—to spare his feelings. To put some of the blame on myself.

"There's someone else. Isn't there?" Tarek accuses, shaking his head back and forth. "That's the *only* logical explanation for this. Don't you realize what you're giving up? I'm a fucking catch—you know that as well as I do!" He stabs his pointer finger into his chest as he tells me this, and I can't help but scoff at the gesture.

He's always been a bit full of himself—just like his father and just like his brother. It's one of the things I can't stand and know will never change.

"Allie, come on," he says, a bit softer. He drops back down to the couch and scoots in next to me, cupping my face in his hands. "I need you." He leans in and brings his lips to mine, his tongue forcefully snaking into my mouth. I place both hands on his broad chest and push him away, but he pulls me back.

He kisses me hard, his hand on my thigh, his fingers squeezing. And for a single moment, I give in. I relax into him and allow my lips to move with his.

But as his hand snakes further up my thigh, I remember. I

remember why this doesn't work, and why it needs to be over. I pull away, breaking the kiss, wiping the back of my hand against my mouth as if I can erase the taste of him.

"I'd like you to leave," I say, my head lowered. I can't look at him and say this, not with that lust in his eyes.

Tarek stands.

He exhales, and for a moment I think he's about to hit me, but Tarek would never do that. I flinch anyway, and close my eyes as he roars in frustration, a guttural sob of sorts filling the space around us. He stomps through the dining area and into the foyer, mumbling to himself as he does so.

"You're making a big mistake!" he hisses. The front door opens and slams closed and finally—finally—he's gone.

CHAPTER THIRTEEN

Allie

Sunday, June 7, 2015

Breakups are a tricky thing. It doesn't matter whether you're the dumpee or the dumper, apparently they're a fucking headache. And mine still isn't going well. It doesn't help that it's Sunday Funday, and I'm starting to second-guess everything. The guilt is mounting just like the laundry piled in the corner of my bedroom.

Tarek is hurting, and it's *my* fault.

I'm trying not to let this become my problem, but I can't help it. I care, okay? To a fault, I give a damn about people and their stupid feelings. Even the ones who don't always give a damn about mine.

Wine glass and cell phone in hand, I step out onto the balcony overlooking the courtyard and call home. Mom answers on the first ring, as she often does.

"Hi, sweetie! How are you?" she says, her voice pitched and motherly.

"I'm doing good, Mom. It was a busy week."

"Work overloading you again, hun?"

"Yeah, for the most part. I'm on a deadline, so Franklin's freaking out a bit, as usual."

"Well, don't stress out too much honey, I know how you get." I picture Mom waving her finger in the air, her other hand on her hip. I smile at the thought. "How's Tarek?"

"I don't know, Mom…"

And somehow it feels like she knows; like she saw this coming and it makes me love her even more that she's pretending she didn't. "There's no sense staying in a relationship after all this time if it's not serious, honey. Why are you leading the poor man on?"

I take a deep breath. "I'm not, actually," I start. "We… broke up last week." It feels good to say it out loud, to get the weight off my chest.

"Oh, honey…" Mom sighs. I hear the disappointment in her voice—she's always liked Tarek. "Tarek's a good man. I hope you let him down gently." I nod, as if she can see me, but a noise outside catches my attention, and I peer over the railing. There's nothing there, but the sun's gone down and the street lamps haven't turned on yet, so it's hard to see. I grab my wine glass and go back inside, locking the sliding door behind me and then slumping down onto the couch. I set my phone on the coffee table and tap the speaker button while Mom continues.

"Your brother and Sophie are coming for supper on Saturday. You should join us."

"That sounds great, Mom. I think I will."

"Really? Oh, that's wonderful! I'll even make your favorite—Tater Tot Hotdish!"

My stomach grumbles in response and suddenly I can't

wait to get home. It's been far too long since I've been home, and I need the escape now more than ever.

"That's perfect, I'll see you Friday."

"Okay honey, I love you."

"Love you, too."

I end the call and lean back against the couch, flicking on the table lamp. It's a full moon tonight, so I open the curtain a little to let in the light. It's breathtaking and haunting. I grab a novel from the bookshelf and find a seat on the couch. I read a few chapters and eventually drift off to sleep, the glow of the moon overhead, my mind finally settling at the thought of spending the weekend at home.

CHAPTER FOURTEEN

Owen

Sunday, June 7, 2015

I've been here before, in this strange state of loneliness. It confuses me, terrifies me in a way, to feel so close to someone, yet so damn far away. To watch, but not touch.

She tucks a strand of hair behind her ear and a tiny smirk hits her lips, like she's read something funny in the book she's reading, but not quite funny enough to make her laugh.

I want to hear her laugh.

I'd give anything for that right now. God, I want to hold her more than anything. Being close to her is everything I've ever needed. Everything I've always thought impossible. A man like me? A woman like her? No. These things don't happen. She's the queen of the castle and I'm what? A peasant? The kinda guy who hooks up with bartenders who work in sleazy bars for shit tips and go home with strangers because of the off-chance the guy's well-hung and can rock her world for the night.

No.

Men like me don't get to have a woman like Allie.

But that's going to change. *I'm* going to change. I can do that for her, I know I can. I'd give anything to be good enough for her. To feel her skin. To smell her perfume or the shampoo in her hair.

I wonder if she can sense my presence, if she can feel me near. How would she react? Would she be afraid? Would I smell the fear seep from her pores if I were close enough?

She moves so gracefully, and I'm mesmerized by her beauty. By the way she walks.

The sound of her voice, her laugh.

I want to make her happy, to hold her at night while she drifts off to sleep.

But I need her to feel these same things for me, to want me. To crave my touch, the feel of my lips on hers. The feel of my erection against her backside in the morning as she wakes.

It's the little things, really.

I don't think I'm asking for much.

She's asleep now, on the couch, and she looks cold. She shouldn't be cold, not my Allie. I tell myself not to do it, not to go in there, but I can't stop this urge. I can't.

I check the area behind me. The street to the left. The right. Not a car in sight, not a dog walker for miles. It's safe, so I go. I start walking across the street and when I get there, I stay low to avoid the street lamps.

Nothing to see here, folks. Just a fellow neighbor going for a stroll in the middle of the night.

I make it to the courtyard on the far side of the building and check for signs of life again; it's quiet, so I climb the fire escape, and when I get there I cup my hands against the glass and look into Allie's bedroom window.

No movement.

I pull off my shoes and shimmy the window open—she always forgets to lock it—and wince when it squeaks a third of the way through. But nothing stirs, so I climb inside, careful not to disturb anything as I make my way through her room and into the hall. I walk to the living room, and my heart is thumping like a snare drum.

There she is, my Allie.

She's so peaceful, and she's snoring these little tiny child-like snores that just melt my heart. I want to lie with her, to hold her, but I know that I can't, so instead I pull the Afghan from the back of the couch, and I drape it over her. She stirs slightly and I freeze, but she doesn't wake up.

I lean down and smell her hair and hope that her scent never leaves me. There's a noise in the outside hall, probably that stupid neighbor of hers that likes to come home drunk all the time. I've seen him come and go, but he's not a threat. Too much trouble with the bottle to ever be a viable witness to anything.

Still, I know it's time to leave, and I don't want to, but I do.

But first I leave her a note. I scribble it quickly and leave it there on the end table for her. She loves my notes. She saves them, I've seen it. She always puts them in the top drawer of her desk.

She loves when I come to check on her in the night.

CHAPTER FIFTEEN

Allie

Sunday, June 7, 2015

I startle awake to a dark room, and it takes a moment to orient myself. I must have fallen asleep on the couch, which I rarely do, but it's been a stressful week and I've been tired, so it doesn't really surprise me. I don't recall grabbing my grandmother's blanket, but it's covering me, and I pull it from my body and drape it haphazardly over the back of the couch.

The curtains are still open, the full moon shining brightly in the star-filled sky. I push myself up from the couch and cross the room to close them. Something catches my eye, a dark figure moving across the street.

There's a shadow beneath the street lamp, and it's moving quickly like it's been startled. My eyes dart left and right, up and down, but it's gone as suddenly as it came. A deer, perhaps.

The night is otherwise quiet, but still I check the locks on the windows before drawing the curtains. I reach to turn off the light on the end table, but there's a note stuck to the surface. I pick it up, the residue on the back sticky on my fingertips.

Sleep well, my love.

The paper falls from my fingers, almost as if in slow motion. This wasn't here before, I know it wasn't. *Was it?*

I turn and look around the room as if expecting Tarek to be sitting in the corner chair. But he's not. No one is. The room is empty.

The deadbolt on the front door is secured.

There truly isn't anyone else here.

It must be an old note from Tarek. Maybe I just didn't notice it before. I walk to my desk and slide open the top right drawer, placing the note inside. I'm not sure when he started leaving them for me, but I find them all the time—in random places in my apartment, in my car, the gym. A couple times at work, even. I smile, despite the small ache in my chest, and tell myself I'm doing the right thing—that Tarek and I aren't meant to be together, and I didn't make the biggest mistake by breaking things off with him.

Sleep well, my love.

The note's message lingers in my mind as I climb into bed. It replays on a constant loop, reminding me of my guilt while I drift off to sleep.

CHAPTER SIXTEEN

Owen

Thursday, June 11, 2015

I shouldn't know that noise.

I shouldn't know what's happening in that room, but I do, and I don't know what to make of it. What I'm supposed to do.

He's grunting, and she's pretending to like it, using her fake moan that only I know means she's not really enjoying the fuck. That she just wants it to be over.

I never know what to do when this happens.

I set my book bag down next to the couch and stick my hands in the pockets of my jeans. I pace the room. I mumble under my breath.

"What do I do?" I ask nobody.

The moaning grows louder, and the headboard bangs against the wall. Bodies smash together, and it's disgusting because I know what it means. I hear a crack, and it echoes like a slap across the cheek, followed by a cry. My feet move before I tell them to.

I stand against the door and turn the knob. It's locked, but I plant my feet on the ground and square my shoulders. I ram the door and it breaks the old frame, sending me tumbling into the room.

Two figures on the bed stop what they're doing and look up at me, like deer in headlights. I grab a vase off the dresser and raise it over my head. The man pulls his dick out of her and shakes off the tip. It drips onto her stomach.

She clutches her cheek and pulls the blanket over her naked body with the other hand. She doesn't seem to care that his sticky goo is getting all over the covers.

"Who the fuck are you?" the man bellows. He's big and burly, with curly black hair all over his chest. It looks like his pubes and I know this because I can see those, too. His voice booms in the small space because there's nothing in the room other than the queen-sized bed and a small dresser. Nothing on the walls, not even blinds to cover the rotting window.

"Her son. Get the hell out." I say it calmly, but inside a fire burns in my chest.

I want to kill this man for hurting her.

I want to cut his body into bits and pieces and then shove them into a trash compactor.

He steps toward me and stands directly in front of me, his tall frame looming over my childish one. I'm tall for thirteen, sure, but there isn't much meat on my bones.

There's a lot of meat on his bones.

I raise the vase again, prepared to smash it over his ugly head if I have to. It'll make a mess I won't want to clean up, but I know Mom won't do it so I'll have to. I hope he leaves without a fight.

He smirks and then steps back, snatching his clothes up

off the floor. He stands there naked. Doesn't even cover his junk. Lets the remaining juices drip onto the floor.

"Your mom's all dried up, son," he says. "You'll have to start turning tricks yourself to keep food on the table around here."

I don't understand what his words mean, but I know they can't be good, so I hock a wad and spit it in his ugly face. He rears back and I know he's about to hit me, but I duck at the last second and his fist goes through the drywall behind my head.

I shove him and he falls to the ground, his arm dangling from the tattered Sheetrock.

"Get out!" I scream, louder than I ever have before, because maybe for once someone will hear me.

"Fuck this," he barks. He rips his arm from the wall and gets to his feet. I keep hold of the vase just in case, and watch him stomp out to the hallway and get dressed.

"Owen..." Mom croaks, sitting up and leaning against the headboard. She reaches for a menthol and lights it, blowing out a puff of smoke. "Go after him! He didn't pay yet."

Pay for what? I wonder, but I don't move, because whatever he didn't pay for isn't my fucking problem, and haven't I done enough for her?

"He's a john. Go collect." She waves her hand casually, as if I'm her secretary or some stupid errand boy she's sending on a coffee run.

"Are you hurt?" I ask, staring at the palm-shaped welt across her cheek.

"No, I'm not fucking hurt, boy! Some of 'em like it rough. Now go get my damn money."

. . .

"Owen? Are you listening?"

My eyes snap open and take a minute to adjust to the lighting, or lack thereof. There's just a small bedside lamp on, and the room has an amber glow to it. I must have dozed off while she was yammering, and I haven't a clue what the hell she was talking about.

"Hmm?" I mumble.

Millie glares at me and rolls her eyes before settling her head into the crook of my shoulder. I didn't mean to tune her out again, but how is it my fault she can't hold my attention?

She snuggles closer against me, curling her naked body into my side, and all I want to do is push her off and go home. But I don't. Women remember shit like that, and I can't have her going and remembering I'm an asshole when all is said and done. I need her to forget about me and move on to the next schmuck.

Problem is, I keep showing up at her place.

And we keep ending up in bed together.

It's been a month of this back and forth, and already she's getting attached. Shit, maybe I am, too, if I'm being honest—the sex is hard to pass up. But I can't keep doing this to Allie; cheating is wrong, and my girl doesn't deserve it, so I need to end things with Millie before Allie finds out.

Before Millie ruins everything.

"You're off in la-la land again," she says, bringing her hand to my face. She softly drags her fingers along the edge of my jaw, and it sends a shiver straight to my groin. "Are you here with me?"

"I'm sorry. Yes. Just tired." I try to pass it off, make it less of a deal, just in case I want to come back tomorrow and repeat this process all over again.

"Well, there's no reason I can't help you relax…again," she teases. She winks and her upper lip curls. I want to hate it, but fuck if it isn't sexy as hell. Her hand slides down my torso and under the blanket that rests at my hip. I feel her hands on me before I have a chance to turn her down, to drag my idiot ass out of this bed and go home, never to return.

Instead I watch her kiss her way down my stomach.

I watch her tongue slide down the length of my dick.

And then I close my eyes and imagine she's Allie when she takes me in her mouth.

CHAPTER SEVENTEEN

Allie

Friday, June 12, 2015

The drive home to my parent's house is usually exhausting; ridiculously long and boring, despite being less than two hours on a good day. It wasn't so bad when Tarek was with me—sometimes Court if he couldn't make it—but I've always struggled to make the drive alone. Today it's cathartic and couldn't have come at a better time. My thoughts are all over the place right now, my head immersed in a thick fog.

I slept with Tarek last night.

I shouldn't have, I know, but I couldn't get those love notes out of my head. They were so sweet, so thoughtful. And when he dropped by unexpectedly after work and smooth-talked his way inside, it just…happened. I've been mentally kicking myself ever since, and it wasn't easy getting him to leave this morning.

It won't be any easier telling him it was a mistake either but doing so is inevitable.

Just not today.

I blast the radio, belting out every song on Journey's *Greatest Hits* album. With the windows down, I feel the wind in my hair, hearkening the start of summer, and find myself wondering why I don't go home more often. I suppose that's common for adult children after they move away, but still I feel a pang in my heart and vow to put in the effort to make the trip more frequently.

Lincoln's silver Dodge Ram sits in the driveway, and I pull in and park beside it. I'm only half tempted to key the giant monstrosity out of spite. My brother, the charming fella that he is, has a love for flashy things. He and Tarek got along well in that regard.

I try not to fault him for it, but today it hits me hard. Lincoln and I are close—in age, being that we're only thirteen months apart—and also as siblings. Nearly Irish twins, we are.

He often dated my friends, and before college, I dated his too. It was kind of the thing we were known for and quickly became a common jab in our group of friends. Some days I think he and Court will end up together, but then I remember Linc has no desire to move out to the Twin Cities—and Court's not wired for country living.

I purposely park considerably close to his Dodge, to the point where I couldn't open my passenger door if I wanted to, and chuckle to myself—he'll have to crawl through from the passenger side of his truck to get to the driver's seat.

Sucker.

I should feel bad, but I don't. In fact, I can't help but chuckle at myself as I make my way to the front porch. Harmless sibling rivalry keeps us young, right?

"Is that my girl?" Mom coos from the kitchen when I step

inside. She trots to the front door, drying her hands on a dish-towel like the classic suburban mother that she is.

And I love her for it.

"Hi, Mom!" I drop my bags to the floor and she pulls me in for a rib-crushing hug.

"It's so good to see you, sweetie," she says, pulling away and using the towel to dab her eyes.

"It's good to see you too. Where's Dad?"

"Awww, come on!" I hear the shouting from the living room, and Mom and I smile at each other. Dad and Linc are obviously watching some sporting event, judging by the ruckus.

Mom turns and heads back toward the kitchen. "Well, come on in, sweetheart! Leave your things there; I'll have Lincoln take them up to your room in a bit."

I follow Mom to the kitchen and she puts on a pot of coffee as she gabs about the weather and turns her attention back to the casserole she's making.

"Where's Sophie?" I ask, looking around the kitchen.

Mom sighs and gets a sad look on her face. She shakes her head, and even though I don't need her to say more, she does. "She didn't come. I think they broke up," she whispers.

"Ah," I say, and my heart pangs a bit for my little brother.

Looks like we're in the same boat.

After dinner I find myself in the backyard on the love seat swing Dad hung in the oak tree when I was eight. Linc and I used to fight over it, over whose turn it was to use it—because God forbid we share the dang thing—and sometimes we'd stay out here for hours without any other care in the world.

Simpler times, I think.

Linc comes up behind me and clears his throat. "Room for two today?" he asks. I scoot over to make space, and Linc puts an arm around my shoulders, pulling me in for a side hug.

"How ya been, Allie? For real, not the sugar-coated version you gave to Mom and Dad." I half smile; he knows me too well.

"You've heard from Tarek," I assume confidently.

He nods. "I have. The guy is a mess."

"Linc—"

"I know, I know..." He puts his hands up defensively. "I'm just saying. He's not doing well."

I drop my head and stare at a spot in the grass. "I can't live my life trying to please everyone else," I say. It comes out harsh, but Linc gets it. He nods. "I'm sorry about Sophie," I add. Linc shrugs but doesn't say anything.

We don't speak for a few minutes, but it's not awkward. It never is with Linc. He picks up a stick and starts to peel back the bark, dropping the shavings to the ground. I can't help but wonder if I should have stayed in Brainerd...if moving to the cities was a mistake and maybe it's time to come home.

"Do you ever wish you'd gotten out?" I ask.

He shrugs, considering it for just a moment. "Not really. I've always liked it here."

And I knew this; it's kind of how I hoped he would answer. My little brother, content with a simple life. With a house in the country, not a neighbor for miles. A dog napping on the porch, no need for a leash. "You, though? You were made to do bigger things, Al," he says, nudging me in the shoulder.

I smile against my will, and he tosses what's left of the stick across the yard. I'm half tempted to run after it like a dog, as I once forced Linc to do, but somehow manage to control myself.

"Anyone up for Canasta?" Dad asks when Linc and I make our way back inside.

"Sounds great," Linc and I say at the same time. Mom grabs a bottle of wine and two glasses from the cabinet in the corner as each of us resumes our positions at the kitchen table —the same ones we've had since there were four of us. But it's good; it's reliable.

Mom and I share the bottle of wine while dad and Lincoln nurse a couple beers and dig into a bowl of potato chips. *It's good to be home*, I think, suddenly realizing how poorly Tarek and his money fit into my family.

CHAPTER EIGHTEEN

Owen

Saturday, June 20, 2015

I find myself in Millie's bed again tonight. I didn't mean to come here, really, but I did, and we've done what we've done. I can't take it back, I can't pretend it never happened.

Nights at home in my empty bed are harder every day, and even though my heart aches for Allie, for this horrible and unfair betrayal, I needed this.

A warm body next to me.

Someone to satisfy these urges.

I shove this remorse deep down into my soul. I'll deal with it later. Millie steps out of the en suite bathroom, a towel wrapped around her, her blonde hair wet and messy around her face. She has that look in her eyes again, the one that tells me she wouldn't mind going another round. And I consider it, but instead I slide out of the bed and grab my clothes off the floor.

"Ah, really?" Millie pouts. "You're leaving?"

"Got somewhere to be in the morning, Mil," I reply, avoiding her eyes because the disappointment is too much. I'm always letting someone down, and I can't bear the thought of it anymore.

Millie was supposed to have moved on by now. Found another barfly to take home. But she hasn't. She keeps texting, and I keep showing up.

I didn't expect to like her as much as I do. I'm an idiot, I know.

I finish getting dressed and pull Millie over to me as I sit down on the edge of the bed. She leans into me and I hold her, taking in her fresh scent, her shampoo, and it's nice. Fuck, it's nice to feel wanted for once. I linger a moment, unwrapping the towel from her body and exposing every inch of her. I hold her naked body and kiss the tops of her breasts. Her neck. Her stomach. I grow hard again when she moans in my ear and fuck—just one more time.

We can do it *one* more time.

I growl and lift her, tossing her onto the bed, and she bites her lip as she spreads her legs. I strip out of my clothes again and bury my face in her as she bucks against my mouth.

I stay just a little too long, a little too late into the night, but once she's asleep beside me, I slide out from under the covers and get dressed. I kiss her cheek and silently walk out of the bedroom, promising myself this will be the last time.

I drop my car off at home and walk through the path in the woods toward Allie's, my head hung low because I know what I've done is wrong.

I know I've failed her.

But I go to her, anyway.

I need to see Allie.

CHAPTER NINETEEN

Allie

Saturday, June 20, 2015

His hands are rough, calloused and scratchy against my skin. His eyes are dark, filled with anger and possession as they bore into me. He breathes erratically, puffs of air landing on my face. They linger in my mouth.

Hot. Rancid.

Unfamiliar.

I feel pain everywhere, like needles stabbing into my flesh over and over. If it weren't for the pain, I'd think I was having a nightmare, watching as if from outside my body.

On my face, arms, my ribs. It hurts to breathe.

It hurts between my legs.

A drop of sweat lands on my cheek and rolls downward, onto the pillow beneath my head.

I can't move, but I try anyway. I swing my arms and swat at his rough hands as they roam my body. I swat at his face. I kick as violently as I can, but I don't know that it does any good. I have no strength, no fight left in me as I continue to drift into the darkness.

I want to scream, but his hand juts out and cups my mouth hard, pressing my head into the pillow. He's speaking, but I can't make out the words. I see his mouth moving. He licks his lips, and I think he just called me by my name, but he can't possibly know my name.

I don't know his.

There's something about his eyes...there's something, and I can't...the pain is too much.

The room spins, and I'm dizzy. So dizzy.

It's so dark.

AFTER

CHAPTER TWENTY

Allie

Friday, June 26, 2015

I wake with a start and sit up abruptly in bed, forgetting the broken ribs inside me, the sudden movement causing a sharp pain in my stomach. I wince and pull the covers from my body, my head clammy and streaked with sweat. My breaths are heavy, and I forget for a moment where I am and why I'm here. I wonder what time it is or how long I've been asleep, and I try to breathe, but it feels like my throat is closing in on me. It's still scratchy and dry, and I know I must have been screaming in my sleep again.

The nightmares are relentless.

I drop my legs over the side of the bed and my bare feet hit the floor. I tell myself to move, to get up and walk, one foot after the other, but it takes a moment for the command to reach my limbs. When it does, I pad slowly to the bathroom and splash cold water on my face, careful not to get the bandage over my left eye wet. It does little to shake the movie-like images from my brain.

Eyes so dark they're almost black.

I don't want to see him, but I know that I have to. I need to remember his face, his smell, his body. I try to, but nothing more comes.

The detailed images are always lost as soon as I wake up.

I lean over the counter and force myself to look in the mirror. The puffiness in my face has gone down, but the bruises remain. I hardly recognize myself. The woman staring back at me isn't the same woman from last week. She's not the same woman from a month ago, or even last year.

She's someone new.

Someone broken and scared.

Someone afraid of her own shadow, of tiny foreign sounds in the night.

He did this to her.

He changed her irrefutably.

I pull away from the mirror, suddenly ashamed to look at my own face, even though there's no one here to witness my weakness. Just the stranger reflected in the glass.

Six days can change a lot about a person.

I grab my phone, unlock it, and open the Notes app. My fingers somehow tap the right buttons to form cohesive sentences that I can relay to Detective Feeney. The nightmare gave me so much, yet so little, and all I manage to record is that his eyes are dark, that his body is big and ripped with muscles that held me down against my will.

"This is nothing," I mutter to myself, frustrated that I can't pull any more from my memories but these nightmares.

It's not enough, and may very well be considered useless, but for some reason it still feels significant to me and doesn't let me go.

A knock at the door startles me as I settle back into bed, causing yet another jolt of pain from my ribs. The hospital is driving me crazy with all its sounds—the beeping and monitors and constant visitors.

I just want to go home.

"Good morning," Mom says, popping her head in the door. "You're up."

"Barely," I mumble. She holds two paper cups of coffee in her hands, and suddenly I don't feel so grouchy. "Caribou, even?" I say, grateful she remembered my love for the Midwestern coffee chain.

"Just for you, honey." She hands me the cup and sets hers on the bedside table, taking a seat in the folding chair beside me. I adjust the bed until I'm upright, wincing as it moves, and Mom reaches over to cover my legs with the thin blanket.

She looks over at me sympathetically. "How are you feeling this morning, sweetheart?"

I sigh, internally wishing I could lie to my mother and tell her I'm magically feeling better, that I'm choosing happiness. I hate how much this hurts her, and for some reason, I feel responsible. But I can't do that to her. I can't lie to her. I know it's not what she wants, anyway. She wants honesty.

She wants to help.

"I'm really sore," I tell her, sticking to the physical aspect of my recovery and sparing her from the reality that I'm also anxious and terrified and don't want her to leave me alone in this room again. She takes my hand and squeezes twice.

She always squeezes twice.

One more look from her and the tears flow like a waterfall. I can't hold them back, and instead fall into a fit of violent sobs that does little to ease the pain in my ribs.

She holds me and rubs my back as we cry together.

Mom and Tarek switch shifts around lunchtime. This has been their daily routine, according to Mom. Tarek comes from work, taking half-days and staying through the afternoon until Dad or Linc or Court can tag in. Darcy says he's been here every day since I was brought in. This surprises me, considering I'm no longer his girlfriend, although Tarek doesn't seem to think that's the case.

It's like *he's* the one with amnesia.

I've certainly been a bit disoriented since coming to, so it's possible I'm not remembering things right, but I do know we broke up a few weeks before I ended up here.

Courtney even confirmed it.

So I know he's been trying to win me back, that he's been bringing flowers and leaving me love notes. And for now, I just go with it, because I don't know what else to do. He's hurting, so I let him stay. I also know I went to bed alone that night, the night of the attack. Although, I don't actually remember going to bed.

I just know I was alone.

Tarek sits in the chair next to my bed, playing some warcraft game on his phone while I stare at my Kindle screen. The words are blurry, but it gives me something to do, mindlessly paging through something in Kindle Unlimited.

Another knock at the door, and Dr. Nelson steps in.

"Are we ready to go home today?" he asks, a warm smile on his face. I knew he'd been pleased with my progress, but didn't realize he was pleased enough to send me home.

"Really?" The thought excites me, but then I remember that I may not be able to go to my actual home. "Um, home-home or home to my parent's place? Has Detective Feeney been back?"

"Not that I'm aware of, but you could give him a call."

"No need, I've spoken with him," Tarek chimes in, setting his phone face down on the side table. This is the first I'm hearing of his conversation with the police.

Tarek takes my hand and kisses it before placing it back down onto my lap and looking down at me. "Your apartment is ready to go."

"How?"

"Detective Feeney signed off on it yesterday, and I went by and cleaned it up. You won't have to see it a mess, and it'll be just like new when I bring you home this afternoon."

"You did that for me?" A tear threatens, and I swipe it away with my finger. "Thank you."

"All right," Dr. Nelson resumes. "So, we'll get one of the nurses in here to check your vitals, and if all is good to go, we can get started on your discharge paperwork. We've got you all set up to start therapy next week, and we'll also need to see you back for a checkup with your primary, Dr. Regan, okay?" I nod, and he flips the chart closed, stuffing the pen into the pocket of his lab coat.

The thought of returning home weighs heavily. What if it's not the same? What if somehow, I can still feel *his* presence in my room? In the hallway…

I can't breathe.

"Hey, hey…babe, it's okay." Tarek leans in and takes my bruised face in his hands. "I'll stay with you until you're comfortable." He smiles. "Maybe it'll be a nice little test for us to see how well we would do living together." He winks, and I manage to smirk in response.

He's been so kind, I remind myself.

"Yeah…sure," I say softly, my voice barely above a whisper. I struggle to form the words, and as much as I don't think Tarek should stay, I know I don't want to be alone, so I accept his offer and reach for my phone to text my parents and let them know I won't be staying with them after all.

"I'll start getting your things together here. Get these flowers and cards and stuff down to the car."

"Okay. Thank you, Tarek. You've been wonderful."

"I want to, babe. I was so scared when I got that call. I didn't know what to do, what to think. I wanted to kill the guy who did this to you."

"How did you find out? Who called you?"

"Lincoln called me actually. Said he thought I'd want to know."

Why would Linc have called Tarek? He knew we'd broken up. I'd told him the weekend I went home. I make a mental note to have some words with my little brother.

Court meets us at the hospital as I'm being discharged, her demeanor solemn, like she was hoping for a moment alone with me, but Tarek is rushing to get out of here.

"Can I swing by in a bit?" she asks.

"Maybe tomorrow?" I offer, grimacing when I try to bend over to grab my purse from the table. Courtney steps in, grabbing it for me and slinging it over her shoulder. She eyes Tarek as he steps out of the room, his arms full of flowers and gifts sent over the last couple of days.

Courtney puts an arm around my shoulder and pulls me close, her eyes filled with concern. "Listen, Allie, I know Tarek has been super helpful since you've been here and all, but please…" Her eyes dart across the room, making sure he's out of earshot. "…be careful, okay?"

I know where this warning comes from, and I smile at my friend, because she knows me so well. "I will, I promise. I know he's trying to get back together. And maybe…maybe that's what's best, huh?"

"Did you see his hands?" she whispers, her eyes darting back and forth.

"What about his hands?"

"They're bruised, Allie…" She leaves the statement hanging for a moment, then waves her hand in the air, brushing it off like she meant nothing by it. "I'm just worried about you," she continues. "Promise me you'll let me come by tomorrow and check on you? I'll come over in the morning."

"It's a date," I confirm, and she nods before lowering me to a wheelchair.

His hands…I can't stop thinking about his hands.

My home doesn't feel like my own anymore.

It's tainted somehow, less like a sanctuary and more like a prison.

But I breathe, and I tell myself everything will be okay. Tarek will stay with me overnight; he's insisted, and I don't argue because I'm not ready to be alone here.

I shower slowly and dress even slower as Tarek unpacks for me and orders dinner from the Chinese place we love.

"Detective Feeney stopped by," he tells me when we sit down to eat. He's intentionally nonchalant, like he didn't actually want to tell me the detective stopped by, but knew he had to.

"He did?"

"Yeah, when you were in the shower. He wanted to know if you had some necklace—or maybe it was a bracelet?" He waves a dismissive hand. "I can't remember. He said to have you give him a call."

My hand instinctively reaches for my neck. *My necklace.* The one my dad gave to me for my thirteenth birthday.

It's missing.

"I'll give him a call now." I push up from my chair, sliding the plastic container of takeout to the middle of the table, my appetite lacking. "You can finish that if you want," I tell Tarek, pointing to the chicken fried rice I've barely touched.

"Allie, you need to eat." He dabs his mouth with a napkin, frustration settling on his face.

"Maybe later, okay? I'm not really hungry."

In the bedroom, I pull Detective Feeney's business card from my purse. He answers on the second ring.

"Detective Feeney…"

"Detective, hi. It's Allie Mason. Tarek mentioned you stopped by?"

"Miss Mason, hello. Yes, I was hoping to ask you a few follow up questions. Do you have a moment now?"

"I do." I sit down on the bed, suddenly aware that this is where it happened. My throat tightens, and I hold my breath, silently counting to three and forcing myself to find peace in this space.

One.

"First things first," he starts. "Have you remembered any additional details about the night of the attack?"

Two.

"Miss Mason, are you there?"

Three.

"I'm here. Sorry. I…I don't think there's been anything new, no. I've had some nightmares, but that's about it."

"We were able to lift some prints off the window sill in the bedroom. They still haven't turned up any matches, but we'll continue to run them through the system. We might get lucky and this guy will turn up."

Fingerprints.

Not in the system.

"Any unusual activity around the building since you've been home?" he asks.

"No. Not that I know of, anyway. I haven't been here long though."

"Any sign of the necklace you're missing? Silver with a heart pendant, right?"

I sigh, sadness washing over me. That necklace means so much to me. "No, not yet."

"Well, let me know if it turns up," he says before taking a pause. "Please…let me know if *anything* else comes up. You can reach me at this number any time, text or voice."

"I will, thank you so much, Detective."

I push to my feet and Tarek appears in the doorway. He leans against the frame, and I walk to him, stopping with my arms at my side. He presses his lips to my temple and wraps his arm around me carefully, and I let myself be held by him. He's comforting, familiar.

But now he's still kissing my face, my neck. He's rubbing my arms and lower back and his hands are dropping lower… lower…his lips find mine, and there's an urgency there, desire.

I pull away and shove him forward, the acidic taste of blood on my tongue as I bring a hand to my mouth. He's kissed me so hard the cut on my lip has reopened.

"No," I whisper. But he doesn't realize his mistake. He

doesn't know this is too much for me, that it's too soon and I'm not ready at all.

I may *never* be ready for this.

"Allie? What's wrong? What is it?" he asks, and I see the confusion in his eyes—the hurt. The torture of being rejected again.

I feel pain everywhere, like needles stabbing into my flesh over and over.

"I can't! Please, don't touch me like that."

"Baby, I'm sorry, I wasn't thinking…" He bows his head in shame, and when he looks up, there are tears in his eyes. My hands shake, but he steps forward and holds them.

"Did you see his hands?"

I don't flinch, because this touch is okay. I remind myself that this touch is safe.

But is it?

"Tarek?"

"Yeah, baby?" I lift our hands, still held together, and rub my fingers over his knuckles. He pulls away, but only a little, as I lift them higher to get a closer look at them.

They're bruised, the knuckles. Slightly purple and greenish.

Like week-old bruises.

"What happened to your hands?" I ask, barely able to get the words out, suddenly not wanting to know the answer. He pulls away, runs his damaged hands through his hair and bows his head. "Tarek?"

"I got mad, okay? When all this happened with you…it's embarrassing, but—" He takes a step back and motions to the wall next to the dresser.

To the fist-shaped hole adjacent to the light switch.

"I punched the wall," he says, looking up at me with tears in his eyes. And it hurts, this fear inside me that had me convinced his wounds were a result of something else. I take his hands in mine again, and he pulls me close. I breathe him in, his scent, and I kiss his lips softly. Just a little bit; only enough to show him I'm sorry for asking.

He leads me to the couch in the living room and we fall asleep together, his arms holding me because I can't bring myself to sleep in my own bed yet.

I make a mental note to buy a new bed, and then I drift off to sleep, images of dark eyes flashing in my mind.

CHAPTER TWENTY-ONE

Owen

Friday, June 26, 2015

I sit on the porch steps and wait for my mom, certain I'll hear the clunk-clunk of her muffler before I even see the rusty car coming down the road. Dad and Amber left an hour ago for their honeymoon, and Mom was supposed to pick me up at the house. She's late, and I don't know where else to go.

I consider walking down the block to my friend Nick's house and asking to stay there for the night, but the thought of admitting that my dad left and didn't trust me to stay alone in his house is too embarrassing, and I brush off the idea. Instead, I make a mental calculation of how many miles it is to Mom's house.

At least fifteen, give or take.

I give her another hour, but she doesn't show, so I shrug my bag onto my back and start walking, hopeful that I'll get there before the sun sets and that I won't make a wrong turn.

It's after 9:00 p.m. when I finally make it there. It's been dark for over an hour, chilly for May, and I wish I'd thought to pack a jacket. There aren't any lights on inside, and all I can do is hope Mom left the trailer unlocked.

She didn't, for once, so I climb in through the bathroom window, tossing my bag in first and then heaving my body up and through. I scurry to the sink and turn on the water, drinking from the faucet like a thirsty camel.

I make my way to the living room, and it's littered with takeout containers and empty pizza boxes, cigarette butts stubbed out in the overflowing ashtray. The stink is enough to make me plug my nose. And I can't help myself, I grab a garbage bag from under the sink and I start cleaning.

I'm grateful when Monday comes so I can go to school. There's no food in the trailer, not even a loaf of bread, and I don't have any money. Dad's the only one who puts lunch money in my account, but I don't know if there's any left. Sometimes the lunch ladies let me help with dishes for free lunches, though, so maybe I'll have to do that.

This cycle continues the entire two weeks Dad and Amber are in Cabo. Mom never comes home. Dad doesn't check in. By the start of week two, the principal gives me a form to apply for state-sponsored lunches. There's a line for a parent signature. I crumple up the form and toss it in the trash.

It'd be kinda nice if someone gave a shit about me.

The picture of Allie and Tarek is gone, removed from the frame and replaced with a photograph of Dr. Simms and her husband.

"You seem distracted, Dr. Simms," I say, fishing to see if she'll crack.

"Hm? No, no, everything is fine, thank you." She waves

me off, settles into her chair across from me and crosses her legs. “How have you been?”

“Not the greatest,” I admit with surprise. I don’t plan to open up to her, especially not today, but the words are out before I can stop them.

I can’t stop thinking about Allie, how her face was covered in blood and she looked nothing like herself.

“Let’s talk about why you’re really here, Mr. Riverson,” she starts, and I’m alarmed at the fact that she just referred to me using my last name. She doesn’t typically do that. She pulls a file out from under her notebook and flips it open. “Two counts of assault by the age of seventeen,” she reads from the page.

I sit up straighter and clear my throat. Dr. Simms pulls her reading glasses off her face and holds them in her hand. She looks at me with confident eyes, like she’s excited the shoe’s about to drop. She’s proud of herself. “In juvenile court, you approached the bench without cause, threatened the judge…”

“I didn’t *threaten* the judge,” I interrupt, my temper flaring.

“It says here that you did,” she says, pointing to the file.

“Well, it’s wrong.”

“And what about the fact that the charges filed against you were claims made by your father?”

I bite the inside of my cheek, withholding any physical reaction to what Dr. Simms feels the need to remind me of. “What about it?”

“You told me your parents were dead, Mr. Riverson. That they died in a car accident. Do you remember that?”

“Yep.”

“Why would you do that?”

“I didn’t feel like talking about it,” I say, my arms folding across my chest. “I still don’t.”

"That's fine, but lying to me will get you nowhere. If you're going to waste my time I can recommend someone else, seeing as you're required to be here."

"I have anger issues, big deal."

"Yes, anger issues that haven't been resolved through traditional anger management, despite the numerous attempts and leniency you've been granted because of your father. So you're here. You might as well get something out of it, don't you think?"

Without a word, I stand and leave Dr. Simms's office, shoving my way through doors and down the stairs, out onto the sidewalk, and I'm so angry I could explode.

Who the fuck does she think she is?

What gives her the right to talk about my father like he's worth the breath?

The Sunday of the second weekend, Dad's supposed to pick me up at Mom's. The phone in the trailer has been disconnected for as long as I can remember, so I can't call him to find out if their flight has been delayed. When he doesn't show by late afternoon, I grab my bag and walk home.

The front door is locked at the house, but I don't have my key, so I walk around to the backyard where Dad and Amber are having dinner on the patio. Steaks and baked potatoes, an expensive bottle of wine between them. They're tan and smell like salt water.

My stomach grumbles when I get a whiff of the T-Bones; I haven't eaten since school lunch on Friday. I drop my bag on the ground and stare at Dad, willing myself not to cry.

"You're home early," he says. No mention of the fact that I'm covered in sweat and smell like raging teenage anger.

The anger bubbles up inside me, and I get the urge to stab a steak knife through his hand.

"She. Wasn't. Fucking. There." I spit the words out, grinding my teeth. "The whole two weeks, Dad. She never came home. There was no food."

Amber sets her fork down and pulls out the chair beside her, motioning to it like she actually wouldn't mind if I join them. "Well, sit down, Owen. There's plenty of food here. Right, Mitchell?

Dad scoffs, shoves the chair Amber's pulled out right back under the table.

"What is it with you and your mother, huh? Always demanding money like you've done something to earn it." He takes a bite of his steak and chews it slowly.

"I'm fourteen."

"Old enough to get a job, if you ask me."

"Mitchell..." Amber hisses. She kicks him under the table, but he waves her off. She doesn't want me here anymore than he does, but at least she's humane enough to offer me dinner.

She may have married him for his money, but even she can see he's an asshole. Most lawyers are, though.

"Go on up and take a shower, why don't you? Use up some of that free water for a change. You can make yourself a sandwich or something once you've washed off the trailer park stench."

I swipe the steak knife off the table and stab it hard into the wood. I glare at my father as he pushes to his feet, this man who means nothing to me. Who would love nothing more than for me to run away and never come back.

I don't give him a second to react; my fist connects with his cheekbone, ripping the skin on my knuckles open. Amber screams, covering her mouth with her hands as Dad stumbles backward. The shock of my aggression renders him speechless as he wipes blood from his mouth.

Amber cries out and runs inside, pressing the phone to her ear.

"Get out," Dad growls.

I don't move an inch. I have nowhere to go.

The police arrive a few minutes later. Dad decides to press charges, so I end up in juvenile detention for the first time.

It's another three hours before I get something to eat.

After leaving Dr. Simms's office, I go straight to Allie; I don't know what else to do. Her chaos always seems to calm mine, and I want nothing more than to be around her.

I settle into my spot, grateful she's left the curtains open, yet also concerned considering everything she's been through. I wonder again if she knows about me—I'm fairly sure she saw me the other night, but I can't be certain.

CHAPTER TWENTY-TWO

Allie

Monday, June 29, 2015

Nothing is really quite as it seems anymore. My physical wounds are healing, but I haven't even begun to scratch the surface on psychological ones yet. I'm not sure I ever will.

My apartment feels unsafe. All the locks on the doors and windows are secured, the blinds and curtains drawn, but I still have a nagging feeling that someone is watching me, that I'm not quite alone.

This isn't my home anymore.

Detective Feeney says the crime scene investigators swept for bugs—not the literal kind of creepy crawlers, but the electronic device sort. It took me a moment to accept the weight of that statement. In the end, they found nothing, but that doesn't mean they're not here. I keep reverting back, feeling like someone is watching me, invading my space. I shiver at the thought and goosebumps trickle up my arms and down my neck. I rub my hands up and down my arms, trying but failing to warm myself. To calm my nerves.

I can't relax.

No hair.

No fibers.

No foreign DNA, other than the blood on the broken window and a few fingerprints that have no match.

No cameras.

There *has* to be something I'm missing, something they're *all* missing.

This paranoia is nearly killing me, but I heard somewhere that paranoia is often instinctual. As in, I wouldn't be paranoid if there was nothing to be paranoid about. So, the paranoia stays. It's constant; it lives here with me now, making the space feel too small, claustrophobic.

The wall clock ticks across the room. It's the only sound I'm able to register, other than the constant whooshing that remains in my left ear that Dr. Nelson says may never go away.

I lean forward on the sofa, listening intently, trying to pick up on something else. I don't know why, other than that I can't bring myself to do much of anything other than this.

Mom keeps calling, and I have to answer every time she does, because if I don't, she and dad will surely hop in the car and drive out here. Not answering her call could mean I'm in danger, that I'm hurt.

I can't bring myself to contribute to those fears; my parents don't deserve that. But I'm exhausted. I'm tired of pretending I'm okay, even though I'll never admit that I'm not. I don't want to host that pity party. It's like I'm some broken doll that everybody wants to sew back together, but nobody has the right color thread and the needle isn't even sharp enough to poke through the surface.

Each day is a repeat of the one before, the only difference being the date on the calendar or the time on the clock, but even that repeats itself eventually.

Just like my thoughts—I have the same anxious thoughts over and over, day in and day out.

I keep feeling like someone is watching me.

I can't shake it, and the fear lingers no matter how hard I try to convince myself that I'm safe—that no one is watching. But I keep noticing things—little things here and there—that are making me question it.

My keys aren't hung on the hook by the front door.

Did Tarek move them?

The TV was on when I woke up this morning.

Did I forget to turn it off? Was I even watching it?

The lid was left up on the toilet seat.

Definitely wasn't me. Tarek?

Over and over these things happen, and I overanalyze them. When Mom calls around lunch time I send her to voicemail, because I don't have the capacity for her pain today, I'm already filled up. I shoot her a text to let her know I'm okay, that I just need some space.

And that ambient feeling hits me again. I know someone has been here. Someone has been in my apartment, and they may still be here. My heart hammers in my chest, panic rising in the form of bile, but I can't be sick right now, because I may have to ward off an intruder.

But my eyes are heavy, and I can't keep them open. I can't fight right now.

Let them come.

CHAPTER TWENTY-THREE

Allie

Tuesday, July 7, 2015

Fear comes in all shapes and sizes. Whether it's imaginary or vibrant, it's there. And it lingers. It lingers like you wouldn't fucking believe. It's a constant cloud of darkness hovering in my mind, in the beating of my heart. Whether it's irrational or warranted, it's debilitating.

It's hard to live with and even harder to overcome.

These are things I keep trying to remind myself. I don't know whether my fears are warranted or simply unconscious illusions meant to keep me awake at night.

All I know is that I'm afraid.

I'm vulnerable.

I shouldn't be; I should be okay by now. The odds of something like...*that*...happening again are slim to none, right? So, why can't I just shake it off? Why can't I move on without this gut-wrenching fear tearing me apart from the inside? Something is eating me from the inside out. I don't know who I am anymore; why I'm here and why I survived what happened to me. I wonder when it will end, this grieving —this fear—or if it ever will. I hate the vulnerable *thing* I'm becoming, but nothing seems to be capable of pulling me out of this slump, so here I sit.

My phone chimes from the coffee table and I scoop it up, even though all I want to do is ignore it and toss it in the trash bin. It's Tarek again, wanting to know if I'd be up for dinner. "Not tonight," I text back, placing the phone back on the table face down.

I've started spending some nights alone. Tarek was reluctant to leave, but I need this. I need to prove to myself that I can move on, that I can live alone without being afraid of my own shadow. I push up from the couch and pace the living room, unable to form a coherent thought. I don't want to be here, but I can't imagine being anyplace else either.

I saw a man across the street last night. At least, I think I saw him—and then he left, and I can't help but wonder if he was the man Detective Feeney warned me about. *The stalker*, he called him.

But his features are somehow seared into my brain, what I could see from a distance at night feels so real, so certain. His dark hair—sticking out under a black ski cap—and piercing eyes that practically flickered under the glow of the street lamp.

Of all things to be afraid of right now, he should probably top the list. He should be considered a threat. I move to the window and peel back the curtain, using my fingers to separate the slats of the blinds. I'm hoping he's standing out there now, but I know he won't be.

Not in the daylight.

I sigh heavily, disappointment marinating inside me. I

don't want to want him near, but I feel a pull in his direction, drawing me in as if through some magical superpower.

He doesn't feel like a threat.

But that doesn't make sense, because this man is stalking me, I'm sure of it. Watching me from across the street, never once uttering a word to me, yet I can't get him out of my head.

How long has he been watching?

I wrap my arms around myself, imagining his hands on my torso, his breath on my neck, his lips trailing my ear lobe.

My thoughts are interrupted by the doorbell, and I shudder at the thought that it might be Tarek, having ignored my rejection to dinner and taking it upon himself to come over anyway.

I walk slowly to the intercom, wanting to know whose finger pressed the button to my apartment, yet not wanting that person to know that I'm home. I don't imagine I could have it both ways, so I hit the 'speak' button and hold my breath.

"Who is it?" I ask through gritted teeth.

"Allie? Babe, it's Court. Let me in, I've been calling."

A sigh of relief escapes my lips and I hit the unlock button to let Courtney into the building, and then dash over to the entryway mirror to fix my hair.

I just remembered I promised her I'd shower today.

Yikes.

"It's my mission to bring the real Allie Mason back," Courtney announces as she sets several bags of groceries on my kitchen counter. She waves her pointer finger in my direction. "This look is *not* working for you, my dear."

I tug at the hem of my T-shirt, my lip forming into a pout. She's not wrong, I know she isn't, but still I take offense.

"Who pissed in your cereal bowl this morning?" I mutter, running a hand through my disheveled hair.

"Allie, come on. Let's get you cleaned up. At least a shower, and then we can see where the day goes."

"I—"

"Enough," she scolds. "Sweetheart, I know you're hurting and you're healing, and I want to give you time to do that, but you still have to take care of yourself. You have to keep living." Courtney takes my hand and lures me down the hall to the bathroom. I plop down on the toilet seat while she reaches in to turn on the water and draws the shower curtain.

"Hot," I request, and she turns the knob further to the left.

"Come on. Up you get." She slides her arms beneath mine and lifts me carefully off the toilet, pulling my shirt over my head and tossing it to the floor on top of the mound of week-old clothes that already litter the space. I wrap my arms around my stomach self-consciously, even though it's just Court and I have no one to impress.

I'm really just hiding the bruises that linger beneath these ratty, dirty clothes.

She stops abruptly and waves her hand at me. "Do I really have to do this for you?" she asks, doing her best to ignore my wounds. But I see the sudden look in her eyes, the fear that I'm really as broken as I look. It's subtle, but it's there.

I sigh and remove my sweatpants, trying to remember when the last time I changed my clothes was. Steam fills the room and Court scoops my dirty laundry up off the floor as she backs out of the bathroom. "Get in there," she gestures with her chin, pointing it toward the shower.

I sigh and climb in. The hot water scalds my skin, but my God, it feels so good.

Why did I wait so long to do this?

I run my fingers through my hair as the water saturates it, my arms still sore enough that I can't quite get the right one up over my head. I quickly wash my hair, foregoing the conditioner, because it's not like I plan to brush through it anyway. I rinse and let the hot water run over my face.

A shower feels nice, and I try to remember why I put it off in the first place. It always feels amazing once I'm in, but it's like pulling teeth to get here.

Court knocks and pops her head through the door a few minutes later as I step out and wrap a towel around myself. "You decent?" she asks.

"Would it have stopped you if I wasn't?"

"Aha! There she is," Court teases. "Welcome back, Mason. Nice to see ya again." She winks and then sits down on the toilet. She reads me the takeout menu from Jersey Mike's and I'm not all that hungry, but I know I need to eat, so we settle on splitting a turkey and provolone, and she leaves to place the order.

I dress in black leggings and a T-shirt that I'm pretty sure is clean and then meet Courtney in the living room. She's tidied up and I can't say I'm mad about it. This place was a pig sty.

"Thank you," I say to my best friend. She sniffles and holds back a tear, even though Court isn't one to cry, and I understand.

"I'd cry, too, if my best friend walked out of the bathroom looking like this," I joke. And it's inevitable after that...Court barrels into my arms—careful of my still-healing ribs—and we cry. We stand there holding each other, and we cry like toddlers.

Because what the fuck would she have done without me?

Our food arrives and we take it into the living room, both of us snuggled onto the couch, watching *Guy's Grocery Games* as we eat.

"So, what's your plan?" Court asks, her mouth stuffed with a chunk of her sandwich.

"I'm not sure yet," I admit.

"Are you going to come back to work?"

I shrug. "Eventually, yes."

"Franklin keeps asking about you, about how you're doing. I think he sent flowers again?" I nod and gesture to the console table.

"Pretty," Court says. And then, "Not that it's any of my business, but what are you doing for money right now?"

"I had some saved…" I trail off. Court nods, taking the hint that I don't really want to talk about it.

"Want to watch a movie?" she asks.

"Not really."

"Cards? We haven't played Rummy in a while…"

"No, thanks, Court. I'm really not feeling up for anything more than this right now."

"Okay, fine. It's settled then," she sets the remnants of her half of the sandwich in the wrapper on the table and pops up from her seat, heading down the hall. "I'm giving you a pedicure!" she yells. She opens the linen closet and pulls out a foot bath and a pedicure kit and I chuckle at the fact that she knew exactly where those items would be.

"I'm not even going to argue with you," I say, leaning back against the couch. "These feet are outa control." I wiggle my toes and Court sits down on the floor in front of me.

"Well, shit, I didn't really think this through, did I?" she says, grimacing. "What are friends for, huh?" she shrugs and holds up a couple bottles of nail polish. "What color do you want?"

I smile, and nothing else matters right now. This is exactly what I need.

"Surprise me," I say.

CHAPTER TWENTY-FOUR

Allie

Thursday, July 9, 2015

I shower and dress in jeans and a T-shirt, throwing my hair into a messy bun on top of my head. I check the locks on all the windows several times, and then close all the curtains before making my way to the front door. A bright yellow sticky note covers the peep hole and I lift it, peering through the tiny hole to make sure the hallway is empty. I don't see anyone, but still my breath catches and goosebumps line my arms.

I don't want to open the door.

You need to do this, Allie, I chide myself.

Deep breath in, deep breath out.

My hand hovers over the deadbolt, and somehow I manage to flip it to the unlock position, but I flip it right back immediately after. I do this another half dozen times before I eventually leave it in the unlock position.

Now the knob. My hand rests on it, but doesn't move, the

effort seemingly too large. I breathe. I inhale deep breaths, I exhale.

I do this another half-dozen times before I eventually turn the lock on the knob, and now I'm sweating. There are actual beads of sweat forming on my forehead, and I hate them.

My front door is unlocked.

Anyone could get into my apartment right now.

I lift the sticky note again. I peer through the hole. There's no one out there. The hallway is empty, and no one is going to push their way in here and—

My cell phone rings in my purse, scaring the living hell out of me. I jump, and I'm pretty sure I scream a little.

Instead I turn both the deadbolt and the lock on the knob to the lock position and fumble through my purse for my phone.

Unknown Number.

"Hello?" I answer. An unknown number is no longer a rarity for me these days, not with the investigation going on.

Someone is breathing softly on the other end of the phone.

"Hello? Is anyone there?"

Silence.

Aside from the breathing.

Aside from the pounding in my chest.

"Is anyone there?" The silence sends my heart rate into the stratosphere and I feel slightly faint.

I end the call and stare at the screen for a moment before dropping my phone onto the floor and dragging the console table over from the wall. I shove it against the door and double-check the deadbolt.

I have everything I need right here at home.

The next morning I'm repeating the process, but this time I make it through the front door. I lock up, my eyes darting back and forth, making sure no one is in the hall. When I finish, I hold my keys in my hand while I walk briskly to my car, the tip of my car key poking through between my pointer and middle fingers.

Prepared for attack.

I tap the unlock button on the key fob and slide in, immediately re-locking the doors. I breathe. I try to find my zen, because I have to do this. I have to be able to leave my apartment and live my life.

I stick the key in the ignition and turn, it starts and the sounds of *Dave Ryan in the Morning Show* fill the small space. I jump and then push the knob to cut the radio. I adjust the mirrors, because Tarek was the last person to drive my car, and then check the gas gauge, pleased to see the tank is half full. I secure the seatbelt and then shift into gear.

Everything is okay.

I walk cautiously into the police station, my purse closely secured against my hip while my eyes continue to scan the parking lot. I turn and look behind me a few times, making sure no one is lingering behind. My heart thuds predominantly in my chest, and before I know it, I'm sprinting to the door.

I'm greeted by the desk sergeant and ask to see Detective Feeney. I'm lucky he's in. I hadn't thought to make an appointment, focused as I was on actually getting here.

I'm led to an interview room and left alone with the door closed. I set my purse on the table and take in my surroundings. It feels stale, cold, and generally unlike the man who will soon be sitting across from me.

Detective Feeney gives off warm vibes, like a protector. I can't help but wonder how he can work in such a stagnant space, how he juggles working with sometimes violent criminals.

"What can I do for you, Miss Mason?" he asks, stepping into the room and taking a seat across the small table.

"I think I have some information."

I tell him about my recurring dream, about the man I see and his dark eyes.

"How sure are you?"

"I know what I saw," I snap back. Detective Feeney sighs and hunches his shoulders, crossing his arms over his chest.

"Allie, I know you want us to catch this guy. But I can't go after a needle in a haystack."

"I'm telling you, he has dark blue eyes and dark hair. I saw it..." I trail off, losing confidence by the second.

"...in a dream." He punctuates my sentence as if it's his own, and I can see the remorse in his eyes. He wants to catch this guy as much as I do. He wants me to be right.

"Yes," I whisper.

Detective Feeney clears his throat and raises his hand to his forehead, rubbing it as if it's a magic lamp about to grant him three wishes.

His tall frame somehow hovers over me, even from across the table. He stands, pacing the small space, and I almost back away, but remind myself that he's not a threat. He's here to help, and I came here on my own volition.

"You're sure there's no lingering ex-boyfriend somewhere?" he asks skeptically, his pace slowing. He reaches for a manila folder on the table—my file, I presume—and opens it, pulling out a sheet of paper.

"I'm sure. Tarek and I broke up before the...attack," I manage to say, still not quite comfortable calling it what it was. "We were together for about six years, and the guy I dated before him was at least a year before that. There's no one else."

Feeney shakes his head, clearly thinking I'm missing something. "How are things with Tarek?" he asks, his tone almost accusatory.

I suck in a breath, struggling to contain my surprise at the question. "Fine," I say. "Things with Tarek are fine."

I see it then, Feeney's dislike of Tarek. And that's okay, he can dislike him, or anyone else, for that matter. But that doesn't mean Tarek was involved in what happened to me. I keep the thought to myself, my silence enough as Feeney moves on to the next question.

"There has to be *something,"* he says. "A stranger attack doesn't make sense, not anymore. This feels personal. Specific. There are no known serial rapists—or otherwise—with this MO known to the area, either. It doesn't fit a pattern." He glances down at the paper in his hand, squinting at the words on the page as he tries to make sense of them. I know he's already telling me more than he should, but there has to be something we're not seeing.

"Well, they all start somewhere, don't they?" I argue, certain that nobody I know is capable of doing something like this.

"Where were you that night?" he asks after a brief pause.

"Home."

He arches an eyebrow, his face a solid tell that he doesn't quite believe me. "Before that?" he asks.

"Home," I say again, my voice sturdier than the first time I uttered the word.

"You never left your apartment?"

I shake my head. "No."

He sighs and sets the paperwork down on the table, frustration dwelling. "Someone *had* to be there, Allie. Someone you know. Who?"

"I'm telling you, I was alone all day."

"How do you know that if you don't remember anything about the attack?"

"Right. About the attack, no. But I know I was home that day. I know I worked for a bit that morning, and then I had groceries delivered. I unloaded them and put them away around one o'clock that afternoon. I took a nap, and then read a book on my couch. I literally did nothing else, unless you want to go over my bathroom habits, too?"

He frowns, and I instantly regret my sarcasm.

"Hold on," he says, an idea clearly dawning on him. "Where did you order groceries from? Who delivered them?"

"Instacart…and I don't know. It's someone different every time."

"Did you eat or drink anything that was delivered?"

"Well, yeah, I—oh, my God…you don't think…"

He nods, his hand swiping over the sweat on his upper lip as he takes a seat and starts flipping through my file. He pauses on a page a few sheets in. I'm left staring at my hands, massaging my fingers mindlessly while his brain works through the seemingly new information I've given him.

"You didn't know the delivery person, right?" he asks, and I shake my head no as he continues. "What if something you ordered was tampered with? Something that was delivered that day. I need to know everything you ate or drank after that delivery." He reaches for a legal pad across the table and flips to a blank page, readying a pen I never saw him pick up.

"I…"

"Come on, you said you remember everything before the attack. What did you eat?"

I think back, stumped that the answer isn't coming to me easily, that it's not readily available. I open my mouth to speak, but no words come out, and I need another moment to think. Detective Feeney watches me intently, and the room feels like it's caving in on me. My breath hitches, my palms now moist.

"It's okay, Allie. Concentrate. You can do this," he coaches.

"Salad!" I shout, pointing at nothing in particular. "I had a salad. Caesar, one of those pre-made ones."

"Okay. What else? Did you have anything to drink?"

"Coffee that morning…and just water, I think." I rack my brain, trying to recall. I know I opened a bottle of water, and I'm fairly certain I drank the whole thing, plus one or two more.

"Water?" He pauses and grabs a document from the file. "From the tap, or a plastic bottle?"

"A plastic bottle."

"Was the case damaged at all?"

"I…I don't think so, no."

"How about the seal on the bottle? Had it been broken?"

"No, I think it was sealed."

"You think?"

"I don't know, Detective. I can't remember, but I think it was sealed."

"Okay, I need to find out who delivered those groceries. I'd like to have a chat with the delivery driver." He shoves the papers back into the folder and stands, motioning for the door.

"Wait, what? That's it?" I scoop my purse up from the ground and follow him to the door.

"For now," he says. "I need to look into a few things." I grip the strap of my purse tightly, because for some reason my pulse is racing again. Detective Feeney looks back at me, likely wondering why the hell my feet aren't moving so he can get out of here and start tracking down the delivery guy.

"What's wrong?" he asks.

I shake my head, unsure. I don't want to leave the safety of this room, despite the fact that less than a half hour ago it threatened to swallow me whole. "I'm scared," I admit, shame-faced.

Detective Feeney's face softens, and he steps closer, placing a hand on my forearm. I don't flinch like I expect to, but the contact startles me all the same.

"Do you want me to have an officer drive you home?"

"No, I…can't ask you to do that. You guys have more important things to do, I'm sure. Maybe just give me a minute?" He nods, and steps out of the room.

When I work up the courage to do the same, twenty minutes have passed, but Detective Feeney leans against the wall across the hall, his keys in hand.

"Ready?" he asks, pushing off the wall. We walk together and say nothing, something unspoken yet understood between us. And I'm grateful.

I don't have to drive home alone.

CHAPTER TWENTY-FIVE

Owen

Friday, July 10, 2015

I follow Tarek to a bar in Uptown. I don't know why, but I do. Allie went to bed hours ago, and I wasn't tired, so I figured I'd see what the asshole was up to.

Three shots and a few beers in, he's pretty hammered, and I wonder if Allie has any idea this guy still parties like he's in college, like some jock whose daddy pays the way so he can get away with anything he wants.

My jaw clenches, and it takes every muscle in my body not to go over there. Not to pummel his face into the sticky concrete floor of this bar.

He doesn't deserve Allie.

He doesn't deserve a fucking thing.

"Owen?" I turn and see Millie behind me, dressed in her typical skank-wear, yet somehow still fuckable beyond belief.

"Oh, hey," I shout over the music. I attempt nonchalance, but it's insincere. I haven't seen her since the night of Allie's attack, and I'm suddenly reminded that I never even told her things were over between us. I blocked her number after the first missed call and then the first text the following evening when she invited me over.

"Haven't seen you around much," she says, her bottom lip in a pout. "What happened between us?"

What a loaded question, Millie.

I shrug, not in the mood for this conversation. Her face drops, and I see the hurt in her eyes. "Look, I'm sorry…it's just not a good time," I say.

"Whatever," she stiffens, squaring her shoulders, and turns on her heel. I check out her ass as she stomps away, suddenly recalling what she looks like naked and nearly chasing after her to beg for forgiveness.

But I don't.

I need to stay focused for Allie.

I stay and watch the sleazeball for another half-hour or so, eventually ditching him and heading home for the night. I intend to go to Allie, but the noise from the bar has left me with a headache, so I don't.

I strip out of my clothes and take a quick shower, rinsing off the smell of the bar, and then climb naked into bed. Sleep comes easier than usual, but the ache in my heart never settles.

CHAPTER TWENTY-SIX

Allie

Saturday, August 1, 2015

"It's been weeks, but I still can't stop thinking about Feeney's comment, his face when he asked about Tarek. His line of questioning was unexpected, and while I do think he's wrong, he made some valid points." I look down as the words come out, unsure what Court will say, but certain she'll think I'm off my rocker.

"Allie…really? You think Tarek had something to do with this?"

"I don't know, Court! I don't know anything anymore." I lay my head in my hands, holding back tears I know will come anyway. "I just want answers."

"I know, honey, really. I do. I can't begin to imagine what you're going through, but leave it to the police. They'll catch this guy."

"It's been six weeks…"

"It has. You're right about that, but think about the

evidence; the blood that doesn't match Tarek, the fingerprints. How do you explain that if Tarek was involved?"

"I can't. That's just it; I can't explain any of it, and it's so frustrating. I just want this to be over."

Court scoots closer and wraps her arm around me, pulling me close. I fight the tears, desperate to make it through one day without crying.

"I know you'll disagree," she starts, "but I think we should go out tonight. You and me, like old times."

"Oh, I don't know, I—"

"No excuses!" Court says, popping up from her seat on the couch. "You *need* this. You've been sitting around here doing next to nothing, stewing by yourself about this horrible *thing* that's happened to you. And it is, it's horrible. But, Allie, I miss you. I miss my friend, and I just want you to be happy. It'll do you some good to get out."

I shake my head no, but Court feigns ignorance. "Come on, I'll even do your hair and make-up like old times." She smirks and bats her eyelashes and I can't help but giggle. She used to give me that look all the time, and it's the first time I've seen it in a while. And then, because she knows she still hasn't sold the idea, she says, "Diamond Back is playing…"

"You should have led with that." I huff and fold my arms across my chest. "Fine. But let the record show that I'm doing this against my own will and better judgment."

"Let the record show as well that I don't give a damn," Court counters, her hand on her hip. She winks and grabs my arm, pulling me off the couch and down the hall to my bedroom.

"Good luck finding anything other than sweatpants and T-shirts in there…" I say to Court as we stand in front of my closet. She winks and starts pulling garments off their hangers.

"Challenge accepted," she says.

People filter in from all angles, the crowd growing larger by the minute, and I feel a shift in my mood. I don't want to be here around all these people, but Court's having fun, and I'm supposed to be, too. Somehow she managed to pull together a little black dress and three-inch heels for me, and despite my apprehension, this is the best I've felt about myself in weeks.

"I'm going to grab a drink!" I shout to Court over the music. I feel the bass from the speakers in my chest, the beat of the country cover song rattling inside. Court nods and continues dancing to the band.

I make my way to the bar, cutting couples and trios in half when they don't move out of my way. I signal the bartender and, to my surprise, find an open stool. My purse clutched to my belly, I dig inside for a twenty and slap it onto the bar top, but there's a deep voice in my ear before I can even signal the bartender. I jump.

"Buy ya a drink?"

I'm fully expecting to turn around and see Tarek, but luckily it's just some random stranger; two sheets to the wind and looking for somebody to go home with.

"Oh, I'm here with someone. But thank you," I say semi-politely.

Court counts as "someone", right?

"So?"

"Excuse me?"

"It's a drink, not a marriage proposal." He huffs and downs the rest of his drink. "Get over yourself." He pushes off the bar and saunters off like the thirty-something man-child that he is. I shake my head and brush off the intrusion, signaling for the bartender. He finally takes his eyes away from a rather large set of boobs leaning over the bar and nods in my direction.

"Rum and diet, please."

"Six-fifty" is all he says before reaching for a clean glass and returning his attention to the chest in front of him.

I feel another presence, but when I turn, there's no one within a two-foot radius. I shiver, suddenly cold, as I sip my drink and scan the room.

And then *he's* there.

We lock eyes and he doesn't look away…his stare is intense, but non-threatening.

I can't shake the feeling that I've seen him before, that I know this man. I peel my eyes away and search for Court in the crowd. She's gyrating against the guy who offered to buy me a drink, and I can't help but chuckle at the irony. I'll have to let her down easy and tell her he's an asshole, but I give her a few minutes to dance in the meantime.

When I turn back, *he's* gone.

My stomach rumbles, and suddenly I'm dizzy, light-headed, even though I've only had a couple sips of my drink. For a moment I imagine I've been roofied, but that thought quickly dissipates as I remind myself no one has been near my drink.

I suddenly don't want it anymore, and I slide it onto the bar top, motioning for the bartender again. "You all right?" he asks?

"Water…" I manage to squeak out. I sit on the stool for a moment, and he hands me a plastic cup of ice water, which I down immediately.

My stomach in knots, I slide off the stool and trot toward the restroom, pushing my way into an empty stall and leaning over the bowl. I vomit violently, my insides on fire.

CHAPTER TWENTY-SEVEN

Allie

Wednesday, August 12, 2015

I don't feel like myself.

I can't seem to shake the feeling that something else is wrong with me, something physical. Medical, like internal bleeding or something that'll surely kill me.

I double over the toilet, my hands gripping the seat so tightly the tips of my fingers turn white. The acidic vomit burns in my throat and I gag, but nothing more comes up. I drop to the floor and scoot back against the wall, still close enough to the bowl in case I need to be sick again.

My ab muscles burn from the pain of vomiting, my ribs not yet fully healed. Everything hurts.

I fall asleep on the bathroom floor, the tile cold against my cheek.

An hour later I wake up cold, but not from the chills. Simply because I've fallen asleep over the air vent and the AC is blowing on my feet. Despite my cold toes, I feel perfectly fine and pull myself off the floor and into the shower.

I eat dinner.

Three bites in, and the nausea hits me again and I'm running to the toilet. I heave, my ribs on fire as I'm gutted once again. This time it hits me like a ton of bricks. Goosebumps trickle down my arms, and with my face resting on the toilet seat, I just know.

I'm pregnant.

"You're about eight weeks..." Dr. Regan says, her face twisted with concern. She knows what eight weeks means. She knows the terror this brings, the possibilities it threatens.

My baby is measuring on target and with a solid heartbeat at one-hundred-forty-eight beats per minute. And while I can stand to gain a few pounds, the baby is perfectly healthy.

Perfectly healthy.

It almost seems unfair, doesn't it? While so many women in the world are suffering miscarriages, still births, infertility, and literally praying for a child of their own, that I would somehow end up with one that I don't want.

One created by a monster.

I haven't had a chance to accept this yet.

I'm not ready.

This baby is not mine—it's *his*. Regardless of who *he* actually is.

I need more time. For what? Who the hell knows. An abortion? I'm not sure I could go through with that. I'm all for pro-choice, but now that it's me? Now that it's *my* body? I don't have much time to decide, which doesn't help—I can't make this decision lightly.

Eight weeks.

Since my attack.

Since my life was ripped away from me.

I draw in a breath, my hand instinctively covering my mouth. My eyes fill with tears, and before I know it I'm bawling like a baby and being held by my primary care physician.

It's not her fault, yet for some reason I have to fight the urge to hit her.

"We can discuss your options," she says, but I know that's pointless. I know I have no choice but to carry this baby to term. The other option isn't something I'm wired to do and therefore isn't an option at all.

I won't have an abortion.

"A prenatal blood test can be performed to determine paternity as well," she starts, but I struggle to digest her words, and she doesn't push it further.

This is all too much.

"Is there anyone I can call for you?" Dr. Regan asks, seemingly ready to give up her position as my shoulder to cry on. I don't hesitate.

I give her Courtney's number, and she leaves to have her nurse make the call. I sit on the exam room table until there's a soft knock on the door over a half hour later. Court enters, the nurse lingering behind her. I'm sure they need the room for another patient, but still I sit, hospital gown open at the back, my ass crack exposed to anyone walking by.

But I can't care.

It's nothing in comparison.

Court's arms wrap around me tightly. She says nothing, just smooths the hair on the back of my head and holds on for dear life. She knows; the nurse has told her, and I'm grateful, because those words aren't ready to fall from my mouth.

She cries with me, loud heavy sobs that neither of us could hold back if we tried. She knows what this means, what it changes.

Through snot and sniffles, Court finally pulls away. She grabs us tissues from the counter and we wipe our eyes. We grab new tissues and wipe our runny noses. We say nothing, just console each other through facial expressions.

She grabs my clothes from the chair and hands me my jeans before extending her hand. I take it, and she pulls me to my feet. Dropping the hospital-issued gown, I dress in a zombie-like state. I pause when Court draws in a breath and places her hand over her mouth, her eyes drawn to the scars on my skin, still lingering after all this time.

"It's…not…right…" Court chokes out. She drops to the chair and reaches for another tissue, hanging her head low and shaking it back and forth.

"I know," is all I say. It's all I can muster.

Nothing is fucking fair anymore.

The possibility exists that my attacker is the father of my child.

This is the gut-wrenching thought that repeats on a loop in my brain. Over and over and over again. Nonstop since the moment Dr. Regan confirmed my pregnancy.

The thought makes me sick.

Even though Tarek and I slept together not long before the attack, the logic still points to my attacker being the father of the child growing inside of me. Tarek and I used protection, so it can't be his.

It has to be the other guy.

Right?

I don't know what to think, how to feel.

I don't want a child with either of these men, and I'm not ready to be a parent, let alone a single parent at that. I climb onto the bed and crawl under the covers, curling into the fetal position, my tears soaking the pillow.

I have to tell my parents.

I can't imagine what this will do to them after the pain they've gone through since my attack. Mom has been worried sick, sending casseroles and food over with Lincoln every time he stops by. She's begged me to come home, but knows I'm too stubborn to do so, and my apartment is too tiny for her to stay.

I have to do this alone.

CHAPTER TWENTY-EIGHT

Allie

Thursday, October 15, 2015

Everywhere I go, I feel like people just *know*. Like there's some invisible sign plastered to the back of my shirt that says, **THE BABY'S FATHER IS A RAPIST.**

The feeling hasn't gone away since the day I walked out of Dr. Regan's office. Maybe it will once the baby comes, when there's no longer any evidence of my pregnancy. Of course, then it'll probably just be replaced with a new sign: **I GAVE MY CHILD UP FOR ADOPTION BECAUSE THE BABY'S FATHER IS A RAPIST.**

I sigh and tell myself to snap out of it, but the screaming in my head refuses to cease.

Tarek is here. He's always here, ever since I told him the news. He hasn't said much about it, other than that he wants me to keep the baby.

That he wants to raise it with me.

I'm not sure what to do with that yet, but one thing I do

know is that I can't do *this*. I can't have this baby and act like nothing is wrong. Like this child was conceived out of love.

I haven't told my parents yet, or Linc. I'm not sure how to, and honestly, I'm not ready to have the discussion of 'what's next' with them. For now, though, I'm going through the motions. I'm eating healthy, exercising when I can, and trying to do my part.

Today that part is a routine check-up to make sure the baby is developing as expected, that the heart rate is normal. I'm sure it is, but mine? Mine is not. I take my seat in the waiting area after checking in for the appointment and pull my Kindle from my bag.

"Really?" Tarek asks, looking offended.

"What?" I shrug, my eyes darting around the room.

"You're going to read right now? Instead of talking to me?"

Ah. There it is. The classic *Pay Attention to Me* game Tarek loves to play. I don't have the patience for it on a good day, let alone now, while my hormones are all out of whack. There are only so many conversations you can carry on in the waiting room of a clinic as it is, and small talk has never been my idea of fun. It's not like we can sit here and talk about what's very obviously on both of our minds—the two elephants in the room.

Elephant A: I'm only here because I was raped, not because my boyfriend/ex-boyfriend—the man sitting beside me—rocked my world one night and now we're the oh-so-happy expecting parents.

Elephant B: Tarek didn't ask to join me for today's appointment, he simply came with. I mean, he drove me here, which I appreciate, but I had other options. I realize this is something any loving boyfriend would do for his pregnant girlfriend, but again, I'm not his girlfriend, and this is not his baby.

It's complicated?

Sure, let's go with that.

And then there's the fact that the results of the prenatal paternity test are still sitting unopened, tucked safely under my mattress. Out of sight, but never really out of mind.

I can't bring myself to open the envelope and haven't even told Tarek about the test. I'm not sure he would be pleased with the fact that I plucked a few hairs from his head while he slept. I needed his DNA but wasn't ready to talk about it yet.

Now here we are.

After today's appointment, when it's time to leave, Tarek and I walk silently out to his car. We heard the baby's heartbeat today, and I wanted nothing more than to smack the smile off Tarek's face as the sound filled the room—because, yes, he came into the exam room with me; my insistence that he stay in the waiting area did *not* go well, and I wasn't about to make a scene.

Allowing him to share that moment was a mistake, one that will make tonight's conversation harder than it already is.

"Should we stop and grab a bite to eat?" Tarek asks, opening the passenger door for me. He's hovering, like I might break right before his eyes. A likely scenario, I suppose.

"Sure," I say, ducking under his arm and into the seat.

"What you hungry for?" He climbs into the driver's seat, securing the seatbelt over his chest before looking over at me. "What's wrong?" he asks, his eyes full of concern.

"Hm? Oh. Nothing. I just—"

"It's okay, baby, I'm here. Everything will be all right," he places his hand on my thigh. I flinch, but only slightly, and he pulls away abruptly. "I'm sorry, I know you don't like to be touched yet."

"It's okay."

I'm not even sure what caused me to flinch. If I don't remember the attack, why would a familiar hand to the knee trigger that response?

"Maybe we should order in instead?" He's being generous now. I know he doesn't want to order in, he's probably fucking sick of ordering in. He prefers a home-cooked meal.

But I nod anyway.

After dinner, I clean up the kitchen while Tarek watches the MLB playoffs on TV, his feet up on the coffee table and his arms behind his head.

He's gotten comfortable here again.

"Tarek?"

"Yeah, babe?" he calls back, his eyes still glued to the television screen. I roll my eyes and make my way over to him.

"What are you doing?" I ask, and his brow creases like he's confused. He gestures toward the TV with the remote in his hand.

"Watching the game…"

"I see that. I mean, what are you doing watching the game *here*?" I have his jacket in my hand and I set it down on the arm of the couch. He watches, his jaw slacked open.

I know this isn't like me, being so forward with him, but we've been here before, and it doesn't work. I can't do it again, not when there's life growing inside me.

"What are you saying, babe?" he stands but doesn't walk toward me.

"You should head home," I suggest.

"Are we really doing this again, Allie?" He steps forward. "After everything I've done for you?"

I take a step back, restoring some of the distance between us. My voice shakes, but I say the words anyway. "I just think it would be best if we move on—separately—before one of us gets hurt," I say. I know it's lame and sounds stupid, but it's all I can manage at the moment.

"I *am* hurt, Allie. Right now. Can't you see that?"

"Tarek, I can't do this. I truly *cannot* do this." The words feel wrong coming out of my mouth; I'm not sorry, but I feel like I should be, especially after all he's done for me. After the worry and the anger, the nights of holding me and sleeping next to me, next to my bedside, unsure if I'll wake up or if I'd be the same person once I did.

I'm not the same person.

And I don't want this—this relationship we've been faking for weeks—anymore.

"We can be something—a family. Don't you see?" Tarek pleads. "This baby is a second chance for us." He turns and paces the living room, running his hands through his hair, a labored sigh escaping his lips. I don't mean to hurt him, I really don't.

"No, Tarek. It isn't."

"It is! We can raise this child together. We can be happy." He says these idiotic words with a smile on his face, as if he actually believes they're true. As if we haven't gone down this road and that a rapist's child isn't growing in my womb.

"No."

I turn away and find myself heading to the kitchen, because I suddenly want copious amounts of coffee, but I'm not sure if it would be insulting to brew some right now with Tarek sulking in the next room. I'm pretty sure he's about to burn a hole through my area rug with the level of pacing he's working through.

Fuck it, I'm making the coffee.

I reach for the coffee filters and tin of coffee and silently remind myself that it's okay to feel this way. It's okay not to want him. It's okay not to want this baby.

The baby.

Shit.

I can't have the coffee because I'm out of decaf. *Of course, I am, because why wouldn't the universe take one more thing that I love away from me?*

I slam the lid back on the coffee grounds and shove the container aside. There's no rule book that teaches you how to deal with this shit. How to "get over" being violated in such a way that all you actually want to do is curl up in the fetal position and either cry or simply die. I like to think I'm stronger than that, but we never truly know how much we can handle until we have to handle it.

Tarek comes up behind me and snakes his arms around my waist, his hands settling on the baby bump forming beneath my shirt. He drops his chin to my shoulder.

"Allie, please—" he pleads. And I have to tell him. I have to tell Tarek what I've decided, without ever needing to know the results of the paternity test.

It's easier not knowing.

"I'm giving the baby up for adoption," I announce, nearly whispering.

"What?" Tarek barks, releasing his hold on me and taking a step back, his face full of torment as I turn and face him. He deserves eye contact for this. Why? I don't know—in case the baby is his?

"I'm meeting with an adoption agency tomorrow," I say.

He stews for a moment, silently at first. and then slams

his fist onto the counter. I jump in surprise. *"No*. This is wrong, Allie. It's...how can you give up *our* child?"

"Stop saying that! It's not *our* child! You have no idea what this is like, Tarek...no idea how terribly hard this is."

"I'm trying to help! I'm offering you the out that you need, here. Marry me. We'll raise the baby together. You don't have to do this."

"We broke up! Remember?" I say through muffled tears. "Before the...before all of *this* happened. Why don't you understand that?" My voice is barely above a whisper, but it's all I can do not to break down right now.

He takes my hands in his and I let him, because this is even harder than it was the first time. "This is our chance to start over, Allie. We can be a family. I'll raise the baby like it's my own, I swear to you."

"I can't...I don't want this. I don't want...*us*. This baby. This isn't a way to start a family and this child—despite whoever his father is—deserves a chance at a good life. I can't give him that."

Tarek's face softens and he lets go of my hands, running his fingers over the stubble on his chin.

"Him?"

Shit.

"It's a boy?" his mouth curves into a crooked smile.

"I didn't mean to tell you that, but yes. It's a boy." *Ninety-five percent likelihood,* according to the sonographer.

"Honey, *please*...don't take this away from me—from *us*. We can give this child a good life."

"Don't take this away from *you*? Tarek, what the hell don't you understand here? The baby might not even be yours! Do you have any idea what you're asking me to do? You're asking me to raise the child of a *rapist*!" I spit the word out, hoping it sounds as rancid as it tastes. His hands cup my face and he draws me closer, too close for comfort.

"Baby, don't you see that that doesn't matter to me? All I've ever wanted is you and me together, with kids and a dog and…I don't know what else, but it's always been *you* in that picture with me, Al."

"But it matters to ME!" I scream, absolutely fed up. He'll never understand.

I don't want this.

Not one part of me wants this.

The baby.

Tarek.

A family.

I feel like everything inside my head is kicking and screaming, throwing a fit and begging me to put an end to the misery, but I can't. I don't know how to do this, how to please everyone. Tarek, my parents, Court. Even Detective Feeney. Everyone expects me to just move on, to let it go.

I can't accept that the seed of a rapist may be growing inside me.

I run from the room and lock myself inside the bathroom, breathing heavily. I try to catch my breath, but my chest hurts and my eyes water.

Tarek yells from the hall, "Life isn't one of your fiction novels, Allie. *Fuck!* You sit here expecting some great love story and when I try to give you one, you don't want it!"

The front door slams and I slump against the wall, my head in my hands, the shame too prevalent to ignore.

CHAPTER TWENTY-NINE

Allie

Monday, October 19, 2015

On Monday morning I oversleep, which really is a daily occurrence at this point. The seconds, minutes, and hours tick by slowly while I lay down to sleep, but sleep rarely comes, and when it finally does, it's not long before I need to wake up again.

I'm still on extended leave from work, so it's not like it's a big deal most days, but I try not to sleep the day away.

And today, of course, I have somewhere to be.

Somewhere I don't care to go, but promised my parents—and Court—that I would, so I guess I'm going. I picture my adult self being dragged out of the car and through the parking lot kicking and screaming, tears soaking my cheeks, as my mother forces me into the therapist's office. Tantrums may have worked for a hot minute when I was three, but I don't think they'd get me anything aside from a trip to the loony bin today.

So I get out of bed.

I drag my ass into the shower, despite the fact that I showered last night. I brush my teeth, and flip my long hair into a chignon at the top of my head, and then pull on a pair of jeans and a hoodie. I'm keeping it simple with no makeup, because I'd be a fool to show up at the therapist's office looking put together. The poor woman would assume she's got an easy patient—someone who isn't there for any reason other than to flush money down the toilet.

I'm not an easy patient, and I know that.

Mariëtte Simms made that clear to me last week when she left me a cryptic voicemail insisting I see someone to discuss what happened to me—when she offered to put in a referral, since seeing her would be a conflict of interest, but this way she'll still be able to claim credit once I'm all fixed up.

I know her phone call was Tarek's doing. As if seeing a therapist would suddenly make me realize I've made a colossal mistake breaking up with him.

I switch off the light in the bathroom and toss my wet towel into the hamper. I stand in the doorway for a few seconds and try to remember why I'm going to this. Why I'm subjecting myself to something that'll do nothing more than upset me again. Just when I start to feel okay, something else pulls me back.

I realize a moment later that my lollygagging might be more about having to leave my apartment than it is about seeing a therapist.

It's not like it's any safer here.

It's supposed to be getting easier, but instead it all seems to be getting harder.

And as this realization comes to light, I suddenly can't breathe.

I dial the clinic's number and cancel my appointment.

Two days later, on Wednesday afternoon, Court takes an extended lunch break and drives me to my rescheduled appointment.

I pick at the fringe on the pillow, unable to focus my attention on Dr. Ellison. I don't want to be here, but I promised.

Dr. Ellison looks at me with compassionate eyes, her tone soft and almost comforting, which I realize is the goal to get me to open up, but it does nothing to put me at ease. I'm rigid, and I swear if it gets any colder in here I'll have icicles coming out of my nose by the time this torture hour is over.

She seems to be handling me with care.

As if I'm broken.

As if I'll further unravel and her efforts will have been for nothing.

"Do you remember much about the night of your attack?" she asks, adjusting the ballpoint pen in her hand. She hasn't made a single note on the page, and I wonder how much of this performance is just for show.

"No. Not really."

"What's keeping you up at night?"

"Really?" I'm incredulous. Annoyed that she would ask such a stupid question. "Isn't it obvious?" I ask, pointing at my protruding belly.

I hadn't expected it to grow so quickly, but there's a definite bump. I know, because I'm resting my hands on top of it, twiddling my thumbs and willing myself not to cry.

"A pregnancy is not always an obvious factor in sleep deprivation," she shares. "In fact, some expecting mothers report they sleep *better* during pregnancy."

"Good for them," I mutter, unintentionally rolling my

eyes. I don't mean to be rash, but my emotions are all over the place, and I seem to have lost control of my temper.

It wasn't supposed to be like this.

She ignores my snapped response and moves on to the next question. "Have you made any decisions about your baby?"

Her pen finally starts to move on the page, her eyes cast downward as she writes. "I've met with an adoption agency," I say. I hadn't intended to share that tidbit, but the words are out of my mouth before I can take them back.

"That's good. Good," she makes another note. "And, how are you feeling about that decision? It's not one to be made lightly."

"No, I suppose it isn't," I agree. I cross my legs at the ankle and refold my hands across my stomach. The baby is kicking, and I don't know what to make of it. I'm glad to feel movement, despite my desire to get this pregnancy over with. "I'm...I guess I don't really know. Nervous. Scared."

"Both are to be expected. And what about the baby's father?"

"You don't know?" I ask, baffled that Mrs. Simms didn't lay the groundwork for me. She shakes her head no, and I have no fucking clue where to start. We sit in silence for a few awkward beats, and as I'm opening my mouth to speak, she speaks first.

"We don't have to go over it today if you're not comfortable, Allie. Is it fair to say perhaps the father is no longer in the picture?"

I nod, sighing in relief. "Yes."

And it hits me then; I see it in her eyes the moment they change. It's subtle, but I feel her judgment. Despite her years of training and working in this field, she can't hide the emotions on her face. She doesn't understand why someone my age, perfectly healthy with a stable career, would give up their child, their own flesh and blood.

"Why do you feel that you're incapable of raising the child on your own?" she asks finally. I glance at the clock on her desk, and because I know we only have a few minutes left of our scheduled session, and because I've read enough books to appreciate a dramatic ending, I loop my arm through my purse and push myself up from the couch as gracefully as I can.

"I was raped," I say.

And then I leave her office.

Court drops me back off at my place, but doesn't walk me to my door since Franklin needs her back at the office. She missed a client meeting just to drive me today, and neither of us are sure Franklin would understand why it took both of us for this one measly appointment.

We don't talk much on the drive back, but Court reaches over and squeezes my hand before I climb out of her car.

It's happy hour night, and since I don't feel comfortable going out—and can't drink anyway—Court usually comes over to keep me company. I'm grateful for her and don't know what I'd do without her at this point, but I can't help feeling like I'm holding her back from something.

She's not a nurse and shouldn't be taking care of me like this. "Court, I'll be fine," I say, smiling genuinely. "I need to start spending some time on my own."

"You know I don't mind hanging out, Allie."

"I know, and I love you for it. I couldn't have made it this far without you. You're amazing and I love you. But I need to get used to doing things on my own again. I can't live my life in fear or else he wins."

"Wow, your appointment must have gone well today."

I chuckle, because of course none of this is the result of my therapy session. "It went fine, and thank you for taking me today. You're the best, Court."

We hug again, and she agrees to check in with me in the morning, to give me the night to myself with strict instructions to call at any hour, no matter what, if I need anything.

I trudge up the three flights of stairs, even though I'd much rather use the elevator, but because I'm trying to produce a healthy baby, I choose the physical exercise.

I turn the key in the lock and make my way through the door, dropping my keys onto the console table and reaching for the light switch.

But all the lights are already on.

My apartment is basking in lights I know I didn't leave on. I should be terrified, but I shrug it off. I know there's no one here. To think that there is would be indicative of paranoid thoughts, and I'm working on divorcing those.

I flick off a couple switches and head into the kitchen, opening the refrigerator and pulling out a bottle of water. I remove the cap and chug half of it before recovering it and placing it back in the fridge. I pause when I spot a half-eaten sandwich on the shelf.

I didn't eat that sandwich.

Certainly, I made that sandwich. I made it, and then decided I wanted chocolate ice cream instead and stuck the sandwich in the fridge. I didn't eat it, and I certainly would have remembered if I had. I close the fridge door and lean against it, convinced that pregnancy brain is real and I'm losing my fucking mind.

CHAPTER THIRTY

Owen

Wednesday, October 21, 2015

She's been gone a while, and I'm officially annoyed.

I didn't trek over to Allie's apartment just for her to spend the day somewhere else, somewhere I'm not even privy to.

What was she thinking, leaving like that?

She could be anywhere—it's not safe. I start pacing, my feet pounding out a rhythmic aggression on the pavement.

"Where the fuck is she?" I mutter to myself. I know I need to stop muttering aloud, someone could hear me, but then again I suppose they could hear my feet hitting the concrete just the same and what the hell good does that fucking do? None.

I raise my binoculars to my face and aim them at Allie's living room window; the curtains are open, but she still isn't home. She always opens them during the day, even after the night she was almost taken from me. It's almost embarrassing how naive she can be, and I don't know what to make of it, but I can't really force her to be more careful either.

I've always liked my women stubborn, I guess. I shrug, as if having a conversation with myself, and can't seem to shake the memory that I was with Millie just hours before my angel was nearly killed.

Fucking Millie.

If that bitch hadn't distracted me with her tits, this never would have happened. If I hadn't been busy thrusting into her like a hormonal teenager, I would have been on time to see Allie and stop that fucker before he ever laid so much as a finger on her perfect body. I can only imagine what it must look like now: tarnished, her flawless skin riddled with scars because of him. I hope he hasn't ruined her, but deep down I know better than to assume he hasn't.

But Millie won't distract me anymore; I've made sure of that.

My pocket vibrates, and the jolt stops me in motion. I shove my hand into the pocket of my jeans and retrieve the not-so-smart phone, audibly groaning and wishing I hadn't brought the fucking thing with me to begin with.

My mother's ugly face flashes on the screen.

There's no way she's out of money again.

I ignore the call and shove the phone back into my pocket. Fuck her. I don't have time for her incessant requests for drug money today. I need to find Allie, and I won't go home until I do. I continue pacing, my heart rattling at warp speed inside my chest cavity. A few more paces, and the hum of the vibrating tone strikes again. I ignore it for a second time and then power off the device, a mild action considering all I really want to do is smash it into a million tiny pieces. I already replaced one cell phone this month and don't need to replace another.

Mother can wait.

I'm startled by a noise behind me, the rustling of leaves or some shit, I don't know. I turn and to my annoyance, it's just a squirrel looking for a nut. I chuck a rock in its general direction and watch it scurry away.

Finally I spot her. She's with Courtney—which explains why her car was still here, but she wasn't inside—and they pull into a parking space in front of the building. I hunker further down in my hiding space, I can't risk being seen as she exits the vehicle. Allie clutches her purse, and keeps her keys in her hand, no doubt extending a key through her fingers to use as a weapon if necessary. I'm glad to see she's smartening up a bit. She surveys her surroundings before slamming the car door and nearly sprinting to the entrance of her building.

She's spooked, and I can't help but blame her. My poor angel. If only she knew I'm here, and that I'll never let anything happen to her again.

I resettle into the space, stretching out my legs a bit and look up to her apartment just in time to see her walk through the door. She pauses for a moment, then moves to turn off some of the lights I accidentally left on. I'm grateful though, that she doesn't draw the curtains and I can still see her.

I raise the binoculars again and span around me, searching for anything out of place, anything suspicious. All seems calm, so I relax and settle back against the bush while Allie sits down on her couch with a book.

I love to watch her read.

At dusk, when I spot him walking up to her building, I know there's no way I'm letting him inside. She's asked him to stop coming by, to stop sending her gifts. I've heard it with my own ears. Seen her throw out those same gifts time and time again.

She doesn't want him.

I toss my binoculars into my shoulder bag and lower my ball cap, making my way to the other side of the street quickly. He's standing at the door buzzer, but I can see Allie's shadow through the curtains, and she's still sitting on the couch. She hasn't gotten up to answer the ringer, yet somehow the door is opening and Tarek's making his way inside.

"How the fuck?" I mumble.

I pick up the pace and manage to catch the door before it closes again. I hold it so it doesn't click shut and then scamper off in the other direction until he makes it up to the first landing and then I follow him up. I'm not sure what the plan is, but I need to protect Allie, and that means I'm following this fucker until he leaves.

I stop at the landing on the third floor and peek around the corner down the hall. Tarek is standing at Allie's door, staring at it as if his eyes have the power to will it open.

He doesn't move for the longest time.

So I don't either.

CHAPTER THIRTY-ONE

Allie

Friday, November 6, 2015

My mind reels from lack of sleep, the nightmares too vivid to sleep for long. I wake covered in sweat, panting, my heart ready to burst through my chest.

I can't move, but I try anyway. I swing my arms and swat at his rough hands as they roam my body, at his face.

I can't shake this feeling of unease. It takes effort, but I sit up in bed, my belly a nuisance I have yet to get used to.

I kick as violently as I can, but I don't know that it does any good.

Lights flash outside and illuminate the room for a moment. I'm seeing shadows, like I'm being watched. The notion that someone's here makes my skin itch.

I have no strength, no fight left in me as I continue to drift into the darkness.

I climb out of bed just before 5:00 a.m., abandoning the

warmth of my blankets. Anxiety bubbles in my chest and the nightmare lingers as usual.

There's something about his eyes…

"I think I need to leave town for a bit," I tell Court later as she helps unpack my groceries. She hands me a box of noodles, and I stuff them into the cupboard label side out.

"What do you mean you're leaving town? Where are you going?"

"I don't know yet," I shrug. "I just feel like I need to get away for a little bit—maybe even just the weekend. This is all...too much."

"Allie, I get it. As much as I possibly can from the outside, I do. But you can't leave. I mean, you need support right now. And what about Franklin, huh? I thought you wanted to come back to work soon."

"I do. But you know I can work from anywhere. And like I said, it may even be just for the weekend. I need a change of scenery; some time alone."

"What about the investigation?" she asks. "That detective that keeps asking questions…what if he has more? What if they catch him and you need to testify in court or something?"

"Okay, for one, that's not happening overnight. And two, they have nothing, Court. Literally nothing. No leads, no suspects. Feeney says they're still investigating, but…" I pause, letting the sentence hang for a moment. "I haven't heard from him in weeks. There's nothing new, and I can't keep sitting here feeling like someone's watching me all the time."

"Where will you go?"

"I'll figure that out later. I just need to go."

Silence fills the room, our words dangling between us, and I see the change in Courtney. The way she's turned into Mama Bear, a protector. I'm lucky to have her.

"Thank you…" I say, turning to her and placing my hand over her forearm. She tilts her head, tears welling in her eyes. "I don't know what I'd do without you." We hug and let the issue rest for now.

"So…Feeney, huh?" Court says after a few minutes.

"Detective Feeney," I clarify.

"Mmhm. You're almost on a first-name basis, I see." Her lip curves, and I see what she's doing, what she's implying, but I'm not ready to bite.

"Oh, shut up." I toss a bag of marshmallows at her, and she giggles. I grab us bottled waters from the fridge, but not before inspecting them to make sure they're sealed.

You can never be too careful.

After Court leaves, I decide to pack a bag for the weekend. Where I'm off to, I have yet to determine, but maybe I can get a last-minute reservation somewhere. A knock on the front door startles me and I sigh, wrapping a throw blanket around my shoulders. I cross the room with a groan.

"Who is it?" I ask, looking through the peep hole. I'm not expecting anyone, but it hasn't been long since Court left so maybe it's her.

"It's Tarek."

I stifle a sigh. I don't have time for this right now. But I unlock the deadbolt anyway, as he already knows I'm home.

But every part of me wishes I hadn't gotten up to answer the door.

"Hey," he says, as I open the door, his shoulders drooped and his hands tucked into the pockets of his designer jeans.

"Hi," I reply, leaning against the door and blocking his way in.

"Can I come in?" He places his palm on the door, pushing slightly, but I push back.

"It's not really a good time…" I trail off, glancing at the clock on the stove. The last thing I want to deal with right now is another argument with Tarek. Letting him down gently didn't go as well as I'd hoped, and I'm tired of having the same conversation over and over.

"I'll just be a minute. Please, Allie."

I release a breath and take a reluctant step back, because I'm the *yes girl* so that's what I do. The door opens further, and Tarek steps inside. He's somber, clearly depressed and disheveled, and looking at me like his emotions are my fault. My responsibility.

He reaches forward and pulls me into a possessive hug, holds me so tightly I can barely breathe through his grip. "Tarek…" I push off his chest and separate myself from him.

It's then that I smell the alcohol on his breath.

And mint.

"Allie, baby. Please don't do this. We're supposed to be together," he pleads, holding our hands together between us.

"Tarek, no. I'm sorry, I know this has been hard. But I can't do this anymore. We can't keep having the same conversation."

"You don't mean that." He reaches for me again and I back away, his hands slipping from mine. He turns and runs his hands through his hair aggressively, and I see it now.

He's drunk.

"This is…so fucked up!" he yells. "It doesn't make any sense!" I can't tell if he's talking to me or himself, he's turned and facing the wall. "Look at you…" he says, his hand over his mouth. "Look at your belly. It's…*our baby* in there."

I reach for his forearm, "Tarek—"

He swats my hand away and turns abruptly. "You are *mine*, Allie. Mine! Who is he? Who else are you fucking? That's the only thing that makes any sense, but it can't be true, right? Because you would *never* do that to me. Is it true?" He paces, and a darkness washes over his face as he asks the question that's been on his mind since the day I first ended things between us.

He doesn't deserve a response, but I give him the truth anyway. "No, there's no one else."

"Then what the fuck is it?" he demands. He stomps back over to me and grabs my wrists, squeezing them and shaking my arms in front of me. "What is it?"

He's yelling now.

Tarek doesn't yell, so I don't know what to make of this.

"You're hurting me," I whimper.

"I don't give a fuck!" he barks "I didn't want to have to do this—" Tarek pulls a set of handcuffs from his back pocket. I flinch and try to step back, but his other hand is still holding my wrist, and he's squeezing so hard and I'm not quick enough to allude him, even in his drunken state.

His eyes are dark. He doesn't look like himself, and I don't know what to do, but all I can think is that I have to protect this baby.

"Shut up!" Tarek bellows, gesturing down the hall. "Get in the bedroom," he says more calmly, shoving me down the hall.

"What?" All I can do is hope I've already screamed loud enough for one of the other tenants to call the police. But suddenly I can't remember if I have, and I look toward the door, then back at Tarek, my eyes darting back and forth because this can't possibly be happening.

It can't.

The lock on the door isn't secured, and I try to gauge his reflexes.

If I can knock him down for a minute...

"You know, you sure are ungrateful sometimes," he slurs under his breath.

I want to argue back, to defend myself, but I don't do it. I say nothing, because anything I do say will only upset him more.

"Everything I do is for you—for *us*—and you don't give a shit. I tried to *show* you that you were meant to be a mother and that we could have a family, and you're throwing it away like we're *nothing*!"

He tried to show me?

He's quiet for a moment before speaking again, and when he does, his words take my breath away.

"Your birth control pills were placebos, did you know that?" He laughs, his eyes wide and crazed. "You wouldn't stop taking them, so I had to *do something*." His eyes turn dark, and he shakes his head, nearly chuckling under his breath. "Poking holes in the condoms wasn't working...and then you just *had* to go and tell Courtney that you needed more *spice*, right? More *passion* and *excitement* between us." He reaches for his belt buckle, loosening it and then unzipping his jeans and thrusting at me. "Is this enough fucking excitement for you, Allie?"

He throws the secrets I shared with Courtney back in my

face like they're poison, and I can't quite make sense of what he's telling me.

"Did you like it when I fucked you from behind, Allie? Hm? Was that more to your *liking*?"

I flinch at the harshness of his words, the hate in his tone. I can't process what he's telling me. I can't make sense of these words and whether they're true or just the liquor talking.

Then it hits me.

His breath on my face, panting as he hovers over me.

"Tarek…what are you saying?"

His mouth curves into a sadistic smile, and suddenly everything is so clear.

The feel of the calloused hands that groped my body hard enough to leave bruises .

"Ah, my little amnesia patient finally remembers, huh?" He taps a finger against his temple, taunting me, his eyes dancing as they graze up and down my body. I gasp, bringing a hand to my belly, my breath catching as panic rises in my chest.

"You…it was…*you*?"

"You gave me no choice, Allie. I had to drug you to get you to stop fighting me," he grunts as he shoves me into the mattress and holds my wrists so tightly they feel like they're about to shatter. "It's just Rohypnol, don't worry. Nothing that'll cause long-lasting effects."

"Please..." I whimper. A tear slides down my cheek, and I know I won't be able to fend him off much longer. He's too strong and I'm growing weaker by the minute.

The water.

He drugged the bottled water when he grabbed it from the fridge.

Tarek climbs on top of me, his hands tearing at my clothes, exposing every private part of me before his mouth is on my neck, his teeth sinking into my skin. I scream, the pain searing through me like a volt of electricity.

I feel his breath on my cheek as he whispers in my ear. "I told you we will always be together, Allie. We are meant to have a family, a baby, and I will make sure you give me all of it."

He slaps me and my cheek stings, but I don't scream again because I know it'll only anger him more. I try to fight back, but I'm so weak. Drowsy. My head is a cloud of fog, and Tarek's face blurs in front of me.

"Stop resisting me, Allie." He almost begs, but I see it in his eyes, they're so dark they're almost black.

And they're filled with rage.

I don't understand what's happening, how we got here, but all I can think is that I'm about to die. The last thing I hear before I pass out is the zipper of his jeans being pulled down.

I try to scream, but nothing comes out.

"Of course it was *me*, Allie." He chuckles to himself again like I've said something funny. I can't breathe for a moment as his words ring in my ears. "I mean, I never meant to hurt you like *that*, really. But you made me so mad, I…I couldn't stop."

He comes at me quick, grabbing me and dragging me toward the hallway, toward the bedroom, and *oh my God, this can't be happening again.* A guttural sound erupts from my mouth and I try to kick, to shove—anything to stop what's happening—but my strength is still no match for his. I'm too pregnant to fight the way I want to, but unlike last time, I'm perfectly sober and he's the one incapacitated.

"You ungrateful bitch!" he shouts as he pulls. He grabs onto my hair and tosses me to the ground and this…this is where he fucks up.

Because despite my cantaloupe-sized belly, I'm still in shape and I'm still quick on my feet. I pop back up, ignoring the dizziness in my head, and level my stance.

Tarek's stare is menacing, but he's unsteady on his feet, swaying back and forth as if he can't possibly walk a straight line.

"Why are you doing this?" I ask, a crack in my voice. And somehow it's enough to distract him, to bring emotional pain to his face, and he looks hurt, like the words physically pain him and he doesn't really want to do what he's doing right now.

And the second he lowers his guard, the second he looks like he's about to back down and beg for forgiveness, I lunge forward and shove my knee as hard as I can into his groin.

And then I run.

I don't even check to make sure he doubles over on the ground, I just fucking run. I sprint to the door, swiping my purse from the table and running down the hall, down the three flights of stairs—all the while looking behind me to make sure he's not closing in. I run through the main door and down the sidewalk, faster than even I expected in my condition.

I don't know where I'm going, and I can't afford to waste time getting to my car, I just keep running. Down the street and then left, my bare feet pound the pavement as instinct kicks in.

"Allie! Don't run from me, baby!" Tarek's voice echoes

somewhere behind me, and my heart thuds in my chest. I have no idea if I can outrun him, no idea if running is even the smartest thing to do, but I can't stop now.

His feet thud on the ground behind me.

I look left, then right, but I keep running straight, checking behind me as I go.

My lungs burn from the chill in the air, and my breath clouds in thick bursts, but the wind is knocked out of me as I crash into something solid. It knocks me backward, pushes me off balance. Strong hands stop my fall and drag me from the sidewalk and into the alley.

He's caught me.

I kick violently and drag in a breath to scream, but a hand clasps over my mouth so tightly I can't even open it to bite at the flesh that's blocking my airway.

How the hell did he catch up with me?

"Shh, stop, Allie. He'll hear you," a voice whispers.

It's familiar, but I don't recognize it. I know it's not Tarek, and for some reason that calms me, and I stop kicking, my body going limp in this man's arms. I'm pulled further back behind a dumpster, and I need to turn around to see who's holding me, but I'm too terrified to look. My heart trembles in my chest, and I can't seem to steady my erratic breathing or the movement in my stomach.

I mumble into the hand that's holding me silent, promising myself I won't scream, but nearly certain I'll break that promise. He holds me against his chest and we breathe together, his chest rising and falling against my back.

"I'm going to remove my hand, okay?" The voice comes out a whisper, but it's masculine and protective. I nod against his palm, my cheek now moist with tears I couldn't stop from falling.

"Don't scream, I'm not going to hurt you." He removes his hand slowly, and I turn with apprehension.

I recognize the face that stares back at me, the shape of his build.

He's tall, dressed in all black, a ski mask pulled low over his brows, his face masked by a well-groomed beard.

Dark blue eyes full of worry stare back at me.

He looks just like the man who's been stalking me.

CHAPTER THIRTY-TWO

Allie

It takes me a moment to realize he called me by my name back in the alley, and once I do, the notion to run hits me again. Every ounce of me fully believes that this is the man who's been stalking me for months.

I've seen him.

But for some reason, I'm not afraid of him.

I feel safe, despite the creepy vibes I'm getting from being inside his house. It's dark, and not just because we're hiding out here. The curtains were drawn when we came in.

I think they're drawn all the time.

We sneaked through the alley and then through the woods to get here, like it's a path he's more than familiar with but never shares with anyone.

There's an air to this space; it's soothing, calm-like with light brown and dark chocolate tones. The furniture appears new and well kept—it smells like leather. The hardwood floors are swept, the surfaces free of dust.

This man keeps an impeccable home.

He gives me space to explore, tells me to have a look around and make myself at home. I run my pointer finger along the mantle above the fireplace, looking at the tip as I pull it away. There isn't a speck of dust left behind.

There are no pictures, no childhood memorabilia or even knickknacks. Just a few house plants and a bunch of hardback books. I scan the titles, surprised to see they were all published by Franklin Books & PR.

They're all books I edited.

The man hovers in the space between the kitchen and living room, two steaming mugs now in his hands, and I realize he's been watching me in silence. I didn't mean to snoop, but I couldn't help myself.

"Do you read?" I ask him.

"A bit," he says, dropping his eyes to the floor and moving toward me. He places both mugs onto coasters on the coffee table, twisting the handle of mine toward me and then gesturing to the couch. "Sit," he offers.

I clear my throat and sit. The couch is firm and feels barely sat in, and I wonder if it's new or just hardly used.

"Have some coffee. Yours is decaf." He lifts his own mug to his mouth and takes a sip, swallowing before saying, "I made it to your liking."

I look down at the mug. It's a Rae Dunn, and I can't help but wonder if that's a coincidence. Reaching for it, I thank him and take a sip. It's delicious, brewed to perfection, not burnt, and mixed with just the right amount of Italian Sweet Cream.

To my liking, as he said.

I don't ask him how he knows my coffee preferences, and instead take a second sip and then set the mug back down on the coaster. We stare at each other for an awkward minute, his eyes studying me intently.

"Who are you?" I ask quietly. He doesn't flinch or offer any kind of reaction. Surely he anticipated the question, but he ignores it and asks his own instead.

"You seem comfortable with me—why?" he asks, his blue eyes penetrating my own. I know I should look away, but I can't. I'm drawn to him for reasons I can't put into words. Perhaps fear?

"I'm not sure," I say finally.

"I won't hurt you, you know." His fingers reach mine, just at the tip, and the soft brush of skin-to-skin contact sends a shiver down my spine.

No, definitely not fear.

"Why did you bring me here?"

"He's looking for you," he says, as if that's enough information.

"I know."

"Your boyfriend is an asshole," he says as if he knows anything about him. It dawns on me that he might, actually, if he is the man I believe him to be, but I don't want to consider the reasons why.

"I don't have a boyfriend." I lean forward on the couch, crossing my feet at the ankles, my hands folded over my belly. As I do, he does the opposite, leaning back against the cushion.

"Well, you do—*did*—but that's beside the point," he argues, waving a hand in the air. "You're not safe with him, so now you're here."

He watches me again, and I want to ask more questions, so I do. "What's your name?"

"Owen."

"I like that name."

"I don't."

"Owen, why do you think Tarek is after me? Do you

know something I don't?" I can't help but feel there's some truth to his statement; to the notion that Tarek's done something to upset this man. That he's not willing to let me go, and maybe that means he'd do something he normally wouldn't.

"Yes."

He was watching that night.

He knows.

"Will you tell me?"

He says nothing as he stands and heads toward the window, peeking behind the thick blackout curtain. I can't help but admire his physique; he's built of lean muscle, his biceps flexing even from the minor effort of opening the curtain. The T-shirt he's wearing is taut against his stomach, tattoos hidden beneath the sleeves. He removed his ski cap after we arrived, and I was surprised to see a full head of dark hair.

I imagine running my fingers through it.

He pulls a set of zip-ties from his back pocket and turns to me.

I inhale sharply, surprised to see the restraints, but somehow I had known he would since the moment I realized he's the man who's been stalking me.

"Please…those aren't necessary," I whimper.

"I can't…I need to tie you up for a bit." He turns, his eyes meeting mine at the precise moment a tear rolls down my cheek.

I should have known this man is dangerous.

I don't fight him, instead I lift my arms as he loops the zip-tie around my wrists and secures it loosely. He helps me off the couch by my forearm, but he's not forceful and he averts my eyes. Like he doesn't want to do whatever he's about to do.

"I need to go out for a bit. I've set up a room for you, and you'll be safe here until I get back." He leads me down a hallway and into a small bedroom. A massive, king-sized bed covered in white linens nearly fills the room.

There's no window, just a small desk lamp illuminating the room from a small dresser next to the bed. I'm led inside, and he leaves me standing at the foot of the bed. He turns and exits the room, locking the door behind him, and I hear the click of a deadbolt from the other side, followed by a loud bang immediately after, like he's breaking things.

I lower myself to the bed, my wrists already aching from the plastic restraints. This is the moment I realize I'm not built for captivity. Not that any of us are, but I know with absolute certainty that I'll do just about anything he asks if it means I will get out of here alive.

CHAPTER THIRTY-THREE

Owen

Saturday, November 7, 2015

I don't know what possessed me to bring her here, to my house. Why I didn't bother to blindfold her, or take a roundabout route that would be sure to confuse her should she ever try to explain to the cops where she's been taken.

I don't know why I felt the need to restrain her. I think she would have stayed, even if I hadn't. But fuck, I don't want her to leave. She could live here with me forever, and I'd never ask a damn thing from her.

We'd be happy together.

She'd be mine.

I drag my hands through my hair and try to figure out what the hell I'm going to do. I don't really need to go anywhere, even though I told her I did. But I need to catch my bearings, figure out my next move. And to do that, I had to remove her from my presence so I don't scare her or try to kiss her or some stupid shit like that.

Fuck.

She's so beautiful, with her plump lips and gorgeous brown eyes. I couldn't stop staring at her like an idiot, and fuck if that's the first impression I intended to give her. I smack myself hard on the side of the head, muttering aloud.

It's hard to control the urges being so close to her. Smelling her and breathing her in. I adjust myself in my jeans. I need to think about what to do next. I can't keep her tied up in that bedroom. The poor thing is probably terrified and crying, thinking she's all alone.

I never want her to feel alone.

"It's okay, my love, I'm here," I whisper.

I hope she knows I would never leave her, that I'd do anything for her.

I groan and before I can stop myself, I've unzipped my pants and my dick is in my hand. I stroke it as if the answer will spew from the tip. I need this moment to refocus my energy, and it doesn't take but a few minutes to find the release.

I can't believe she's here.

I grab a tissue from the end table and clean myself up. Shame hits me like a ton of bricks, but with my head back in the game and my dick back in my pants, it's time to come up with a fucking plan.

I give myself an hour before going back to Allie. When I unlock the door and enter the room, she's draped across the comforter, snoring softly, and I can't help but admire the woman before me.

She's asleep on her side, her dark hair over her face and

her arms in front of her. A pillow tucked between her thighs. Her baby bump resting against the mattress.

I don't want to wake her, but I need her to know I'm here, so I nudge her foot with my hand and clear my throat. She startles, and scoots back on the bed defensively.

"Sorry," I say, and I am because she looked so peaceful and now she's back to being afraid. She says nothing in response as she gets herself to a seated position, somehow making it look effortless even with her hands tied. "I can take those off." I gesture to her wrists.

She nods and holds her arms out in front of her. I pull a knife from my pocket, and she flinches as I release the blade and step toward her. "I won't hurt you," I remind her. She nods again and watches as I slice through the plastic, rubbing her wrists once she's free of the restraints.

"Why did you tie me up?"

"I didn't want you to leave." I fold the knife and stuff it back into my pocket.

"I would have stayed."

I know I shouldn't, but I believe her. I nod, then shrug. The shame washes over me again. "Are you hungry?" I ask, and to my surprise, the corner of her lip pulls up and she half smiles.

"Very," she says.

I reach out and take her hand to help her off the bed. She adjusts her clothes, smooths her hair, and follows me to the kitchen.

I leave her there for a moment, and she watches me head back down the hall. I turn into my bedroom and pull a pair of sweatpants and a T-shirt from the dresser, because the clothes she's wearing are covered in dirt and dust.

"Here," I say, handing the stack to her as I return to the kitchen.

"Oh…thank you, I…I guess I look a bit disheveled, huh?" she says. She's embarrassed, but she doesn't need to be. It's not her fault she's dirty. I point in the direction of the bathroom, and she scoops up the clothes from the counter and goes to change.

In the kitchen I pull a carton of eggs, a package of bacon, and shredded cheese from the fridge. I know she loves omelets, but I don't tell her I know that. I just make her one.

When she's back, my breath catches. She's so beautiful, and I can't stop thinking how cute she looks in my clothes.

She takes a seat at the breakfast counter and watches me crack eggs into a glass mixing bowl, careful not to get any shells in the goo, because they're a bitch to remove and I want her to know she won't be chewing on eggshells.

"Do you like to cook?" she asks once the bacon is sizzling on the stove.

"I don't mind it," I say. The truth is I rarely cook. It's just me here, and it's a lot of work for one person. But I'd cook for her every day of the week if she'd let me. I know how to make all her favorite foods.

She's quiet again for a little while, so I focus on the omelets, frying the bacon to the crispy texture she likes—almost burnt, but not quite—and whipping the eggs in the bowl. I grab the carton of milk from the fridge and add a dash to the bowl, along with salt and pepper and then give the mixture another quick whisk.

When our omelets are ready, I slide the plate over to her, dressed to perfection, her omelet even sprinkled with the parsley I remembered to pick up the other day.

"This looks delicious," she says, smiling up at me. She picks up her fork and cuts into the omelet, placing the bite into her mouth and closing her eyes like she always does when she takes that first bite. "Mmm…this is really, *really* good, Owen."

"Thank you." I give her a half smile and sit down next to her, my plate in front of me. She turns to me and watches me take a bite. She's right, this is a damn good omelet.

"Where did you learn to cook?"

"The Food Network."

She giggles like she thinks I'm joking, and it's endearing.

"My mother…she wasn't around much, and I had a taste for good food and wanted to learn how to make the most of minimal ingredients." I pause and sip my orange juice. She watches me intently. "I learned everything I know about food from watching cooking shows. Survival of the fittest, I guess."

"Or something like that," she says. She smiles again and takes another bite. I can't stop watching the way her fork slides between her lips. "Owen?" she asks, catching me staring.

"Sorry." I stand and clear my plate, setting it in the sink, and then start cleaning up the kitchen. She stands next to me for a moment, the silence screaming so loudly I wonder if I may break. When she finally steps back, we work together to clean up the mess—she washes the dishes while I dry and put them away. It's a domesticated task I've never once had the opportunity to share with a woman, not even my mother.

And I've just shared it with Allie.

CHAPTER THIRTY-FOUR

Allie

We finish cleaning up the kitchen and take coffees back to the living room, sitting on opposite ends of the couch.

"You know what happened to me, don't you?" I ask Owen again. I can't overlook that he evaded the question when I asked earlier. I need to know.

I know this man had something to do with that night. I know he knows who raped me, who fathered the child growing in my belly.

For a brief moment I wonder if it's his and think maybe that wouldn't be so bad. It would be such a handsome child.

But Owen nods with indifference.

He doesn't want to tell me what he knows. He doesn't want to admit what he's seen—or done—that night. But I need him to.

"Will you tell me?" I ask, tucking my legs beneath me. He watches me intently, like he has since I arrived, and I wish I could tell what he's thinking, because I can see the pain in his eyes.

He's hurting.

And I want to know why.

"I don't think you'll believe me," he says, taking a sip from his mug and placing it on a coaster on the coffee table.

"I think I will."

And I know it then. I know what this is and why he's brought me here and what he's seen. There's recognition on his face, a sense that I've seen him before and he knows that I have.

But I'd forgotten.

"You're him…" I whisper, my hand covering my mouth. The tears come slowly and roll down my cheek, and I see him notice them. He scoots closer and he takes my hand, rubbing it gently with the pad of his thumb. "You're the man I saw that night, aren't you?"

The one I've been seeing in my nightmares for weeks, months. The man with the dark eyes, the angry eyes that penetrate me and don't let me go. The man in the shadows, the man…

But he wasn't angry at *me.*

He was angry at Tarek.

Owen nods. "Yes," he says, and the weight of his admission is almost too heavy to carry. I feel it deep inside, crashing down on my chest.

CHAPTER THIRTY-FIVE

Owen

The Night Of

I went to her apartment that night, the night it happened.

It wasn't because I have no self-control. It wasn't. I just really needed to see her. She hadn't been to her usual happy hour that week, and I needed to know why. She and that Courtney chick were like clockwork with their happy hours, so it didn't make any sense. And it wasn't fair, because I hadn't seen her in a week, since I was busy fucking around with Millie, and damn it, I missed her.

So I left Millie's and drove home, parking my car in the garage and then taking the path through the woods to Allie's. For a brief moment I wondered if she'd found out about me—if she or Courtney had seen me in the bar and gotten spooked. Or maybe she'd met someone new. She and that boyfriend of hers had broken up recently, and maybe it was because she found someone else.

All these fucking thoughts swarmed around in my head

for days. God, the guilt I carried for spending my time with Millie when I was supposed to be there with Allie. I nearly couldn't stomach it, and I told myself that no matter what, it didn't matter. If she was seeing someone, I would be fine without her for a little while—it would give me time to right my mind. To work on myself for her. But the truth is, I wasn't fine without her, not at all.

I needed her.

I wanted her.

I had to see her.

So I went to her.

I was just going to watch her from my spot across the street—not to scare her or anything. I would watch, like a good, respectful man, at a distance that would leave no cause for concern. She wouldn't even notice me there anyway. What's the harm, right?

I couldn't let her see me yet; I wasn't ready for her, not in real life. And until I was, I had to settle for small doses of her, for my eyes to marvel in the beautiful perfection that she is, while I somehow convinced myself not to pay attention to the constant ache in my dick.

At least not until I got home.

But that night everything changed.

My world turned upside down.

Dressed in all black, I walked through the woods to her apartment and climbed into the massive oak tree across the street, my new binoculars strung around my neck. All the lights in her apartment were off, but I knew she was home. Her car was parked on the curb outside.

My heart hammered in my chest in anticipation, and as I raised the binoculars to my face, my worst fears were confirmed: she met someone.

And they were fucking.

I could see him from the window—she was never one to bother closing the curtains. Why would she? My innocent Allie would never suspect a Peeping Tom in this neighborhood.

Not that *I* was one of those, but you get my drift.

Just as I'd shoved my suspicions aside, told myself there was no way Allie was screwing some other guy already, I saw him. I drew in a sharp breath as recognition hit me. It didn't make any sense—why they would be together? It physically pained me to see him defile her and take ownership of her the way he did. It wasn't right, and it didn't take but a moment for me to figure out why.

Suddenly my body took over, and I lost all control and found myself jumping from the tree. My feet hit the ground and I ran as fast as I fucking could, straight to the door of her building, my fists pounding on the glass until I was sure it would shatter under the weight of my fist.

No one answered, and it was locked.

I sprinted back outside, my feet planted like concrete bricks on the pavement beneath her window.

Think, Owen! Fucking think, you idiot.

I reached up and grabbed the release to the fire escape, somehow managing to pull my body up. I climbed the three stories and stopped just outside her window, my body motionless for a moment too long, admiring her breasts as they rocked back and forth from the motion of his body slamming into hers.

That's when he saw me.

His eyes wide, he pulled out of her, grabbing his jeans from the floor and tugging them on while running in the opposite direction toward the hall.

He didn't come after me; he ran from me like the coward that he is. Rage overcame every ounce of me in that moment.

I screamed and broke the glass, my binoculars a handy tool for such things. Jagged shards of glass sliced through my hand and forearm, but none of the pain registered; I had to get to her.

He was already out of her apartment, the front door slamming before my feet even hit the carpet. I couldn't go after him, not now that I was finally so close to her.

Not after seeing her mangled body like that.

My Allie. My sweet, beautiful, Allie, lay bloodied and beaten, her clothes torn and stained with blood, her hair covered in sweat and matted across her face, her forehead. I pressed my fingers to her neck and found a pulse. She was alive!

I paced and scanned the room. Her cell phone lay face up on the nightstand and I grabbed it, dialing 9-1-1 as quickly as I could before wiping it down and placing it back on the nightstand.

I had only minutes left with her, the cops would be there soon.

I pressed my lips to her forehead twice, my lips burning from the feel of her skin. "It's okay, my love. Help is on the way. Don't let go," I whispered.

Against every fiber of my being, I stepped back to the window and pulled my body through it, and back onto the fire escape.

Sirens wailed in the distance. They were coming.

I climbed down quickly and shoved the heavy ladder back into place before I turned and ran, mentally vowing to kill the fucking bastard who did this to my Allie.

So, yeah. I was there the night that fuck-face forced himself on Allie. The night he tore into her and took something that doesn't belong to him.

And I was jealous.

I was stark raving fucking mad.

The urges became too much to handle, and all I could think about is how vulnerable she looked laying there in that bed. I wanted to scoop her into my arms and lie in the bath with her, to wash her of him, of his semen and his sweat and every other damn thing he did to her.

I wanted to *murder* him.

To drag a jagged knife across his throat and watch him die as he choked on his own blood.

Instead, back at home I stripped out of my clothes and stuffed them into the washer, pouring a generous amount of liquid detergent into the front-loading machine and starting the cycle. I stood naked in front of it, staring, my heart threatening to beat straight out of my chest.

What the fuck happened?

What did I just witness?

I knew I should have been more careful, but I had to make sure the medics would arrive in time to save my Allie. I'd have to deal with the fallout later.

She was alive, and that was all that mattered.

CHAPTER THIRTY-SIX

Owen

I finish telling Allie about that night, and she looks at me with sad eyes. Her delicate features twist in concern. She doesn't understand, can't comprehend what all this means. Her entire world shatters before my eyes.

It hurts to watch her heart break like this. But the nice thing about broken hearts is that they can be put back together.

And that's exactly what I plan to do for Allie.

She hasn't spoken and doesn't know what to make of it all. She looks beautiful wrapped in my blanket, a book on her lap.

I love to watch her read.

I can't help but sneak another peek of her belly. It's cute, and looks good on her, but I don't think she wants it to be there.

I don't think she wants the baby growing inside of her, and even though it's like she's tainted in some way now, I still want to be inside of her, too. I still want to hold her and keep her here, and tell her she's safe with me.

But I don't, because if there's one thing I learned from my fucked-up childhood, it's that actions speak louder than words.

I have to show her.

"Are you warm enough?" I ask.

She nods, but doesn't speak. I can't help but think I've shared too much. That maybe I shouldn't have told her everything.

And I did.

Even the parts about Millie.

"Anything I can get you? Water? Tea?" I ask.

She shakes her head no, mumbles "Thank you."

I pick up the TV remote and offer it to her, but she motions to her book, and I place it back down on the table. I want to hold her, but I resist the temptation and don't pull her to me.

She slides over, though.

She leans against my shoulder, her head resting there, her hand on my thigh.

And she cries while I hold her.

CHAPTER THIRTY-SEVEN

Owen

Sunday, November 8, 2015

In the morning I make waffles from scratch. Allie loves waffles on Sundays. I plate hers with a cluster of strawberries and cut up bananas and then top it with syrup and a dusting of powdered sugar. I slide the plate over to her across the counter, and she looks up at me with those brown eyes I can't seem to get enough of.

"How did you know?" she asks, and I can't tell if she's pleased or if everything I know about her is freaking her out. I know she knows that I know more than I should.

I don't answer, just shrug, and turn back to the waffle maker to make another. She folds her fingers around her fork and pauses to look at me.

I pretend I don't notice, and she cuts into her waffle.

I know I shouldn't have brought her here, but nothing about it feels wrong, and I don't know what to make of that. I'm pretty sure my actions could be considered kidnapping, but it's not like she's tied up anymore or locked in a room she can't get out of.

She hasn't asked to leave.

"I was hoping maybe you'd let me have my phone back today," she says softly. She chews her waffle, and all I can think about is how much I'd like to lick the syrup off her bottom lip. I'm staring and realize with a start that she's asked me a question and I didn't even hear it.

"Sorry, what was that?"

"My phone," she says. "I was hoping I could have it back."

"Oh."

Okay, so I guess I did take her phone. And her purse. But I didn't *steal* anything, I merely hid it from her. Like a grown up game of hide and seek.

I remind myself I did it for her own good. I did it to protect her.

"Please, Owen, my family has been through enough. It's been two days, and I need to let them know I'm okay."

She doesn't know I've been in touch with her family. And Courtney. They know she's safe. I've texted with them daily, acting as Allie, since she arrived here.

But I don't tell her that.

Instead I say, "Let me think about it. He could be tracking you on your phone and you'd never know. You're safe here, Allie."

She stares at me for a beat before nodding and returning her attention to her waffle. I place a glass of pulp-free orange juice in front of her. She reaches for the glass, taking a sip and then setting it down.

"Your waffle's burning," she says, pointing to the cloud of smoke billowing from the waffle maker.

"Shit!" I grab a towel and start fanning it in the air while I open the contraption. It's black and burnt and about as appetizing as a turd on the sidewalk.

See, if she wanted to run, this would have been the moment.

Instead she laughs and takes another bite of her waffle.

CHAPTER THIRTY-EIGHT

Allie

Sunday, November 8, 2015

Owen is quiet and doesn't say much when he drives me home. I know he doesn't want me to go, that he wants me to stay. But I can't. I need to go home.

I have to prepare for this baby and figure out what I'm going to do—how I'm going to get through labor and delivery and whatever happens after.

I picked my son's new parents last week.

I'm still not quite sure what's happened with Tarek or what state I'm going to find my apartment in, but I ask Owen to come up with me to make sure it's safe. When he leaves I'll need to speak with Detective Feeney.

I don't know how much to tell him.

How do I implicate the man I had loved for so long? And how could he have done this to me in the first place?

Suddenly it all makes sense, why Tarek was there with me

in the hospital. Why he wouldn't stop pushing for us to get back together after he brought me home.

Mariëtte wouldn't stop pressuring him. His father wouldn't let it go, the fact that his son lost the one woman who fit so well into their family. At least that's what Tarek had told me, anyway.

That I'd embarrassed him by breaking up with him.

Emasculated him in front of his family and a restaurant full of strangers when he proposed and I said no, walking away and leaving him alone.

He made me pay for that.

He thought I'd come back to him when all was said and done, once I'd healed and given birth to his child. He would look like the hero.

Owen pulls up to the curb in front of my building and puts the car in park. He turns the engine off and I consider going up alone after all, but the moment my heart rate increases I'm reminded that's a terrible idea.

We get out of the car and Owen comes around to my side, meeting me on the sidewalk, his eyes darting back and forth, checking our surroundings.

Making sure it's safe.

We head inside and once upstairs, I'm surprised to find my apartment door closed. I remember I'd darted out rather quickly, leaving Tarek on the floor in the foyer. I turn the knob, Owen at my six—I've always wanted to say that—and push the door open.

I'm startled only slightly by the fact that it's unlocked, because what reason would Tarek have to lock it? Owen pulls me aside and heads in before me, his hand hovering over his pocket like he might pull a weapon at any moment.

I don't know what I expected to feel once I stepped inside, but my apartment no longer feels like home. It feels small—claustrophobic—and I bring a hand to my chest as Owen makes his way down the hall and into the bedroom.

He comes out a moment later, his hands now at his sides, and checks the locks on the windows, on the sliding door. Everything is secure.

The only thing out of place is the mess near the front door where Tarek and I fought.

I breathe a sigh of relief and Owen stands next to me. He takes my hands in his and pulls me to his chest. He hugs me, my belly acting as a spacer between us.

"If you ever need me…" he says, taking my head in his hands.

"I know," I say.

I open the door and Owen steps out, reaching across the threshold and taking my hand once more. I smile sadly. He rubs the top of my hand and then nods before turning and walking down the hall. I close the door, securing all the locks, and relief floods over me.

I breathe.

I ignore the mess by the door for today and make my way to the living room, lowering myself to the couch and pulling my grandmother's Afghan over my lap. I don't reach for a book like I normally would. Instead I grab a notebook and a pencil and start drawing, the thought to redecorate impaling my mind.

It's time to create a new space. Because as my mom always says, happiness is relative.

I'm a good half hour into jotting down ideas for my apartment when I realize I haven't touched my phone since I got home. I dig it out of my purse and see that it's powered off, so I turn it on and wait for the screen to load. I'm taken aback as I page through text messages and see that Owen had been in touch with my family, with Court. Acting as if he were me responding. I can't help but notice how much his responses sound like me.

I could have written them, they're so accurate.

I should have asked more questions, found out more about Owen. But he seemed so…normal. Aside from locking me up the first day that is. But even then, I wasn't all that afraid.

Somehow I knew he wouldn't hurt me, that he was only trying to protect me from Tarek. But it hits me again in that moment—the fact that it was Tarek who destroyed me.

It was Tarek who violated me. Who took my soul and ripped it clean from my body. I press a hand to my belly as I realize again that the child growing inside me does indeed belong to him. I would have been relieved, had I not learned what he's done to me.

No wonder he wanted to keep the baby.

My heart aches at the thought of him doing those things to me—at the realization that he drugged me and tampered with my birth control.

That he raped me.

Beat me.

He'd never so much as pushed me before this. I curl into a ball on the couch, my head resting on a throw pillow, my tears soaking through the fabric.

The child of a rapist.

I certainly can't keep him now.

The ringing of my cell phone jerks me awake the next morning. I've slept through the night for the first time in months, and after a moment of confusion, I right myself and grab my phone from the table. The name on the display nearly sending me into full blown panic.

"Detective Feeney?"

"Good morning, Miss Mason. How are you doing today?" He takes on a professional tone, but his voice is somehow warm and calming as usual.

"I'm all right, Detective. What's going on?" I tuck my feet under me and nervously play with a loose thread on the cushion.

"I just wanted to give you a quick update on your case. Do you have a minute? I tried calling yesterday." I nod as if he can see me, not sure the actual words on the tip of my tongue can manage to roll their way out of my mouth, but somehow he understands and continues. "We got some results back from the lab. On the, uh…"—he clears his throat—"semen sample."

My heart drops, and I know this is the pivotal moment in my case. I know what these results say, what they represent, and I wish I could go back and unlearn what I know he's about to tell me.

"Tell me," I manage to choke out. Because I need to hear it this time. I need to hear the science. The words feel lost in my throat, but I know I've said them.

"It's a match to Tarek."

"You're sure?" I ask, my hand instinctively covering my mouth and mumbling the words.

"Yes. We're still working to find a match on the blood and fingerprints from the window…" he says, his tone hopeful.

"Okay," I say with a sigh, expelling the air from my lungs

as I let defeat take over. Deep down, I knew, even before I really *knew*, that this baby was Tarek's. "What happens now?" I manage to ask.

He doesn't know the rest, I think.

"We'll need to continue pursuing the blood and fingerprints. I'll be in touch, Miss Mason."

"Thank you, Detective."

I end the call with Detective Feeney and set my phone on the coffee table. Despite the time that's passed, I still don't tell him about my pregnancy, and I don't tell him what I learned this weekend. I don't know how to explain any of it. I don't have any proof of what Tarek's done, other than his confession to me, and he'll do nothing but deny that.

And I don't need the DNA results to know who the blood and fingerprints belong to.

CHAPTER THIRTY-NINE

Allie

Sunday, December 6, 2015

I wake from a late afternoon nap to overcast skies, the same ominous shade of gray I feel inside. Snow is coming, the flurries already starting. I sit up in bed, stretching as I do so; the ache in my back getting worse by the day. I pad to the bathroom and relieve my bladder, certain I may as well take up residence on the toilet.

I crave coffee and decide to make a cup of decaf. I finish up in the bathroom, wash my hands, and then head toward the kitchen.

"Hello, Allie."

I scream, the words unexpected.

The figure on the couch stands, turning toward me, and my breath catches, my heart nearly going into shock.

How did he get in here?

I look toward the front door, see the locks are disengaged,

and panic starts to bubble up in my throat. I want to run, but there's nowhere to go.

Talk to him.

"Tarek, what are you doing here?" I ask, my voice shaking despite my attempts at willing it not to.

He's too close, inching closer by the second, but I remain as stoic as possible. I know he can see the fear in my eyes, but I fight it anyway.

"I wanted to see you," he says simply. As if he has the right. I say nothing, the words lost somewhere in the back of my mind as I try to make sense of what's happening. Of why he's here and how he got inside. "Allie, you *have* to get over this. Truly. You're alive, you're *fine*," he says tauntingly, like what he's done to me was nothing. "It's not like you remember anything anyway. Let's start over…be here with me." He holds his arms out as if I'll come to him. As if I want him to touch me.

His act isn't lost on me, but I see it now—that twinkle in his eye that tells me he's proud of what he's done. He thinks he's gotten away with it, that I won't tell anyone what I know.

There are no witnesses, after all.

Vomit tickles the back of my throat and I swallow it down, determined not to let fear take me down. I feel the panic attack coming before it hits, and all I want is for him to leave. My head is foggy, warm. I need to sit down, but I don't want him to witness me struggling—it does nothing more than provide him with a reason to coddle me.

How is this the same man who held me as I cried?

As the very wounds he created healed?

"I need you to leave," I say as confidently as I can muster. I know my voice is shaky, but I can't falter. Fear pricks the back of my neck.

"What?" he barks, somehow shocked. "We have a date."

A date?

"No, we don't." I take a few more steps backward, managing to open the door and hold it ajar for him. He stands there staring at me, and I fold my arms over my chest. "Please, Tarek."

His eyes bore into me, and I know he's angry with me, but I don't care. The right to be angry isn't his, but I can't say this to him because he doesn't listen when I try to explain.

"We're supposed to be starting over, babe," he says, taking a few steps toward me. My body hugs the door instinctively, I don't want him to come any closer, but I know he must to get through the door. "What happened to us, baby?" He shakes his head, and the hurt in his eyes would have killed me before, but I feel nothing. I say nothing, because there's no point in arguing anymore.

He's drunk again, I realize, and his words slip out of his mouth too fast, jumbling together like they're written in cursive. His arms hang loose at his sides, but he lifts one and swipes his hand against his nose.

"Tarek..." I start, but he cuts me off and shoves his pointer finger against my lips.

"Shh...don't," he says. His finger slides slowly down my neck, settling on my clavicle. "I need you."

I start to shake my head, but his hands are distracting as they move freely, his fingertips pressing into my skin. "You and me? We're perfect together. We fit. Our minds. Our bodies. You can't take that from us, Allie. You can't."

"I...think you should go," I whisper.

Now that I know what he's capable of, what he could do to me with all that built-up aggression, I'm terrified. My hands shake. I wish Owen were here, and I realize I'm hoping he's watching, that he comes in to stop Tarek again.

"No!" Tarek barks. His hands grip me tight around the waist and when I jump, when I resist him and try to pull away, one hand slides down my backside and cups my ass. He leans forward and places sloppy kisses on my chest, and I try to push him away, but he's like dead weight and doesn't move.

A tear slides down my cheek.

He's going to kill me this time.

He stops abruptly, his eyes finding mine. "Let's have a drink," he says. I feel him press against me in anticipation. He's pale and looks almost sick, the skin on his face slick with sweat.

"No, thank you," I say, the words barely audible as fear grips me from within.

"Come on, you know you want to. I'll make you another special cocktail." He tilts his head, taunting me with a smirk. His eyes are dark, and it's as if he's someone else entirely. He's not Tarek. He's not the man I loved for six years, the investment banker with dreams of a wife and a house full of children and white picket fences. No, he's the pompous, narcissistic asshole whose girlfriend left him.

And I understand it now. I get why he does this, why he can't stop once the anger takes over.

His upper lip twitches, and I see it in his eyes—how much he wants to hit me. How he wants to hurt me and watch me suffer, because it's the same torment he believes I've done to him. To his family. He's embarrassed and ashamed, and that's because of me.

Because I stopped loving him.

His shoulders slump and defeat glistens in his eyes. He knows this is where it ends. It's a primal rage, an anger deeper than anyone should ever feel because it's so inhuman. So unnatural. He snarls and drops his brows.

But he backs away.

He releases me, and I don't know why or what spooked him, but he walks out the door. He slams it shut, and I hobble over to it and lock the deadbolt.

He's not finished.

He'll *never* be finished.

CHAPTER FORTY

Owen

Sunday, December 6, 2015

I spot him as he exits the building.

Tarek.

In Allie's building, where he doesn't belong.

Shit.

Panic flutters in my chest, and I can't believe I didn't see this coming. I can't believe I wasn't here to protect her. His nonchalance irks me, and I'm torn between running upstairs to make sure Allie's okay and following this dickhead to see where he goes.

Instinct kicks in and I choose the latter, following the dickhead.

He makes a left at the corner and sets off down the alley. It's the same one I grabbed Allie from last time. The same one she ran to when he last chased her down.

The irony isn't lost on me, and I know what I need to do.

I feel it in my veins, in the goosebumps on my skin. The sweat that runs down the back of my neck.

I approach, my boots heavy on the concrete.

He turns when he hears my footsteps, unsure of what he'll find when he looks behind him, but alert enough to know someone is there. That someone is lurking.

"Who the hell are you?" he barks, his face peppered with concern. I look scary, I know. A big guy, dressed in all black, ski mask over my face.

Fists closed at my sides.

I'd be shitting my pants if I were him, too.

"It doesn't matter who I am," I say, my voice low, my tone serious. I point a threatening finger in his direction. "I'm telling you right fucking now, stay away from Allie Mason."

"Or what?" he snaps.

I shove him in the chest, pushing him hard against the brick building. The impact knocks the breath out of him, and his eyes go wide. I get in his face, pinning him to the wall.

"Or the next time you see me you'll be talking through a hole in your fucking neck."

I shove off, prepared to leave. To go check on Allie and forget about this asshole. But the anger boils like lava in my chest, and it takes everything in me to walk away.

Fuck, I intended to walk away, I did.

But that's not what I do.

That's not what I do at all.

He mumbles something, and it sets me off. It ignites a rage inside me that I can't control.

What gives him the right to do what he's done?

I turn in a swift motion. Just a few steps and I'm back in front of him, my body rigid and ready for battle. He flinches, this preppy wad of shit, and puts his fists up like a twelve-year-old boy on the playground. He's no match for me.

I know this.

Even he knows this.

Still, I don't retreat. I advance. Like a predator, I taunt him, and I don't care—I don't *fucking* care—that what I'm about to do will end his life.

This is the only way to stop him.

I pull the switchblade from my pocket and flip it open. The sharp blade glistens against the setting sun, and when he sees it his eyes go wide, his face white as the ghost he will become.

He tries to step back, to deflect, but there's nowhere for him to go. With his back against the wall, he pleads, "Wait, look, fine. I'll stay away from Allie. I get it—"

I raise the knife and his hands cover his face, his forearms protecting his head from a blow, but it won't be enough.

It's simply not enough.

I stab the point of the knife into his carotid artery.

I twist it.

Then I pull it back slightly and slide it swiftly across the length of his neck.

He gurgles and chokes on his own blood. It's thin and pours out with ease, courtesy of however many drinks he had before harassing Allie. His hands wrap around the gaping wound, as if he can stop the blood from seeping out. But it's there, flowing between his fingers and down his torso, onto the ground. He slides down the wall and slumps into a seated position, his leg bent oddly beneath him.

He's heavy against the pavement.

His head slumps to the left.

His chest stops moving, and his arms fall to his sides.

The light in his eyes goes out.

It's disgusting, what I've done. That I've taken a life. Somewhere in the back of my mind, I feel intense remorse. Not for the man I've killed, but for the federal crime I've committed.

The fact that it wasn't planned, and that means I could get caught. That I'd be taken away from Allie forever, and that would be devastating.

But that man? He deserved what he got. To rape a woman—one he claimed to love—to strip her of the right to feel safe and free in her own body, her own home? That's punishable by death, if you ask me. That man didn't deserve to go on living, to continue taunting Allie the way he did.

He nearly killed Allie, I remind myself.

And that's what keeps me from going insane. The thought that keeps replaying in my mind that reminds me I had cause: I had reason, and I had a duty to protect Allie from a monster.

After it's done, I run home. The sun has set, and as I run through the woods, I strip out of my clothes, carrying them in my arms. Naked and cold, I slip into my house through the back door, unseen as usual. I drop my clothes into a garbage bin and run upstairs to shower.

His blood seeps down the drain as it's rinsed from my skin.

He nearly killed Allie.

Once I've dressed and cleaned the shower, I end up back at Allie's. Back in my usual spot, watching her in the window.

This time she comes outside.

She's at the door and she's looking at me, she's waving me over, but I can't go. I can't run to her because someone might see me.

So she comes to me. She knows where I hide now, even though I never told her. And she's standing there, she's right in front of me, and she looks so sad. She steps forward, and I take her face in my hands and just look at her. I can't stop the tears. They've come from nowhere, along with the pain I feel in my chest as I look into her eyes.

I know I don't belong here; I can see that now. All I ever wanted was her love. Her trust. I can't control these feelings, these urges, and no one can fix me. No one can take this ache from my soul.

I wish things were different, I do.

She pushes to her tiptoes and presses her lips to mine, and it's the only thing I've ever needed in my entire life. But this is it; this is all I'll ever get from her.

I know now that this is the end of us.

But still, she lets me hold her while I cry.

She lets me have this one last moment.

CHAPTER FORTY-ONE

Allie

Sunday, December 6, 2015

The man I loved for six years of my life lies dead in the alley a few blocks behind my apartment. I don't know yet that he's there, but as I walk away from Owen, I suspect something has happened and I don't know what to do with that. He motioned toward the alley before I left him in the woods.

Our shared kiss lingers on my lips and I press my fingers to them, confused and filled with longing. I don't know why I kissed him, but for that single second in time, I gave myself to him the only way I know how. When time simply stopped and nothing else mattered, like an unspoken thank you.

I turn to walk back to my apartment, but something pulls me toward the alley instead, like a force I can't control. I don't want to go over there, but I know I should, so I do. I shiver, the chill in the air hitting deep within my bones. I wrap my jacket tighter around my body, my arms holding it together because it won't zip over my belly anymore.

The night is dark, but the glow of the street lamps lures me closer and closer, until I reach the intersection of the alley and stop at its opening. It's dark as I look in, shadows looming against the buildings, and I shudder as a chill runs through me. The feeling nags in my chest again, and I just know.

I have to go in there.

Forward I step, the heel of my boots echoing against the ground, each step like a taunting chord in a symphony I don't even want to listen to.

Step.

Clack.

Step.

His body sits limply on the concrete, his legs folded beneath him unnaturally. He's covered in blood, his face pale and his eyes, as if they're looking right through my soul, open. Lifeless.

Owen summoned me here on purpose, saying nothing to warn me of the horror I would find once I got here, of what he's done. It feels like betrayal, like a trick he's played that I didn't see coming.

I drop to my knees, my skin scraping against the pavement. I reach to check Tarek's pulse, but it's hard to find a space in his mangled neck to put my fingers. When I do, I feel nothing—no beat, no rhythm. The symphony ends with a crash, and there's nothing left but the sticky coagulated blood on my fingertips.

Like dried ketchup left on a plate.

I cover my mouth with my other hand, my stomach convulsing as I muffle a scream and try not to vomit. A heart-wrenching sob snakes its way between my fingers, and I hyperventilate. Shallow, quick breaths I can't control, they come too fast.

Someone runs toward me and like a movie, the encore of the symphony begins.

Step.

Clack.

Step.

I'm pulled to my feet by hands I'm not familiar with, there's shouting and voices echoing around me, more footsteps, but nothing makes sense anymore.

The noises all blur together.

Lights flash.

Blue and red.

And the darkness returns.

I see shapes above me, and they're blurry as I come to. An officer…an EMT. They help me onto a gurney and place an oxygen mask over my head. I inhale as if I've been drowning, and oh my God, the air feels good. I suck it in greedily.

This can't be happening.

It can't.

Tarek is dead.

My head pulls to the left, drawn to the commotion. To the lights, and the dusting of snow that's falling. And I see it then. Officers and EMTs surround his body, covered with a white sheet to hide the gruesomeness that I know is there.

I wasn't done with him yet.

I didn't get to say goodbye, and now the panic is back, and I can't stop looking over at the sheet. I picture his corpse, the flesh and bones that no longer work, and my God, what will his mother think?

Mariëtte will be devastated.

I cry harder at the thought, at the unbearable loss in

front of me. I forget everything I know of the present as I'm bombarded with memories of the old Tarek. The Tarek from college who smiled and laughed and loved me and wasn't like his father or his brother at all. He was free and—

"Ma'am, I'm Officer Bautch. Do you know this man?" the officer beside me asks. I nod, the oxygen mask still over my mouth.

"Are you hurt?" I shake my head no. He reaches for the walkie on this collar and radios for additional backup—a 419.

Homicide.

Oh, Owen, what did you do? I stare at the sheet again, at the linen that covers Tarek's body. At the blood that's seeped through the thin cotton. I follow the trail of dried blood beneath him to the cracks in the concrete where it's settled, and I beg the snow to fall harder to wash it away.

With help, I sit up on the gurney, my feet hanging over the sides. The shadows in the alley shift, and for a second I think I see Owen.

But I don't, not this time.

I'm escorted through the alley and down the street where an ambulance and several police cruisers are parked, the road blocked for traffic. Detective Feeney steps out of his car, and my breath catches.

I didn't expect to see him here, and he looks equally surprised to see me.

My stomach is in knots, and everything hurts. I stumble, my limbs suddenly heavy, and Feeney catches me, pulling me upright.

"I've got her," he tells Officer Bautch as he comes up

beside me. His arms link with mine and he holds me, keeping me upright while I lean against him.

He's looking at me funny.

Like he's trying to hide his shock. I hadn't told him I'm pregnant, and now here I am at the scene of a crime.

"Are you okay?" he asks.

I'm not sure he knows why I'm here or who's down there under that sheet, but I let him hold me anyway. We walk together to a bench and sit, him beside me in jeans and a dark leather jacket, his eyes filled with concern.

"...not okay," I mumble, but I don't have any more words yet, just those.

"Have you been checked out by an EMT? Are you hurt?"

I shake my head, and the fear that was in his eyes drains. He glances around at the people before us, the police cars, the ambulance and the officers milling about. Down the alley they lay evidence markers, but nobody looks under the sheet.

"What are you doing here, Allie?" Feeney asks, and I don't know what to say, how to explain my presence here.

"It's Tarek..." I force out with a sob.

The shock spreads across his face, and I can't tell what he's thinking, but it can't be good because he stands quickly and makes his way over to Officer Bautch. They stand close, speaking in hushed tones, like they're sharing a secret, but I catch some of the words.

"Is she a suspect?" Feeney asks.

"No, not that I know of. We've collected her contact information... follow up tomorrow."

Feeney nods and walks back over to me, his hand extended. "Come on, let's get you off your feet," he says.

We make our way up to my apartment, and I drop heavily into a chair at the table. Feeney pulls a bottle of water from the fridge, somehow comfortable enough around me to do so uninvited.

I don't mind.

"Here," he says, handing me the water. I twist off the cap and take a long drink. Feeney takes the seat across from me and leans over the table, his fingers forming a steeple in front of him. I know he has questions—and not just about what happened today.

"I didn't know how to tell you," I say, gesturing toward my stomach. He nods, but otherwise doesn't acknowledge the admission.

"What happened tonight, Allie?" he asks, his tone gentle but somehow still fortified with authority.

"I…I don't know."

"Why were you in that alley?"

"Tarek was here…before," I admit. "We fought. He was drunk, and I asked him to leave. But his car was still out front when I closed the curtains later, and I…"

I leave the sentence hanging, but it's not all true so it feels like a lie, and I don't know why it rolls off my tongue as easily as it does. But I need it. I need the lie, because if I don't have it then I have to tell Feeney what I know, and I'm not ready to do that.

"What happened next?"

I hesitate, and I don't know how much to say, how much might be *too* much. Feeney senses it, that I'm holding back, and he reaches across the table, placing his hand over mine. His thumb caresses as his fingers squeeze. I see the pain on his face—unexpected and foreign—like he knows I'm involved but doesn't want to believe it.

It shouldn't feel good—his touch—but it does.

It's intimate, but I need it, and somehow, the words fall out, the ones that follow the lie. "I went outside…checked his car, but it was empty. Like he hadn't been in it yet. I heard a noise…by the alley…so I went. I went, and…and…"

My words levitate in the air, unfinished. Semi-nonfactual, but Feeney's cell chimes from his pocket and it pulls us back, pausing the moment. He's needed at the crime scene. The medical examiner has probably arrived. He pats my hand one more time then pushes up from his chair, and clears his throat.

"Are you going to be all right?" he asks. "Alone?" he adds.

I nod, and it's the first time I realize that it's true. That there's nothing more to fear.

Feeney steps forward as I stand and I see the apprehension on his face, I feel it in the air around us. He doesn't want to go, but he has to, so he does.

I lie in bed, staring out the window as if Owen might appear. I picture him earlier, when we stood together before I went to the alley, and I remember the look on his face. The expression that said so much in place of the words that couldn't be said.

Goodbye, my love.

An unexplainable force brought us together in this life. Like the world belongs to him and everything else just orbits around him. I think I orbit around him, too. It's the only reason I can think of to explain why I don't tell anyone what I know.

That Owen killed Tarek.

For me.

CHAPTER FORTY-TWO

Allie

Saturday, January 9, 2016

I can't focus on anything other than the spot on the wall in front of me. I keep seeing his lifeless face, his head tipped to the side against the brick wall.

I close my eyes to sleep, but when I do it's more vivid, the image burned into my brain. And maybe I deserve that, maybe I deserve to suffer a little bit more. Tarek didn't deserve what happened to him and I can't help but feel responsible. Justice should have had a chance to run its course. Instead, Owen sat on the throne of a one-man jury.

While the words haven't been spoken, I know it was him. I know Owen killed Tarek, and it hurts to know that. To not be able to tell Detective Feeney as they worked the crime scene. As the leads dried up.

It's been over a month, and I haven't seen Owen since that night.

My mind is in a constant state of overcast, and I can't

seem to shake the feeling that someone is still watching me. I know who he is now, what he's capable of.

Most days I force myself to leave my apartment, in search of some semblance of normalcy. Dr. Ellison says that's the only way to avoid becoming a paranoid hermit. In nicer words, of course. Truthfully, with everything available at a person's fingertips these days, it wouldn't be all that difficult to lock myself in the apartment and never leave.

But I don't feel alone there either. I don't know where he is. I can't see him. I don't sense him the way I used to. But he could come back at any time.

Tarek's face flashes in my mind again.

I should have known.

I could have helped him.

I shower and manage to make myself a cup of tea and instead of beaching myself on the couch with my favorite throw blanket, I rinse my mug. I put it in the dishwasher. I dress in the only pair of pants that fit and throw on a maternity top instead of the ratty sweatshirt I tend to wear every day.

And then I force myself to dry and straighten my hair instead of lopping it on top of my head in a chignon and even swipe a couple layers of mascara on my lashes. With apprehension I can't explain, I grab my purse and my keys and step through the front door. I walk down the hall and into the fresh air.

And I don't die.

Once I'm on the road for a few minutes, I signal my turn into the Speedway gas station and pull my car into a parking space near the entrance, hesitation overwhelming me, as if I'm trying to convince myself that everything I'm doing is normal.

I pull the keys from the ignition and stuff them into the

pocket of my jacket, my eyes darting back and forth in front of me, and then into the rearview mirror to check behind me, as nonchalantly as possible. There's no one, other than the expected patrons of the convenience store. No one is staring, no one is hiding behind a hooded sweatshirt with a ski cap pulled low over their eyes.

I don't know why I'm afraid, why I suddenly can't breathe every time I step outside. I take a deep breath and slowly let it back out, the air doing little to calm the nerves that have settled over me. But I have no choice; I need to be okay again.

My hand snakes around my purse strap and the other reaches for the door handle, pulling it open as somehow my legs move and I'm standing on the pavement beside my car. I look around again, double checking that my surroundings remain as they were no more than sixty seconds ago.

"This is ridiculous," I mutter to myself. The car door slams shut, and my fingers find the lock button on the key fob. I press it and the horn chirps, signaling that the doors are locked and there won't be any unexpected visitors hiding in the back seat when I come back out.

Once inside, I grab a Snickers bar and milk to satisfy my pregnancy hormones.

"Just this for you, miss? Any fuel today?" the attendant asks, his hand hovering over the touch screen.

"No, that's it. Thank you."

His expression is wary, as if he knows something has spooked me but isn't sure he wants to get involved. I'm certain now that he witnessed my pep talk in the parking lot a few minutes ago. I'm embarrassed for only a moment; the realization that had something happened—had someone been watching me, ready to attack—he would have witnessed it and been able to help.

I smile in attempt to ease his discomfort as much as my own.

"That'll be five sixty-seven," he says as I hand him my debit card.

He motions to the card reader, a do-it-yourself contraption that I have no interest in utilizing today. I stretch the card further toward him, and he finally takes it. He slides the reader over and jams the plastic into the slot. "Usually it's the elderly who struggle with these things," he says sarcastically.

I don't bite, just ignore him and wait for my card to go through. I punch in my pin number and remove my card before reaching for the plastic bag. I turn to leave, no longer interested in what this teenage attendant has to say.

"Hey!" he barks. I turn. "Your keys."

I turn around and scoop them off the counter before darting for the door.

I can't explain this fear, this constant feeling that a threat is near. I can't, and it kills me. I can't speak with the one person who might understand, because I don't know where he is.

I didn't think he was capable of what he's done.

And while I know he did it for *me*, the fact that I didn't see it coming leaves a gaping hole in my chest. And it's there that the fear has settled.

CHAPTER FORTY-THREE

Allie

Tuesday, January 12, 2016

I can't sleep.

At night I lay in the darkness, willing my body to relax, to settle into a dreamless sleep. But rarely does it happen anymore. I'm so tired I can't think straight, and it's three in the morning so I don't want to admit defeat and climb out of bed yet.

I lie on my back and stare at the ceiling, memorizing its little imperfections; the dips and cracks in the plaster that would otherwise go unnoticed. I count sheep and then remember I don't like counting sheep, so I stop. I sing aloud to myself, some song by Ariana Grande that's been stuck in my head for weeks, but all the notes are wrong so I stop doing that too.

I give in; I get out of bed.

In the kitchen I make eggs and bacon and toast and pancakes and I douse them in butter and syrup, and holy hell it looks delicious, but when I sit down to eat I no longer want any of it and I think I'm going to throw up.

I toss it all in the trash and clean up the kitchen. I wash the dishes, I scrub the counters. Then I wipe and reorganize the cupboards, because they could use a good cleaning anyway.

It's still not yet 6:00 a.m.

I need to do something with my hands, I need to keep moving. I consider hopping onto the treadmill for a run, but the baby is due in a few weeks, and I don't think a run will do anything more than kill me at this point.

Three weeks. That's all the time I have left with him, my son, but my body isn't ready to give him up, so here we are. I can't take it anymore, this lack of sleep.

I lay on the couch with the curtains open and the lights off, watching the snow fall outside, the flurries dancing in the glow of the street lamp.

And finally, I drift off to sleep.

My intercom doorbell rings around noon the next day; I'm not expecting anyone, but the doorman has an updated list of visitors now, so I shove the panic-filled thoughts away and waddle to the door. My heart skips a beat, but not in a bad way, as I look through the peep hole and see a familiar face. I smooth my hair as best I can and then pull the door open.

"Detective Feeney?"

"Allie, nice to see you. Do you have a few minutes?"

I step aside and swing the door open to let him in. His expansive frame fills the doorway and pauses in the entry. I peek into the hall on instinct, but no one else is there so I close the door and turn the deadbolt.

Feeney notices, but doesn't acknowledge my force of habit.

"What brings you by?" I ask. My hands are shaking, and I don't know how to stop this nervous twitch. I haven't seen Feeney since the night of the murder.

"I was hoping I could ask you a few more questions," he says, and my heart drops because these aren't the words I wanted to hear.

"Sure, have a seat," I say, pulling out the dining chair for him. "Would you like something to drink? Coffee? Water?"

"No, thanks, I'm good."

I wind up in the kitchen anyway and grab a bottle of water for myself before taking the seat across from him.

"You okay?" he asks. He reaches across the table, but stops before our fingers touch. I feel a pang in my chest. The words are lodged, and I don't know how to speak without breaking down, so I shake my head no.

Feeney clears his throat. "I'll get right to it then." I nod and he leans forward, his elbows on the table. "Does the name Owen Riverson mean anything to you?"

Owen's name on Feeney's lips startles me, and my breath catches. "Should it?" I ask, attempting to mask my surprise.

"Does it?" he repeats.

He blinks.

I blink.

I have to tell him.

"Sure," I say slowly, picking at the corner of the place mat. I look up at the wrong time and lock eyes with Feeney, his expression changing from friend to cop.

"Allie…"

"Okay, I know him. Sort of. Yes. Why?"

"How do you know him?"

"I can't say."

"You can. And I need you to," he says through nearly clenched teeth.

I sigh, my heart pounding in my chest at the thought of telling him what I know, what I've kept from him all this time.

"I stayed with him a couple months ago," I start. Feeney's brows shoot upward. "When I went out of town." I see the disappointment in his eyes, the hurt, and it's all I can do not to jump up and throw my arms around him. *I didn't sleep with him,* I want to yell, but I don't.

"You stayed with *him*? Where?"

"I don't know. His house, I think?"

There's a pause, a silence that fills the room, and it's louder than anything I've ever heard. He's upset, and it's my fault.

"How did you meet him?" he asks after a few minutes. And I can't take it anymore, I need this to be over. I suck in a deep breath and release the words like vomit.

"Tarek showed up here that Friday night. He was upset about our breakup and…he shoved me to the ground. Said I had no right to give his baby up and that we're meant to be together. He wouldn't stop and…he tried to…he tried to force me into the bedroom. I kicked him and knocked him down and just…ran. I ran and didn't look back. And I ended up with Owen. He was there, and I just, ran into him…I—"

"What do you mean he was *there*? Where? At your apartment?" He's yelling and I don't know why he's not asking questions about the night Tarek was killed, why he's focusing on that weekend instead.

"Well, no, a few blocks down, I guess. I literally ran right into him and he pulled me into the alley and told me he saw what happened and that he would take me somewhere safe."

As I say the words I realize how they must sound to Feeney, how stupid I must look.

"Did he hurt you?" he asks. His hands are clasped together on the table, his fingers clenched.

"No! The opposite actually…he took me to his house and let me rest and fed me and…that's it, really. I stayed with him for the weekend and when I said I wanted to go home, he brought me home."

"Allie, were you dating this man?" he asks.

I place my hand over his. He doesn't pull away. "No." I see the relief in his eyes, the way he exhales and his chest deflates. Like the monster in the room is finally gone. He takes a deep breath and delivers the news he came here to tell me, only it isn't really news.

"We believe Owen Riverson is the man who attacked you. His fingerprints were found in your window and on the fire escape outside. We were finally able to match them through juvenile records. We believe that's how he accessed your apartment." He pauses to let the words sink in. "He's the man who's been stalking you."

I don't react the way I should when Feeney tells me about Owen. All this time and his words don't bring me closure. They don't bring Tarek back and they don't bring him to justice.

He really would have gotten away with it.

"Allie, are you hearing me? Do you understand what I'm telling you?" Feeney asks when I don't respond. I nod slowly, the truth on the tip of my tongue.

"Owen didn't rape me," I say quietly, and I watch the color drain from Feeney's face. "*Tarek* did. He told me himself. Owen was just…there. He…he stopped Tarek and chased him off. He's the one who called 9-1-1."

"Wait, what are you saying? What do you mean he was *there*? In your room?"

"I'm saying…you're wrong. All Owen did was try to help."

"We have evidence—*actual* evidence—that this man was stalking you."

"I won't deny that," I say, my head lowered. The shame rests heavily on my chest; it's another burden I'll have to carry.

"Wait a second. You *knew?*" Feeney asks defiantly. "You knowingly withheld information from me? From the department?"

The tears come, and I don't know how to stop them. How to go back and have this conversation a million other ways or to have told him from the moment I found out the truth. I wipe at my eyes with the sleeve of my sweater.

Feeney's eyes search mine for answers, and I don't have them anymore. Everything I say just makes things worse. "I'm trying to help you, Allie. That's all I've done since the moment I met you. Since I took on this case." He runs his fingers over his jaw, the stubble making a scraping noise as he does so. "And you're over here playing house with your fuc—your *stalker*?" He spits the word out like it's rotten, his anger enough to bring him to his feet.

"No, it wasn't like that. I—"

"Enough!" he says, his palm crashing down on the table. "You need to stop speaking. Right now."

"What? Why?" I ask, determined to finish this conversation, no matter how hard it may be.

But the answer is in his eyes.

He's a cop.

And what I've told him changes everything.

CHAPTER FORTY-FOUR

Owen

Thursday, January 14, 2016

I wish I could go back to when she was here; when Allie took residence in the corner seat on my couch, my blanket over her legs, a book in her lap. When she ate the waffles I made for her and laughed at me when I nearly burned the kitchen down.

I would have kept her forever if she'd have let me.

She doesn't notice when I'm not around anymore; she doesn't miss me the way I miss her, and I don't know what to do with that. Tarek is gone, so she's no longer afraid.

Anger festers within me, and I can't contain it—I can't. I pace the expanse of my living room, the carpet sure to be worn through by morning.

Everything is fucking wrong.

This isn't how this was supposed to go, my relationship with Allie. I only wanted to make her happy, to prove to her I could be the man she needs me to be.

But I can't, and it doesn't matter how hard I tried.

I want to scream. To yell. To break down every wall in this fucking house.

You will never be good enough, Owen.

I step outside, the snow falling rapidly. For some reason, all I can think is how Allie must love this, how she must be watching the snow fall from her window, dreaming of building snowmen and making snow angels as a child.

Most children who grow up here get to.

But I didn't.

I pull my shoes and socks off my feet, and fuck, it's colder than I thought it would be. But, I keep undressing until I'm naked, my balls shriveled and seeking refuge somewhere deep inside my body. I spread my arms out like I'm flying, my head tilted toward the sky.

I fall backward, a dead drop like a trust fall, except the only thing to catch me is the mound of snow behind me. I lie there, my arms and legs kicking, waving. Back and forth, over and over, until I can't stop shivering.

The cold rattles my teeth, and I can't get warm, the arctic frost seeping into my veins and chilling me to the bone. I've dreamed of this moment, this unrelenting cold that wraps itself around me, suffocating me from the outside in.

My fingers ache and don't want to move, my hair frozen in the snow, and I know if I were to touch it, surely it will break off.

But something pulls me forward, a force I don't dare try to fight. I sit up, snow wedged between my ass cheeks, and I'm hit with uncontrollable laughter at how stupid I must look, and how there's no one around to see it. I wish more than anything that Allie was here with me. That she was right beside me, making naked snow angels in the cold, just because it's something to do together.

It'd be kinda nice if someone gave a shit about me.

I stop laughing and grab my clothes from the snow bank, tossing them into the dryer when I get inside. I know now what I have to do; what comes next.

It's really the only thing left to do.

CHAPTER FORTY-FIVE

Allie

Sunday, February 9, 2016

"Come on, Allie, you can't keep moping around here waiting for the universe to realign. Get up. We're going to do something about that hair of yours."

My hand shoots up and I finger my hair, looking over at Courtney as if I can't believe she just said that. "What do you mean? What's wrong with my hair?"

"Really, woman? You need a cut. And probably some color, if I'm being honest. Your old lady is showing, Mason."

"Thanks, that's very kind of you," I say with more than a hint of sarcasm. "But, I don't feel like going out, so I'll pass."

"I know you don't. That's why you're going out anyway," Court says, reaching over and swiping the throw blanket from my lap. I swat at her in attempt to steal it back from her, but it's no use, she's on her feet and across the room before I even consider standing from my position on the couch.

Fine. I wasn't cold, anyway.

I huff and fold my arms across my chest, making no further attempt at excuses that I know won't mean shit to my best friend. She sets the now-folded blanket on the coffee table and crouches down in front of me, placing a comforting hand on my thigh.

"Look, I know you're hurting, and I know you want nothing more than to crawl into a hole and become some old spinster with a couple cats and home grocery delivery. But you have your whole life ahead of you, Allie. What happened to you is unspeakable, but what I've been watching every day since then isn't much better, either. I need my friend back. I miss you."

I swipe at a rogue tear and can't help but shove Court playfully in the shoulder. She's not wrong. She never really is. She smiles, and I smile back as best I can. I reach up and touch my hair, looking at the split ends.

"You really think I'll become an old spinster?"

"Not if I can help it," she says. She takes my hand and pulls me up from the couch and into a hug, my belly a barrier between us.

"Come on, let's find you something to wear so we can run to Target and get some hair dye."

I groan, but I follow Court to the bedroom anyway, because Target sounds like a better place to be than here right now.

Court and I pick through several boxes of hair color, finally settling on an amber-brown. I'm not one for boxed dyes, but at this rate it's easier than booking an appointment with my hairdresser, Kate, while I'm this close to giving birth. Plus, it gives Court and me something to do today.

But as we make our way down the aisle, I hear a familiar voice.

All the air is knocked out of me and I grab Court's hand, putting a finger to my lips. We stop walking and duck to the end of the aisle. She's never met Tarek's mother, so I know she doesn't feel the panic in my gut, but I think I'm about to shit myself *and* the floor.

"Steven, I'm going to grab some of those soaps I like," she says.

And wouldn't you fucking know—we're in the soap aisle.

She stops dead in her tracks as she turns the corner, her face flushed and riddled with shock and anger and everything in between those two emotions.

"You," she says, and it's guttural. It's so low it's like a lion's roar. Her teeth are showing as I try to speak and nothing comes out, the words stuck in my throat because this woman terrifies the hell out of me.

Steven comes up behind her, his face an equal mix of shock and anger, but he says nothing.

"You…you *murdered* my son!" Mariëtte screams, and it's the last thing I expect her to say, but she does, and now people are looking. I'm the size of a whale and people are watching, listening as she accuses me of being a murderer. She looks like she's about to attack, and I take a step back, Court's arm around mine.

Mariëtte takes several steps forward, and I'm certain she's about to hit a pregnant woman, but Steven steps in, pulling her back before she gets too close. "Mariëtte, that's enough," he says.

I see the hate in his eyes, too, though.

They've lost a son, and I can't help but feel sympathy.

Regret.

Remorse.

All the guilt builds up and it marinates inside me and now I don't feel so well. My skin is clammy and I'm so hot, but they're still standing there and people are still looking.

The last thing I see before I pass out is the look on Mariëtte's face as she glares at my belly.

Like she wants to cut me open and rip my baby out of me.

It is, after all, her grandchild in there.

CHAPTER FORTY-SIX

Allie

Tuesday, February 23, 2016

He's here again, Detective Feeney. Standing in my foyer—on unofficial business and dressed in dark jeans and a black T-shirt, his signature leather jacket unzipped.

My mind flashes back to the last time we spoke, weeks ago, when he questioned me about Owen. After he left it had taken me a few days to realize he'd only asked about Owen because of his prints and DNA on my window.

Not because they suspect him of murdering Tarek, I'd realized.

They didn't know.

To Feeney, Owen is nothing more than a man obsessed with a woman. A stalker who happened to be at the right place, at the right time.

"We're closing the homicide case," Feeney says, his hands in the pockets of his coat. "...handing it over to the

Cold Cases Division." I can't help but breathe a sigh of relief, but I don't know why or where it stems from. "I just thought you should know," he says.

"So, it's over?"

"For now, I suppose." He knows Owen is still out there, that he's capable of more than even I once thought. But there's no proof. No evidence connecting him to the crime or putting him at the scene.

Feeney stands close to me, his arms at his sides, and I know he feels what I'm feeling, what I've been trying to tell myself isn't there. But he won't do this with me. He won't engage, because he's wired to move forward without looking back.

He's wired to fight, and I know he's still angry; I feel it coming off of him.

I want to touch him, to place my hand on his chest and stand on the tips of my toes to kiss him because I can't deny my attraction to him—despite the trauma I've been through and the fact that I'm the size of a whale at the moment. And now I'm thinking about the song from *Free Willy* and it's all I can do not to sing it aloud to him in hopes that he'll understand...*hold me...*

But I don't, because it's not my place to feel this way. I'm not supposed to want him. Especially not in this condition.

"You're never going to catch him, are you?"

"I don't know," he admits. "We can't catch them all, unfortunately." I can see him fighting the urge, but eventually his eyes land on my belly. At the massive bump. I know I shouldn't ask, but I can't help it, so I do.

"What if it was your wife, Detective?" I pause. "Could you raise a child conceived with her rapist?"

"No."

He doesn't hesitate, doesn't even take a breath or wait for the punctuation to reach the end of my sentence. I nod and stuff my hands into my pockets, ignoring the fact that he doesn't have a wife in the first place.

Freezing rain falls outside, but I don't mind because maybe it'll wash away some of this sadness.

"So, what do I do now?"

"You live your life, Allie. You go on."

It's this moment that I know I'll remember. It's the sadness in his eyes. The kindness in his heart. He doesn't want this to be the end of us any more than I do, but it is. I'm having this baby and giving him away. I won't be the same person when this is over, and he knows this.

I can't stop looking at his lips, his eyes. There's a kindness in them that most people don't carry. Not after the things this man has seen.

"Will I see you again?" I ask.

"I hope so, Allie Mason. I hope so."

He hugs me, and I know it's goodbye. His strong arms wrap around me and they pull, they pull so much it hurts. I cry into his chest and feel it rise and fall as he rubs my back.

His mouth reaches mine, his lips soft. His kiss says everything his words cannot, and nothing will ever be right again. Not after this. Not once I give up my baby.

It pains me to pull away, but I do, and he swipes away my tears with the pad of his thumb.

"Take care of yourself, Allie."

My contractions start the following morning. The pain is so severe I'm certain I'm about to give birth to a bowling ball and all ten pins. I hobble over to the couch, grabbing a sheet of parchment paper off the counter as if it'll save my couch from any bodily fluids that might leak out.

I'm new here, what do I know?

I grab my phone and call Courtney; she answers on the first ring. "Court, the baby's coming," I force out with a grimace, clenching everything tight even though I'm not supposed to.

"What? Oh, my God, where are you?"

"Home. Can you come drive me to the hospital?"

"Yes! Give me ten minutes. Ten minutes!"

I end the call and try to remember what I'm supposed to do now. Do I pack a bag? Is my phone charged? Should I bring a book—will there even be time to read?

I text my parents and Linc; Mom lets me know they'll meet Court and me at the hospital when they get into town.

She doesn't want to miss her only opportunity to meet her grandson.

The nurse stabs an IV into my hand and secures it down with medical tape. I want to punch her in the nose, but only because everything hurts, not because she deserves to be punched in the nose.

I take note of her name, just in case I need to remember it.

Sadie.

Court storms into the room, holding my mother's hand, and the two of them come to my bedside but get pushed away by my new friend, Sadie, the nurse I want to punch.

"Not yet, ladies, we need to check some vitals and get her hooked up. Do you mind taking a seat in the hall for a few minutes?" Nurse Sadie says. Her eyes are kind, so I cut her some slack as she closes the door again.

The heart rate monitor comes on, and I hear the whooshing of his heart, and it's the most magical sound I've ever heard. "It's so fast," I say.

"Mm, it's a great heart rate," she says, pushing some buttons on the keyboard.

She checks my dilation, and I sag in relief when she announces there's still time for an epidural. But then I consider skipping it, going drug-free just for the simple fact that maybe I deserve to feel every bit of pain that's about to come.

But a contraction rips through my uterus, threatening to tear out my insides and surely—surely—I am about to fucking die, because this *cannot* be normal. And just like that, an epidural is no longer a question.

Nurse Sadie brings me ice chips, and I can't help but think it's rude of her not to bring some water, too. I pop an ice chip in my mouth and pretend it's chocolate. "Dr. Regan will be in shortly," she says once all the cords are finally sticking out of me. "Would you like me to let your family back in?"

I nod and lay my head against the pillow. I don't know how much time I have before the next contraction and I want to take advantage of the quiet.

Just for a moment, I tell myself.

The quiet doesn't last long, but I tell myself not to panic when the chaos starts. The true torture doesn't come until after the room goes silent; when the doctors and nurses leave and there's no one left here but me. So I savor the moments, even though they're excruciating and I hate every second of it, because this is all I have left.

Now he's here and this is it.

"Do you want to hold him?" Nurse Sadie asks once the baby has been cleaned, weighed, and measured.

I nod, and Mom stifles a cry. I hadn't planned to hold him. I hadn't planned to see him or smell him or look into his eyes.

Because it was supposed to be easier that way.

He's placed in my arms and he's so beautiful, all seven pounds, six ounces of him. He cries and it's so loud, but I don't care because it's like he's saying everything I'm feeling inside. His tears drip on my skin, and I want to bottle them up and keep them.

"I'll be back in a few minutes," Nurse Sadie announces as she leaves the room.

Mom sits next to me on the side of the bed, her eyes overflowing with tears. I can't help but notice she doesn't ask Dad and Linc to come in; they couldn't do it—be this close to him and know it's the only time they'll ever see him.

So they don't; they're just here for moral support.

"He's so handsome," Mom says, but I barely hear the words, they're so quiet.

Nurse Sadie doesn't stay away for long; she returns with some paperwork and a pen. Something more for me to sign, one last second to change my mind.

But I can't.

The Jamesons are waiting.

I sign the form, and then watch as she scoops him from my arms. I want to strangle her and tell her not to touch him, that she has no right to take him.

But it's not true.

She's gentle as she reaches for him; I even see tears in her eyes, too. But it still feels like she's tearing him from my body, straight from my womb, and there's sure to be a giant hole when she's done.

I kiss his forehead as he's pulled away from me, pressing my lips to his soft skin, and it's not fair—it's not *fucking* fair —how much this hurts.

I'd hit her now for sure if she wasn't holding my son in her arms.

"I'm so sorry." I wail over and over through my tears. Mom pulls me to her chest, and I give in to the grief, sobbing loudly. The snot drips from my nose but I wipe it away with the blanket. I avoid her eyes, because I know she's crying, too. She can't imagine why I'm doing this, and she's trying so hard to understand.

"I'm here, sweetheart," she says, grabbing my hand and squeezing twice.

She always squeezes twice.

I don't get another five minutes with my son.

I don't get a lifetime to watch him grow up.

I only get the nine months I carried him in my womb.

I only get the twenty minutes I held him in this hospital bed.

"It's not enough..." I cry. "It's not enough time."

The clock ticks on the wall, a steady rhythm to fill the silence. Mom sleeps in the cot next to my bed, and I lie on my side and watch her. She looks older, like the last year has aged her.

I watch the rise and fall of her chest, the tiny hairs that have fallen over her face that move as she breathes in and out.

I wonder what she's dreaming of. Her eyes flutter, and I hope things are happier in her dreams than they are here.

I hope she can forgive me.

But I don't know that she ever will, because she's always been the best mom, the kind that lives for her children and would do anything for us, even if it meant she'd suffer instead. She'd take on our pain if it meant we didn't have to.

Maybe that's what I'm doing, too.

This suffering is for me, not for the little boy I said goodbye to today. I'll carry that weight for us so that he doesn't have to. I'll hold onto that pain, even if the weight on my heart becomes too much. Because even though it's breaking and even though it may crack right at its very core and shatter into tiny little pieces, he'll still be okay.

My son will always be *my* son, he just isn't *mine*.

I hope he has a good life. That he is loved unconditionally and without the weight of his parent's sins on his shoulders. That's what I couldn't give to him, what I knew would be his disadvantage in this world if he stayed with me. How could I look at the face of a child whose father raped me and not resent him?

I wasn't sure I could—not even after Tarek's death—so I didn't.

He has his father's eyes, but his mother's nose, and that's okay with me. It's cute as a button, or so his Grandma Mason will say.

The pain in my chest is heavy, almost like I'm grieving a death, like he's not really just somewhere with another family —with his new mom and dad—but he's gone and I'll never see him again.

The grief pulls me under, and all I want to do is curl into a ball and sleep. I close my eyes, my head on the pillow, and let the tears fall slowly.

Silently.

And I picture his perfect little face, his chubby cheeks and little wisps of dark hair.

And I vow silently not to give up, to live my best life and not let this moment define me.

Because one day he might need me.

CHAPTER FORTY-SEVEN

Owen

Saturday, May 7, 2016

I didn't expect the birth of her son to hit Allie so hard. She seemed so disconnected during the pregnancy that it took me by surprise when I saw her crying. I watched her cry every night for days…*weeks* afterward. My heart still breaks for her, and I'm left to wonder if maybe I don't know her as well as I thought I did.

I didn't think she wanted that baby.

I saw the boy's adoptive parents that day, when they walked into the hospital just hours after Allie had given birth. They looked nice enough. They smiled. They cried. They couldn't believe someone had given them such a gift.

It felt unfair, for Allie to suffer while they celebrated.

While she napped in her room, I sat by Weaver Lake and pictured a life with Allie. I couldn't help but wonder what it would be like to raise a child with her, she as my wife. She'd be a great mother, despite her reservations about everything. I know she would. I loved watching her belly grow throughout the pregnancy, the way she waddled around her apartment. How she bent over at odd angles trying to pick dirty laundry up from the floor.

How peaceful she looked sleeping in my guest bed the first night she stayed with me.

Had she been mine, I would have rubbed her feet, given her pedicures. I would have taken her shopping for cute maternity clothes and helped pick out baby things. I would have been involved, present.

But I wasn't given that choice, and who am I to force myself on Allie? She'll come around, I know she will. Right now she just needs time.

And I can give her that, because today's a hard day for me, too. On the boy's birthday, that morning after I watched the Jamesons hold him for the first time, another life ended.

Life's kind of odd like that sometimes, full of surprises. Full of irony and disappointment.

Lung cancer.

The beast that finally took my mother from this world. Not the booze. Not the infectious STDs. Not the cocaine or even the pills.

Fucking cancer.

Of all things.

I kneel down next to the headstone my father paid for but won't ever see. He refused to attend the funeral, his wife Amber claiming she would not allow the formality to delay their annual trip to Cabo. As if the beach won't still be there next year.

Mother never was quite the same after my father left her. He ruined her, and I did my best to take care of her until the drugs took over and there was nothing left of her to care for.

I place a bouquet of flowers in the cast iron vase next to

the stone—daisies, her favorite. The green grass sprouts through the remaining black dirt over her grave and it almost seems fitting—that something so vibrant could grow over something as dark and dead as my mother.

"I'm sorry, Mom," I whisper.

Mother may not have been the Susie Homemaker I always dreamed of, but she was still my mother.

I drop my jacket to the ground and lie down in the dirt, my head resting near the stone, and I trace the letters of her name with my finger.

Robyn Marie Riverson

1952-2016

I cry silently as the sun sets, lying beside my mother for the last time.

FOUR YEARS LATER

CHAPTER FORTY-EIGHT

Allie

Sunday, February 24, 2019

Today is his birthday.

My son.

He's four years old, and I haven't seen him since the day I gave birth to him and handed him over to the Jamesons. Renee and Marc, that's their names. They're his parents now, not me.

Not Tarek.

They seemed wonderful when I met them at the agency. A nice-looking couple in their early thirties who weren't able to conceive on their own. He's an insurance guy, and she's a teacher. Third grade, I believe. Normal. Attractive. Fit. Young. Friendly. They checked all the boxes on my end.

Including one I hadn't anticipated.

They'd pushed for an open adoption.

"Please? In case he ever wants to meet you?" Renee had begged.

I've been silently counting down the days ever since, wondering if that opportunity will ever present itself. If I'll ever get to meet this person I created. He would be older, a grown man by then, I'm sure. I can't help but wonder if I'll recognize him. If we'll see each other again and just know how we're connected.

Flesh.

Blood.

Mother and son.

My cell phone rings, startling me from my thoughts. It's Mom. She always calls on his birthday. I answer, raising the phone to my ear. "Hey, Mom," I say.

"Hi, honey. Just wanted to check in and see how you're doing today. Dad and I would love to have you for dinner." Mom's chipper. *Overly* chipper, but it's all an act, one that we seem to play once a year for the last four years straight just because it makes us feel better. But the outcome is always the same.

I just want to be alone.

"I'm fine, Mom. I'll take a rain check on dinner, but thank you for offering." I feel terrible, of course, letting her down like this. But dinner feels like a celebration, and I'm not feeling very celebratory today.

Mom sighs on the other end of the phone, and I chew on a fingernail while I stare out the window. It's cold today, barely above zero with a light snow falling—typical for February in suburban Minnesota, and a perfect excuse not to leave the house.

"Sweetie, Dad and I are worried about you."

"There's nothing to worry about, Mom. Really, I'm fine. Actually, I have a lot of work I need to get through today, anyway. Franklin has me on a tight deadline with these quarterly sales projections." I stare down at the pile of paperwork on my desk, knowing I won't actually touch any of it until morning. The lie leaving a sour taste in my mouth.

"Well, how about tomorrow night then? Dinner around six? Royce can come, too," she says, sounding hopeful.

"Mom—"

"Oh, I know, I know, Allie. I just…your father and I miss you."

"I miss you too, Mom. I'll call you next week, okay? We'll plan a weekend."

"Of course. I love you, honey."

"Love you, too." I say, setting the phone aside. Mom's is the only call I ever take on this day, mainly so that she doesn't freak out if her calls go unanswered and assume that I'm—yet again—nearly bleeding out somewhere.

I made a cake.

I know I said I'm not feeling very celebratory today, but this is actually my tradition on his birthday every year: I wallow in my own pity while stuffing my face with birthday cake until I'm about to throw up. I've never admitted this to my parents—or anyone else for that matter—because how could I? I don't talk about it, the fact that I gave up my son.

It's too hard.

I head to the kitchen and grab the cake from the fridge. This year I went with a chocolate butter cake, with vanilla cream cheese frosting. I imagine by age four he's probably a huge chocolate fan like me. I grab the box of birthday candles and pull four from the box. They slide into the soft sponge, and I light them with a match.

Still a few minutes to go…I always blow them out at the time of his birth. I fight the tears that threaten, and start to sing.

Happy birthday to you…

But I don't even know his name.

CHAPTER FORTY-NINE

Owen

Saturday, March 9, 2019

I remember the sounds.

Panting.

Grunting.

An IV dripping.

The constant beeping of a machine.

Her screams.

Things came back to her in bits in pieces. I like to think I helped with that. The smells are coming back to me, too. They linger, as if the memories are buried just deep enough that I can't quite reach them.

Sweat.

His breath—tainted with alcohol and mint—warm and labored as I hovered over him, the knife at his throat.

The copper-like sweetness of blood.

I remember the look on his face, the way his eyes went wide as I pushed the tip of the knife through the skin. His neck—when the blood comes, and the wound opens up. The moment his eyes go dark, before his body becomes nothing more than a shell.

These are the moments I live with; the ones I use to help keep the urges at bay.

Now, cold seeps into my bones as I run. My feet pound the ground for the first few miles, but I slow about a mile away, creeping into the shadows so as not to be seen.

Another ten blocks and I finally enter a neighborhood, the cookie-cutter houses and well-manicured lawns reminding me of my dad.

The fucker.

I shake the thought away—no time to dwell on a man that's been dead for the last year—and continue on.

I crouch and stop at the front of a house, the soft drum of the street light above me droning in my ears. I stuff my hands into the pocket of my jacket, my fingers nearly numb from the cold despite the sweat on my forehead. I reach the end of the block, turning into the cul-de-sac. The house on the corner, the one with the tire swing in the front yard—that's it.

The lights are on inside, the blinds open, and I peer through with my binoculars.

People need to learn to close their damn curtains.

I can't help it, I watch. A picturesque family huddles together at the kitchen table. The mother. The father. And the child whose DNA matches neither of their own. The child from Allie's womb, handed over to them by a nurse whose name no one remembers.

I've found him.

CHAPTER FIFTY

Allie

Saturday, June 11, 2019

Court FaceTimes from Chicago on Saturday night, her voice a sound for sore ears. I grab the open bottle of wine from the fridge, along with a glass, and teeter into the living room, giddy at the thought of chit-chatting with my best friend.

"Court! How's Chicago? How's the ritzy new job, Miss Fancy-Pants-Literary-Agent?" I ask, relaxing on the couch with my wine.

"Hey girl, hey!" Court beams, and her smile is as infectious as ever. "Chicago is good, actually. Super busy though. And there are people literally *everywhere,*" she whines, and I laugh, but only because I know Courtney hates people-ing even more than I do some days.

"It kinda figures you'd end up there, huh?" I tease.

"Touché, my friend," she says holding up her wine glass. I lift mine and hold it over the screen. "Cheers!" we say together before taking sips.

We talk for another several hours, into the late hours of the night, catching up for the first time in weeks, and it feels so good.

I smile wide as my best friend launches into a detailed story about her online dating life.

On Monday morning I sign into work, coffee at my side—I haven't had a cup of that decaf crap since I gave birth—and scroll through my emails. Even though Court left for the windy city, I still work for Franklin. And Franklin, the old fool, finally signed the deal with Robert Green, the author I've worked with now for four years after falling in love with his manuscript. His novel comes out later this year, and we couldn't be prouder of the final product. But my load at the office these days is a little heavier ever since Courtney left; the old stickler didn't bother to fill her position and apparently thinks I can do the work of two people. It's fine, really. I prefer to stay busy anyway.

Plus, my husband, Royce, works a lot, so it gives me something to do when he's not around. We've been married almost a year, our anniversary coming up next month, and while I never thought it possible, I've found a semblance of happiness. Royce makes me smile. He makes me laugh. He's good to me; a patient man.

He makes me feel safe.

But still, I've spent the last four years living in a what-if universe. What if I had kept him? What if I'd raised my son? What if I'd just stayed with Tarek and none of this ever happened? Could I have been happy? What if I'd never woken up from the coma? These questions always hover in the back of my mind, the anxiety rumbling like thunder as the dark clouds cast shade over me. Sometimes they explode, sometimes they don't.

But either way, the pain never really stops.

That feeling of being watched is back. Like I'm in the spotlight, acting in some show I don't want to be a part of.

But it's the notes that keep me looking over my shoulder. They keep coming, showing up without warning, and I don't know what to make of them. I've yet to tell Royce. I know he'll be concerned, and I can't say I blame him. This isn't normal.

I don't know who's sending them, but I have my suspicions. Some days I look forward to the notes more than my daily dose of caffeine.

Weaver Lake Park, 1:00

The note was tucked under the driver's side wiper on my car. I'd seen it from the window—a lime green sticky note, his signature color.

I know to look for them now, even though I don't want to.

I shower and dress for the day, in black yoga pants and a gray Lycra top. I don't put on makeup or style my hair, and instead I plop it on top of my head in a messy bun that looks more like a bird's nest, but it doesn't matter, because where I'm going, I don't want anyone to recognize me anyway.

Grabbing my keys and purse from the hook by the door, I glance back at my apartment and then slide my feet into a pair of running shoes. I can't help but picture Tarek smiling and waving goodbye from the couch in the living room, his eyes glistening with love before his attention returns to the Twins game playing on the TV. It was a simpler time, one that I know I will never witness or experience again.

That life no longer exists, and in some ways I'm not sure if that version of Tarek ever truly existed, either.

With a sigh, I turn the knob on the door and back out of the apartment, locking up behind me. My feet are heavy as I make my way down the hall and fight the tears prickling behind my eyes.

I exit the building through the front doors, foregoing my car just for a bit, and make a left on the street. Head down, clutching my purse to my hip, I walk.

And even though I don't know what I'm about to find, I don't stop until I reach the park. My stride slows, and my fingers skirt along the top of the chain link fence, my heart beating wildly in my chest. I'm drawn closer, my feet growing heavier with each step, but steadily moving me forward while my mind begs me to retreat in the opposite direction.

I scan the fields, the play area, until finally I see him. He's right there like the note said he would be, his eyes closed and covered by his own little hands. He counts, and a smile forms behind his fingers.

"One…two…"

He is familiar, despite the fact that I can't really see his face. His blond hair blows in the soft breeze.

"Three…four…fivesixseveneightnineTEN!" he shouts, his excitement building with each number. "Ready or not, here I come!" His hands fall from his face and his eyes come alive, a smile spreading across his face as he takes off running.

He's carefree.

He looks…happy.

"Brady! Time to go!" a woman calls from the other end of the park. She's seated on a bench, a paperback book in her hands, and I can't help but wonder if it's one I've edited. She tucks it into her Michael Kors bag and rises to her feet, her hands on her hips. "Brady, come on honey!"

"Coming, Mommy!" the boy answers. He says goodbye to his friends and skips off toward the woman he calls Mom.

A tear rolls down my cheek, but I don't wipe it away, because it reminds me that I'm alive and this isn't a dream. That he's real.

She hasn't told him yet.

That he's not her son.

He's mine.

CHAPTER FIFTY-ONE

Allie

Saturday, July 13, 2019

"You…killed him," I say, unsure of the words I'm speaking. His face flashes in my mind again, the slit in his neck caked with blood.

Owen drops his head, and the shame is so thick I feel it in my bones. "I did this for you, don't you understand that?"

"I—I didn't ask you to do it," I nearly shout. The argument is weak, but I haven't had enough time to process what he's telling me. This hasn't sunk in yet.

I'm not sure it ever will.

"He was never going to quit. You have to know that by now."

"No, I—"

He steps closer, and for a second I think he's going to touch me, maybe kiss me or pull me to him. But he doesn't. His arms stay at his sides, and my arms stay at mine.

He frowns and stares back at me without a word. I've

rendered him speechless, and I'm no longer sure that's a good thing. I don't know what happens from here, what the next move is, but I feel sick. I taste the bile at the back of my throat and fuck if I can't hold it down for once.

"Allie, there is nothing I wouldn't do to protect you." The corner of his lip pulls up. He steps back, and I see it then.

The tear that falls, that he swipes away.

He turns, and I'm left standing there, at the opening of the woods, my heart exposed to the elements. I watch him walk away until he's so small I can no longer see him.

Soccer fields, Weaver Lake Elementary, Saturday, 10 a.m.

I read the note several times before committing it to memory. It was on my car yesterday when I left work, but I wasn't sure what to do with it or whether to show up at the location. Royce worked an overnight, so I spent the evening over thinking it.

I don't know how he knows they're here, Owen. I don't even know *why* they are. The Jamesons lived in Florida, just outside of Jacksonville, when I met them. They had flown to Minnesota for our interview and stayed for a week before returning to take Brady home several months later. As far as I knew, they left after he was born.

I spend the morning on Google, searching with every keyword combination I can think of in attempt to find out all I can about the Jamesons. I don't find much, not even Facebook pages.

It doesn't take long for me to realize who the random notes are from; what they mean. And it hits me then.

I've been receiving them all along.

Little notes left behind throughout the years. At my office. On my car. Sometimes even in my purse. I once thought they were from Tarek, then Royce, the handwriting having changed throughout the years.

Never once did I consider the possibility that they were from Owen.

But they've *always* been from Owen.

Of course they have.

And now, somehow, my boy is here, in Minnesota—where I least expected to see him—kicking around a soccer ball with his teammates. Less than a ten-minute walk away on a good day. I haven't found his house yet; I have yet to follow them home. I'm not sure I will, but I don't need to decide today.

Owen seems to know their schedule, anyway, and his notes let me know where he'll be. Where to watch from so that I'm not seen or recognized. When the notes started arriving again a few months ago—seemingly out of the blue—I wasn't sure what I was showing up to. And then I saw him.

Brady.

I can't help but chuckle at the irony as I make my way through the parking lot and across the fields. The girl who hates soccer and didn't want to be the soccer mom, but look at me now—look how happy he is.

Maybe I could've done this after all.

But his mother isn't here this afternoon, and that's unusual. She's always at his games. I lower myself to the ground, taking a seat on the grass near the woods. I pull my legs up to my chin and wrap my arms around them. And I cheer silently in his mother's absence, a pang in my gut like you wouldn't believe.

After Brady's soccer game, I run errands in town for the rest of the day, stopping to pick up dinner for Royce and me at Whole Foods before heading home—back to the apartment where my son was conceived, because despite my attempts, I can't seem to part with the space. It reminds me of him, of what I've given up, and helps me feel closer to him.

I spent nine months with him here. Talking to him and singing lullabies, as if he'd remember my voice later on in life. As if I'd stay with him somehow, once all was said and done.

Royce says he understands, which is why when the time came for us to get married, he sold his house in Plymouth and moved in here with me. To him, my fear of leaving my son behind was more than valid, and he didn't hesitate.

I slide my key into the lock and turn the knob, checking the hall behind me, to the left, to the right. *Just in case.* It's a nervous tick I can't seem to shake, but I'd rather be safe than sorry, so I don't let it bother me the way it used to.

"Babe?" Royce calls from the bedroom. "That you?"

"It's me," I answer back, setting the food down on the kitchen table. I slide my feet out of my tennis shoes as Royce comes down the hall with a forced smile on his face.

Something's wrong.

"What is it?" I ask sharply.

"Why don't we sit for a minute." He pulls out a dining chair for me and motions to it. I sit, my hands in my lap, shaking slightly, because I already know what he's about to tell me must be important. Royce never starts a conversation this way unless he has to.

"What's going on?" I ask.

"I have some news, but I don't know much yet. I need to

make a few more calls, but I, uh, I got a call earlier…" He slides a slip of paper across the table, and for a moment I don't think I want to know. I want to pretend whatever's happening right now isn't happening, because that's easier than facing whatever truth this is. I've been doing well, for the most part, and don't want whatever this is to set me back.

"The Jamesons…" Royce continues. "They were in an accident."

"The Jamesons?"

Renee and Marc.

Brady's adoptive parents.

That's why she wasn't at the game today.

"They didn't survive, Allie," Royce says softly, and I tremble as he continues speaking. "Brady—your son—is okay. It says they left behind a son, but he wasn't in the vehicle at the time of the crash." Royce takes my hand that's shaking. He holds it, rubs the soft spot between my thumb and pointer finger. I can't bring myself to look down at the article in front of me. At the smiling faces of Brady's parents, formatted neatly next to an accident scene photo of their wrecked vehicle.

"How…this can't…Royce!" The tears come, as they always do, and all at once everything hurts all over again.

"I've got you," Royce says. He pulls me to him, holding me while I cry. While I scream and push against his chest. Because how can life be so cruel?

How can this world be so un-fucking fair?

"What happens now?" I ask after several minutes of silence. Royce shrugs, and I see the tears in his eyes too. I see the sadness.

"I don't know," he says. "But, look…" He points to the page in front of me again. It's a printed article from a website,

The Star Tribune, our local paper. “They were *here*, Allie. In Minnesota. I’ll do what I can to find out why.”

It’s a punch to the gut as the words register in my ears. I can’t tell him that I already knew they were here.

I just don’t know why.

CHAPTER FIFTY-TWO

Allie

Monday, August 12, 2019

"Allie, hi. This is Tanya Herin with the Crossroads Adoption Center. How are you today?"

My breath catches in my throat. I'm not sure I heard her correctly. She continues when I fail to speak; when the words on the tip of my tongue forget to roll off.

I hear her speak in bits and pieces.

"I'm calling with some unfortunate news…were recently killed in a car accident…no other living relatives…wanted to reach out to you to see if…before he has to go into the system."

My heart pounds in my chest as her words come together. I hear them, but I can't quite process them.

My son.

"Are you there?"

"Yes, I…"

"It's okay, take your time. I know this isn't easy to hear

and we wouldn't normally do this, but the Jamesons had a living will and it indicated the boy should return to his birth mother in the event of their untimely deaths. There's life insurance and everything." She pauses. "He has no one else."

"He…um, where is he now?"

"He's with a foster family at the moment. Temporarily, in the event you're able to take him." She trails off, her voice calm, but filled with apprehension.

"I—"

"I understand this is a lot to take in. It's untraditional and likely wasn't discussed with you ahead of time. Perhaps I can give you some time and call you tomorrow?"

Tomorrow.

"No, I—" The sentences don't form easily. Inside I'm screaming. Inside I'm kicking and hollering and telling this lady how much I need to see my son. How I need to hold him and hug him and love him and give him everything he'll ever need in the world.

He'll be hurting, because his parents just died, and he won't know what to make of that.

He'll be scared, because he'll be living with a stranger.

He'll need his *mom.*

The words are out of my mouth before I can reconsider. It isn't a question. It's a second chance.

"I'll take him, Mrs. Herin."

Brady doesn't come home right away. It takes days, weeks—much longer than I expected when I got that phone call from Tanya.

He's with strangers until then, in a foster home across town. Royce checked them out, and they seem to be okay. A stable home in what can often be an unstable foster care system. Delayed because of paperwork and rules, home visits and interviews.

In the meantime, Royce was able to do some research on the Jameson's move to Minnesota, and after a few phone calls, got a hold of Mark Jameson's former employer—and golf buddy—in Florida. The reason for his resignation? *"Brady wanted to see the snow. And we figured he deserved to know his roots, so we brought him home."*

The sentiment brings a tear to my eye, and I can't help but feel lucky to have known them, to have chosen them for my son.

While the days pass slowly, I do the only thing I can think to do, which is prepare for my son to come home. I make lists. I set up health insurance and dental coverage. I register him for preschool. I'm not even sure that's necessary at his age, but it's on the list, so I do it.

I call my parents. They break down in tears, and we make plans for them to come for a visit once Brady is settled. I call Linc. Even my little brother, the tough guy that he is, gets choked up at the news.

I speak with Franklin and let him know I'll need some time off. I manage to finish the edits on my current project before signing off for an unspecified amount of time. Franklin understands. He knows I haven't been the same, and assures me my job will be there when I'm ready to come back.

I go shopping. Court flies in for a couple days, and we have lunch and go to IKEA. We stop at Bed Bath & Beyond and then we hit up the toy store. I don't have a clue what a four-year-old boy plays with, so I fill a shopping cart with puzzles, board games, coloring books, paints, stuffed animals, trucks, Matchbox cars and the entire Toy Story figurine collection.

I stop at Target and buy clothes. I guess at his size, since I've seen him. I spend the rest of the time preparing his room. I buy a twin bed, a comforter set—sheets, pillow cases, and a duvet—in navy and gray tones. I find a dresser and matching nightstand at IKEA, and Royce helps me put everything together. We assemble the pieces mostly in silence, because we don't know what to say. I won't believe it's all really happening until it happens.

The reality of Brady's return seems to be hitting us both differently. Royce has been quiet, and I've been distant. Not intentionally, but the atmosphere has changed. We're preparing for the storm.

We haven't spoken about Royce's role in all this. I don't know how he feels about my son moving in, and I can't help but think back to our conversation before, back when we were saying goodbye to each other and he told me the investigation around Tarek's murder was being closed.

When I stood in front of him with a swollen, pregnant belly and thought it would be the last time I'd see him. I remember the conversation vividly.

I want to touch him, to place my hand on his chest and stand on the tips of my toes to kiss him because I can't deny my attraction to him—despite the trauma I've been through and the fact that I'm the size of a whale at the moment. And now I'm thinking about the song from Free Willy *and it's all I can do not to sing it aloud to him in hopes that he'll understand...hold me...*

But I don't, because it's not my place to feel this way. I'm not supposed to want him. Especially not in this condition.

"You're never going to catch him, are you?"

"I don't know," he admits. "We can't catch them all,

unfortunately." I can see him fighting the urge, but eventually his eyes land on my belly. At the massive bump. I know I shouldn't ask, but I can't help it, so I do.

"What if it was your wife, Detective?" I pause. "Could you raise a child conceived with her rapist?"

"No."

He doesn't hesitate, doesn't even take a breath or wait for the punctuation to reach the end of my sentence. I nod and stuff my hands into my pockets, ignoring the fact that he doesn't have a wife in the first place.

Freezing rain falls outside, but I don't mind because maybe it'll wash away some of this sadness.

"So, what do I do now?"

"You live your life, Allie. You go on."

It's this moment that I know I'll remember. It's the sadness in his eyes. The kindness in his heart. He doesn't want this to be the end of us any more than I do, but it is. I'm having this baby and giving him away. I won't be the same person when this is over, and he knows this.

I can't stop looking at his lips, his eyes. There's a kindness in them that most people don't carry. Not after the things this man has seen.

"Will I see you again?" I ask.

"I hope so, Allie Mason. I hope so."

He hugs me, and I know it's goodbye.

And yet, here he is, my husband, Detective Royce Feeney, putting together children's furniture, smiling up at me as I hand him another screw and washer set. He uses the drill to screw the remaining pieces together.

I'm terrified that he'll leave when everything is finished.

He hadn't anticipated my son coming home any more than I had.

When Thursday comes, I'm a nervous wreck.

I don't sleep the night before. I drink several cups of coffee and skip breakfast. I sit at the table with Royce while he sips his coffee and works a bagel and cream cheese into his belly. He doesn't like to miss breakfast. He's learned to eat even when bad things happen around him.

He scrolls through the *Star Tribune* on his iPad and chews, before he eventually notices me watching him. He smiles and sets the iPad on the table.

"You okay? he asks.

"I don't know," I say quickly, picking at a crumb on the table.

"Everything will be all right." He reaches across the table and takes my hand, his brown eyes searching mine. "What are you afraid of?"

"So many things," I admit, my cheeks wet. "What if he doesn't like me? What if he's too sad and misses his parents?"

"All of that is entirely possible, sweetheart. You know this. Brady will need some time to adjust, but once he does, I think he'll be just fine. Kids are resilient."

A pause.

"And what about you?" I ask, holding my breath. I may not be ready for Royce's answer, but I have to know before I walk into that room. I have to know if I'm about to lose him.

"What about me?"

I drop my eyes and stare at his hand, at the sterling silver wedding band that circles his ring finger. I stare at the dark skin that covers mine, and I don't want this to be the last time he reaches for me. I don't want this to be over, and my God, *what if this is over?*

"Am I going to lose you, Royce?" It's nearly a whisper, but there. I've finally asked the question. The words are on the table, ready for him to pick them up and decide what to do with them.

"Allie—" He slides his chair closer to me, his big arms wrapping around my shoulders, and he pulls me to him. "I'm not going anywhere, baby."

And those words are everything.

I let it all go. All the pain. All the hurt, I just let go of it all. I cry until the tears dry up. I sob, and he holds me, and somehow when it's over, I stand and I wash my face. I put on a little makeup and I brush my hair. And I slide my feet into my shoes and pick up my purse.

And I kiss my husband at the door, where he takes my hand and rests his lips on my forehead.

And then we go pick up our son.

In the county government center, we're led to a recreational area and left alone. I pace the room, too nervous to sit down. Royce stands back, leaning against the far wall, his hands in his pockets. He looks nervous, too, but I know he knows what this moment means.

Everything changes after this.

When the door opens, my breath catches in my throat, and I think I gasp. Just a little bit, in anticipation.

His eyes are the first thing I notice.

They're a beautiful shade of hazel and big, curious. His blond hair is a bit longer than when I saw him last and hanging at his brow, but nothing stands out to me more than his smile. Despite what he's lost, he's smiling as he comes through the door holding Mrs. Herin's hand.

I dab at my eyes with a tissue as they cross the room and stop a few feet from me.

"Brady, this is Allie," Tanya says. "Can you say hello?"

"Hi, Brady," I say, kneeling down in front of him. His lip trembles slightly, and I sense his nervousness. I want to reach out and ruffle his hair, but I don't.

"Hello," he says quietly. He pulls his hand to his mouth and sucks on his knuckles. I smile and swipe at a tear. He points at me with his other hand. "You're crying."

"Yes, I am. You're crying, too, I see."

He sniffles and shrugs his shoulders. "Na-uh."

"Do you know who I am?"

He nods. "You're my other mama."

Mama.

I never thought I'd hear these words from my son. All the muscles in my body work together to hold back the wave of emotions fighting for release inside me. I want to grab him so tightly and never let him go.

This day was never supposed to come. This day wasn't supposed to happen, and now he's here. He's right here, and he's so beautiful, and I can't believe he's mine.

"Who's that?" Brady asks, pointing to Royce. Royce stands up straight and gives Brady an awkward wave. He smiles. It's his friendly cop smile, and it's beautiful.

"That's Royce."

"Is Royce a superhero?"

I chuckle and look back at Royce and then at Brady. "No, why would you think that?"

"'Cuz he's big and he looks like a superhero."

"I suppose that's true. What would his superhero name be if he were one?"

He shrugs, considering it but not offering up any suggestions.

"Is he a nice guy?"

I lean in and whisper, "One of the nicest in the whole world." And Brady's eyes light up. He smiles, and it reaches his eyes. It's beautiful and innocent and everything I need in this moment.

"Can we go to the park?" he asks, his little hand finding its way into mine. "I like it there."

"I like it there, too," I say.

"Royce can come, too," he says.

CHAPTER FIFTY-THREE

Allie

Present Day, October 26, 2021

We measure so much of life in moments. Moments that change us, moments that make us. From birth to death, we have so many measurable moments. Our first steps to our first words. Our first love to our first heartbreak.

Moments happen every single day, but the ones that change us the most are usually the unexpected ones; the ones that manage to catch us when our guard is down. They sneak up when our backs are turned, some of them good, some bad. But they change the shape of us—like clay or Play-Doh or that weird kinetic sand stuff. As humans, we're just as impressionable as these moldable substances. Every moment changes our shape, every bend and fold and nip and tuck.

Until one day, the mold is complete, and we're the final version of human we were always meant to be. By that time we're old and wrinkly and probably on our death bed.

The defining moment in my life, the one that forever

changed me, was the day my son was born. Nine months after the attack that I thought would always be my single most defining moment. But the day I became a mother, and subsequently gave up the child who awarded me that title—*that* was the day that changed everything. I was no longer a parent, but I would forever be a mother.

So much has changed since that moment, and I'm nothing like the person I was before then. I'm some refurbished version of the person I once was. Not brand new. Used, but good enough for now.

I've learned to be okay with refurbished.

Maybe being refurbished just means there was enough of us left to be put back together. And the glue that held us together was simply strong enough to hold. At least for a little bit.

I know birth mothers don't often get a second chance with the children they give up. At least not until those children are no longer children and want nothing more than to know where they come from—to learn their heritage and maybe have a chance to understand why they were left behind in the first place.

They never will, though, not really. The sense of abandonment will never truly leave them, even if they get the answers they're looking for.

Even the ones who get returned will eventually question everything, as Brady might one day. I don't imagine he will remember much about his adoptive parents, the Jamesons, who raised him for the first four years of his life. For now, he still calls me Allie.

And that's okay.

I think one day I may tell him what happened. If he's strong enough to hear it, to understand.

But I got a second chance, an opportunity to remold. I'm

still not sure why, or whether I even deserved it in the first place. I wasn't ready for my son when he came into this world. I'm not entirely sure I'm ready for him now, either, but I won't turn my back on him a second time.

We make progress every day, whether we realize it or not. Sometimes it comes in waves—in little moments, just like everything else. Some so small we don't even notice them.

Brady and Royce have become best friends. They're two peas in a pod, and Brady would follow that man to the ends of the Earth if he could—asking every question under the sun so Royce can teach him everything he knows. There's beauty in those moments; in the mundane of everyday life. But they add up, and one day they'll amount to something big and unbreakable.

I feel more like his mother every day. I worry. I stress about keeping him safe. Making sure he's loved and that he lives the happy life he deserves. One that lets him know that sad things might happen, but sometimes those sad things humble us and make us stronger.

Like proof that we're human.

I still mourn for Tarek, for the man he once was. I can't regret him or wish him away, because despite the ways he violated me, Brady wouldn't be here if it weren't for him.

Happiness is relative, right?

That's what Brady's grandmother says, anyway.

It's been a while since I've felt Owen's presence, but sometimes I think he's still watching. For some reason that brings me comfort. Whether he has regrets or feels remorse for what he's done, I'm not sure. But I hope he knows that sometimes I smile for him, too.

EPILOGUE

Owen

Present Day, October 26, 2021

Love is such a funny thing, isn't it?

Selective, in many ways, in that not everyone gets to have it or experience it. Some of us—perhaps undeserving for one reason or another—are left to wallow in our loneliness. See, love isn't a one-size-fits-all thing. Not from my perspective, anyway. It can be brutal and unforgiving. Gut-wrenchingly fucking miserable.

Because it has to go both ways.

You can't just choose someone to love and make them love you back. It doesn't work like that. So, like everything else in this world, it comes at a price—usually in the form of one sacrifice or another. We give. We take. Until one day the universe decides that all is either right or all is wrong in the world.

That balance is hard to find, and in some cases—like mine—impossible to hold onto. Sometimes one of us is left stranded on a deserted island, our shattered, bleeding heart dangling in the palm of our hand while the other half of our soul goes on living a life that doesn't exist for the sole purpose of loving us back.

I learned that the hard way, growing up with a mother like mine. I was reminded of it with Allie.

The sacrifices I made for her were not small.

I eliminated the one person who held the power to ruin her.

Then I brought her son home.

I couldn't stand to watch her suffer anymore. I couldn't. I loved her—I still love her—in the only way I know how. I protected her. I kept her safe. Allie never wanted to give up her son, I know that now. I see that now. Had I known it then, I'd never have let her give him up in the first place. But she wasn't ready to be a mother then, and that's okay. I think she's ready for him now, though. I suppose she kinda has to be, since he's home with her.

I wish I could have seen her face light up when she saw him again that first time. When she was finally able to hug him and hold him close, knowing she'd never have to let go again.

It's funny how things work out sometimes, isn't it? How such a *tragic* accident, so devastating and unimaginable, can bring such joy and happiness to others.

Happiness is relative, her mother always said.

At least I still get to talk to her through email. My career as debut novelist Robert Green is just about to kick off. Four years I spent working with Allie to perfect my manuscript. My pen name will serve me well, I imagine. At the very least, it keeps me connected to Allie. And she appreciates my writing more than anyone.

Maybe that's why she fought so hard to get me that book deal.

I finger the silver necklace in my pocket, the one I took from around her neck the night I found her so helpless. I didn't mean to take it, but I couldn't help myself. I trace the outline of the tiny heart pendant with my finger, and it helps me feel close to her. My one reminder that she's always with me.

I'll wait for her if I have to.

Allie may need me again one day, and I'll be here for her just like I have been since the day I saw her photo in Dr. Simms's office. I've watched her for seven years; there's no sense in stopping now just because someone else gets to sleep beside her at night.

I'll wait for her.

Even if it kills me.

ACKNOWLEDGEMENTS

Does anyone else have *Another One Bites the Dust* stuck in their head? No? Just me? **shrugs** Welp! Holy moly, I wrote another book!

To be honest, when I set out to write my first book, *My Only Sunshine*, I was kinda prepared for it to be a one-hit-wonder—maybe sell one thousand copies in its lifetime—and then I'd sit back and bask in the glory of that *one* book I wrote. But this weird thing happened...people actually liked it. And then they told their friends about it. Their mothers, their coworkers...and low and behold, they started asking when my next book was coming out.

insert shocked face here

There was never supposed to be a second book. Which means this book exists because of YOU. Because readers like you not only picked up my first book but went on to ask for another.

So, there you have it.

This book is your fault.

I first want to thank everyone who has rooted for me and continues to do so on a daily basis. Those who encouraged me, and challenged me even when I was certain there was no possible way I could write another book. You guys made sure I never threw in the towel, and for that, I'm truly grateful.

I shall now thank some other people…

To my husband, Taylor, for making sure I laugh every single day and for encouraging me not to be too hard on myself. I appreciate the copious amounts of coffee you made for me while I was locked in my office hammering out this book (even though I shooed you away as soon as the cup was in my hands). Your support means the world to me, and I heart chew (more).

To Denim and Landon, my sunshine on cloudy days. Thank you for helping me find inspiration in the simplicity of everyday life. I love you more than words can say. Also, I hope you never stop believing your mom is cool. 'Cuz she is.

To my parents Pam and Dan, for your continued support and encouragement as I dabble in this whole writing thing. I love you!

To my brothers, Jason and Aaron, who I'm not sure will ever read this, but on the off chance you do, just know I based Lincoln's character after both of you. I thought about naming him Jaron or something weird like that, but as you can see it sounds stupid, so I didn't.

To my good friend Officer Jeremy Bautch, for once again answering my many law enforcement questions (although any and all mistakes are my own). And to his wonderful wife, Sadie, who gets to be a nurse in this book because I wasn't able to include her in the last one. I'm sorry that Allie wants to punch Nurse Sadie in the face!

Special shout-out to my mother-in-law, Debbi. Your continued support, encouragement, and excitement over the unorthodox things I write are so greatly appreciated. I promise Mariëtte's character is *not* based on you!

To all my other close friends and family who were named in the acknowledgments of my last book, ditto. I'm running out of space here and there are way too many of you to list, so thanks. Again!

To my incredibly talented editor, Kiezha Ferrell. I'm so lucky to have the opportunity to work with you again! I know I'm in good hands every time I pass a manuscript off to you!

To the incomparable Lisa Regan, for believing in me and telling me to write epic shit. I can only hope I've done you proud, my friend.

Thank you, as well, to the many other authors I've connected with over the last year or so, who provided encouragement and shared my posts on social media without being asked. So many of you have welcomed me into this wonderful writing community with open arms. Special thank you to Mariëtte Whitcomb, Katie Mettner, Laura Kemp, Colleen Hoover (#FanFriday!), Britney King, Kiersten Modglin (KMod!), and Emerald O'Brien. And a heartfelt thank you to Maureen Downey. I know I'm missing many of you here, and I'm already regretting naming names as a result, but you guys…to be a reader and a fan, and now a fellow author…how cool is this?

To Alessandra Torre and the Inkers group from whom I've learned so much about writing and publishing and marketing and everything in between. To have so many resources available, especially as a newbie indie author, is pretty incredible, and I'm so grateful.

To all the bloggers and bookstagrammers who have embraced me both as a reader and a writer, and who have supported me from the get-go. I wasn't sure how things would go when I decided to go hybrid on the 'gram, but you guys have welcomed me with open arms.

To my alpha and beta readers who were so very patient

and kind to me even when their patience ran out because I couldn't write this bad-boy fast enough: Jenna Torgerson, Mandy Henkelmann (Seesters TIAB!), Ashley Heck (Wifeyyyy!), Sadie Bautch, Sawyer Cole Hobson (insert monkey emoji here), Danielle Renee (my mug bestie!), and Maeh Cukrov. Your consistent f-bombs and shocked-face emojis were greatly appreciated.

To my Jump Street Team and ARC readers—you guys came out in numbers, let me tell you! When I released MOS I had about five (not exaggerating here) ARC readers and no street team whatsoever…but this time around you signed up by the dozen, and holy crap, am I grateful! I can't tell you what it means to hear a new reader say, "I've been seeing this book everywhere!" So, thank you for helping me create buzz and excitement for this book and for believing in my work.

Lastly, to the readers. I'm so humbled that you not only picked up my book but read it and are still reading up to this last page. THANK YOU!

ABOUT THE AUTHOR

Shannon Jump is an avid reader of multiple genres, with a passion for writing and storytelling. She refuses to start the day without the perfect cup of coffee, is a die-hard Minnesota Twins fan and Food Network junkie. She lives in small-town Minnesota with her husband and two teenage kids.

If you enjoyed this book, please consider leaving a quick review—even just a sentence or two will do! Who knows? Your review could be the reason a future readers says "yes" to *Even Though It's Breaking*!

To leave a review, please visit one of my pages on Amazon, Goodreads or BookBub.

I love connecting with readers and hope you'll come say "hello" on social media! I also send out a monthly newsletter that offers behind the story insights, exclusive giveaways, and updates on my upcoming projects.

To sign up for my newsletter, purchase official merchandise, and stay up to date on my upcoming releases, please visit my website at www.shannonjumpwritesbooks.com

facebook.com/ShanJumpMNAuthor
instagram.com/sjump4203
bookbub.com/profile/shannon-jump
goodreads.com/sjump4203

ALSO BY SHANNON JUMP

Don't miss Shannon's debut novel,

My Only Sunshine

"My story is like that of many before me. I am a victim of domestic abuse and marital rape, a battered woman. I fell in love with a tall, dark and handsome man; a self-proclaimed bad boy with an unexpected and worsening drug problem. I was blind to his true colors when I said my vows and I feared there was no turning back."

Set in a small town in Minnesota and spanning over twenty years, Brynn Reeves navigates through an abusive marriage, motherhood and friendship while coming to terms with the unexpected path her life has taken. Based loosely on true events, *My Only Sunshine* is a story of love, determination and strength, filled with raw emotion and kick-you-in-the-gut heartbreak.

They said until death do them part; will Brynn find the strength to get out before it's too late?

Visit www.shannonjumpwritesbooks.com to grab your copy today!

Made in the USA
Middletown, DE
19 July 2022

69500692R00176